The Gandy Dancers

Kevin Murphy

Shining Tramp Press

The Gandy Dancers is a work of fiction. Any similarities between the characters in this book and any real persons, living or dead, is purely coincidental.

The Gandy Dancers can be purchased through Amazon or your favorite bookstore.

Library of Congress Cataloging-in-Publication Data is available on file.

ISBN–13 978–0615460437

ISBN–10 0615460437

This book is dedicated to three departed
friends—former prison guards all . . .

Charlie Tezack
Bob Stockwell
Lefty Hodio

7

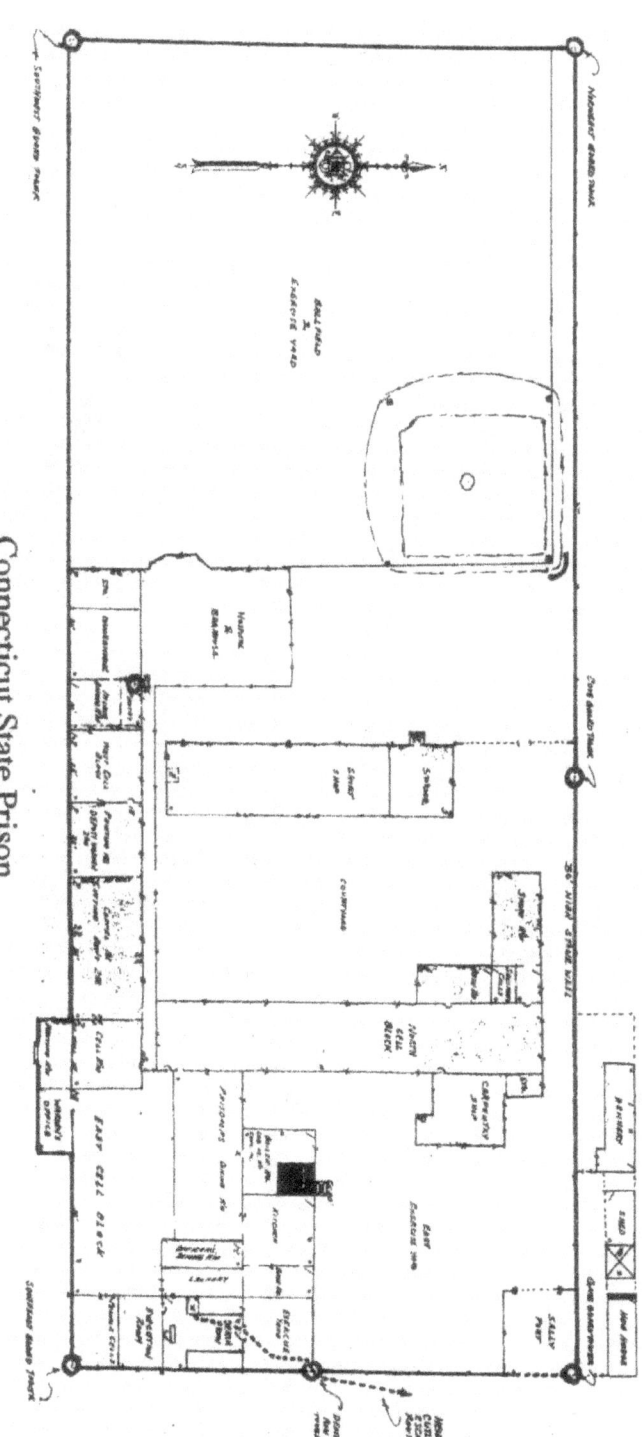

Connecticut State Prison

Introduction

Twelve thousand years ago, Wellesport sat at the bottom of a massive body of water, Glacial Lake Hitchcock, which extended from northern Vermont to southern Connecticut. Slowly, the lake subsided until all that was left was the Connecticut River and its western tributary, the Pompaucau.

Fifteen years after I left Wellesport, a devastating flood steeped everything in the state below forty feet above sea level. The rivers of central Connecticut merged and, for a time, assumed roughly the proportions of the original, ancient lake. At length, the Connecticut River chose a straighter line to Long Island Sound—a course that wiped out the oldest part of Wellesport. The Army Corps of Engineers studied the problem for a year, but drew a blank. The Pompaucau River was gone forever and the Connecticut River at Wellesport became a covetous beast determined to keep the land it had reclaimed so ravenously. Other towns eventually gobbled up the west side of Wellesport, leaving nothing but a meaningless name on yellowing state maps.

All that remains of my childhood are joyful and sorrowful memories of people mostly gone now, and the prison town where we lived. Wellesport was peopled with pleasant folks who hid their faults and prejudices, and gladly tolerated a few smoothies and sharpies. The old neighborhood, ball fields, houses and schools are gone forever, but I feel lucky. Wellesport never suffered the indignities of growing old. It died while it was most alive.

1

A little after three-thirty in the morning, the telephone on Dr. Rory Dunleavy's night table filled the bedroom with an irritating jangle. Having grown used to calls in the night, he scooped up the receiver after only one ring as he swung his feet to the floor. Sitting on the edge of the bed in his pajamas, he whispered into the mouthpiece, "Hello."

Waiting patiently for his answering service to relay the particulars of the emergency, he flicked on the lamp, and retrieved a pad and pen from the lower section of the bed table. Then, pinning the receiver between his ear and his shoulder, he wrote on the thick block of paper.

"Shelly Oleski . . .You say her mother called? . . . Uh-huh . . .Helen Oleski . . . Okay . . . Jackson 9-2665 . . . Right . . . 46 Forked Hill Road . . . Okay, I have it . . . Yes, thank you . . . No, no. That's quite all right. Thank you, Pauline. Good night."

Reaching across his body with his right hand, he depressed the little nipples on the body of the phone to sever the connection. After a brief moment, he removed his finger and listened for the dial tone. He dialed the Oleski's number.

Mother and daughter lived on the west side of Wellesport. Dr. Rory had never known the father. As the woman haltingly explained her daughter's stomach pains, he sleepily formed a mental picture of the abdominal cavity in his mind. The girl was in excruciating and constant pain, and was probably running a fever as well. When he tried to get the girl's mother to tell him more precisely about the pain, she was vague and alternated between English and her native Polish. Trying to form a diagnosis based on Helen Oleski's ramblings was simply impossible.

Messaging his temples with the outstretched fingers and thumb of his right hand, he said at length, "Helen. From what you tell me, it could be almost anything. It also sounds to me like it could be serious. Why don't you bring Shelly to the emergency room at Joan d'Arc as quickly as possible?"

"Dr. Rory, no . . . she . . . she . . . in much pain . . . I no touch her . . . and no car . . . no car."

With this, he realized that he would have to go out.

"Okay, Helen. I'll be there in a half hour. Try to keep her comfortable and put cold washcloths on her forehead," he said. He gently hung up the phone.

His wife, Ann, sat up in bed.

"Do you want me to make some coffee?" she asked. She had asked him this question countless times over the years and already knew the answer. It had become her way of expressing concern and caring when her husband had to go out in the wee hours.

"No, thanks," he said. "I shouldn't be very long."

He got out of bed, threw cold water on his face, brushed his teeth and combed his hair. Then, he put on his shorts, socks, white shirt and tie, plus an appropriate pair of suit pants, and moved quietly out of the bedroom. Descending the back stairs, he was mindful to walk on the extreme outsides of the treads, where they would squeak the least. There was no point in waking the children.

He fished his suit coat and hat out of the hall closet, and put them on. Moving gingerly, he went into his office for his medical bag and traipsed back through the kitchen to the mudroom, where he slid into his shoes and pushed the button for the electric garage door opener.

Arriving at the barn, he started up his new 1958 Buick Special and inched it slowly out into the darkness. Now that he was underway, his mood lifted a little. He enjoyed the new car smell inside his Buick, and he loved September. It was his favorite month of the year. Best sleeping month of them all, he told his kids. The cool night air was such a welcome relief from the heat of August. Until Indian summer arrived, they could unplug the window fans. Some nights, they would need a light blanket.

Wellesport had few streetlights and, once he got off Main Street, the narrow byways demanded increased attention. Only the high beams of his Buick lit the way. Motoring slowly in the darkness, he silently mused about one of his old med school professors, Dr. Nathaniel Root III. At the time, the old gent was at the age when a careful and caring healer turned to teaching if he could find a position. Dr. Root was from a prominent Boston family and was warmly accepted on Harvard's teaching staff, with nothing said about his lack of true academic credentials. During his lectures, he was given to long asides, which were always more interesting than the lesson itself. Root had a favorite expression, which still resonated in the auditory canals of Dr. Rory's ears, "All things being equal, which they never are . . ." The phrase could be used as the preamble to a fascinating diagnosis, or the conclusion to some ironic twist of fate befalling a hardworking general practitioner. One application seemed particularly germane to Dr. Rory's movements this morning, "All things being equal, which they never are, house calls are a very poor use of a busy general practitioner's time. House calls will be only a distant memory in a short time."

From his own point of view, Dr. Rory could not envision the day when he would not be making house calls. Perhaps he was a little too close to the situation, but what would have happened to Shelly Oleski, for example, if he no longer made house calls? The answer seemed grim.

The previous week, Dr. Rory visited an old farmer who absolutely refused to go to the hospital. To make matters worse, Dr. Rory felt a special obligation to the man because he had been one of Dr. Rory's first patients. So, off he went into the night to diagnose an attack of appendicitis and eventually escort the man to the hospital.

"All things being equal, which they never are . . ." he whispered softly as he smiled at the Dr. Root's wry wisdom.

After some searching in the darkness, he found Forked Brook Road, and a short distance later, a new white bungalow with its porch light burning like a beacon. He gathered his bag and strode to the front door. After pushing the bell button, he glanced at the sparsely populated countryside and waited for the door to open. At last, a matronly woman, whose face now seemed vaguely familiar, ushered him in.

"Dr. Rory, I . . . sorry . . . you . . . come . . . but . . . my Shelly . . . she . . . so sick . . . so sick . . . what to do . . . I no know what to do," said the woman.

"That's quite all right, Helen. Where is she?" asked the doctor.

"Oh . . . up the stair . . . bedroom . . . here . . . I take hat," the woman said as she led Dr. Rory up the stairs to a large bedroom.

Entering the bedroom, Dr. Rory noticed immediately that next to the bed, there was a low table piled high with books, magazines, medicines, a water pitcher, and a dozen other items. This was inconsistent with an unexpected infirmity. This young woman apparently had not suddenly taken ill, as he was led to believe.

"Hello, Shelly. How are you feeling?" he asked.

"Lots of pain," she said, grimacing.

She had her knees up, forming a tent of the covers, and was acting strangely. Why was she so nervous? What was going on here?

He felt her forehead. She was hot, but not alarmingly so. Then, he checked her pulse. It was a little high, but that was to be expected anytime he examined a patient. What had him concerned was the amount that she was sweating. Her body was obviously in some kind of distress. Finally, he said, "Let's have a look at your stomach." The girl recoiled a bit, and looked at her mother with fear in her eyes.

Dr. Rory could see that he would have to use some relaxation banter, because the girl was about to jump out of her skin. Soothingly he said, "Now, Shelly. I've examined thousands of patients in my life. I don't think there's anything that I haven't seen before. So, if you just relax, maybe we can figure out what's causing this pain."

His gentle voice quieted the girl, and he slowly pulled back the covers.

He was stunned. Instantly, he could see that Shelly was about to have a baby. She was lying in a pool of amniotic fluid, and would be giving birth at any moment. No wonder this girl was nervous, he thought.

He turned to the girl's mother and said, "As I think you already know, your daughter is about to have a baby. Please get me some clean, dry towels, and some more pillows for Shelly. Then, I'll need some hot water . . . and some washcloths.

He bolted to the bathroom and scrubbed his hands.

Dr. Rory's mind raced now. He wanted to just simply knot the umbilical cord as he had done many times before, but thought better of it. Instead, he would trim back the sheathing, and tie the two remaining vessels together with a surgeon's knot—tighter closure that way. He also knew that in his bag was some five-aught silk to sew up the perineum, should it tear. From there, he would just have to muddle through. He had done fine with the babies that he had delivered in the past, but performing such a procedure so far from the hospital's reassuring equipment and personnel made him nervous. If there were complications, he was painfully aware that his ability to deal with them would be extremely limited.

He summoned his confidence and went to work.

In a short while, he could see the baby's head. Using the fingers of both hands as forceps, he asked Shelly to push as hard as she could. The girl was sweating even more now and screaming loudly. The girl's wailing was distracting him. It was also escalating the intensity of the delivery beyond his comfort level.

Dr. Rory felt the beads of sweat rolling down his back. He tried desperately to maintain a professional detachment and not let his facial expressions reveal any of the misgivings he was harboring inside.

One of the baby's shoulder was hung up, as usual, and shutting down the whole birthing process. He tried to free it as carefully as possible.

When he had delivered babies under more agreeable conditions, he always likened this stage of childbirth to pulling a ship out of a bottle in one piece. Under the right circumstances, this comment was always good for a smile from his patient. Tonight though, he decided to keep such glib comments to himself.

Once he was able to free the shoulder, the baby slid right out. It was a girl.

Turning the infant on her side, he used his little finger to clear the mouth and throat of mucus. At long last, he held the baby up by the feet, and patted her gently on the back and rump, exhaling in relief when the infant started to cry.

Dr. Rory spent the next hour cleaning up the baby and tying off the umbilical cord exactly as he had planned. He knew that there would be no hospital visits for Shelly or the baby. All of the postnatal care for mother and child would fall onto his shoulders.

Fortunately, he didn't have to suture the perineum, and after checking Shelly's abdomen carefully with his stethoscope, he was further relieved to note that there were no other infants waiting to make a surprise appearance.

Within fifteen minutes, Shelley delivered the placenta with the fetal membranes, and Dr. Rory breathed an inaudible sigh. It scared the bejesus out of him to consider all of the things that could have gone wrong, but dwelling on the "what if's" would have given him dyspepsia so, for the moment, he kept his mind on more productive matters.

He left a long list of instructions for Helen Oleski. Shelly herself was too exhausted to do anything, but still he told her to keep an eye on the bleeding. If it didn't stop fairly quickly, she was to call him.

The time had raced by. It was nearing seven o'clock now, and he couldn't stay any longer. He reassured them by saying that he would check on Shelly and the baby during the day to see how things were going. After an enervating three hours, he left.

It was light outside when he started his car, lit a cigarette, and motored back to the old part of town. As he drove, he and pondered the enormity of what he had just done.

Rather than bear the shame of illegitimacy, Shelly Oleski was willing to hide out until the very last moment, and then roll the dice by calling the doctor in the middle of the night. What if he had been away? Would Dr. Packard or his friend, John Gale, have been willing to go out at four in the morning to attend a young girl who wasn't even a patient of theirs? These two women had taken a gamble the likes of which he had never seen before. Could a woman's reputation mean that much? If there were complications, the baby surely would have died. At least at the hospital, there were respirators and incubators, not to mention a reassuring supply of drugs. Was her reputation worth the life of the baby? Or her own?

Forever thereafter, when he got a call in the night from a woman with abdominal pain, he would ask slightly more pointed questions for his own peace of mind.

Dr. Rory returned to his home on Main Street in Wellesport some time after seven in the morning. Although the previous three hours or so had been exhausting, in the final analysis, they represented just an unusually early start to an otherwise ordinary day.

When he walked in the back door, his wife, Ann, was cooking eggs at the stove, while their three kids were gathered around the breakfast table in the inimitable, early morning stupor of school children. Between mouthfuls of poached eggs, they sleepily sorted and piled their books and papers for school. His wife turned and studied him for a while.

"That's got to be the longest house call you've ever made," she said quizzically.

"Complications," he said in an absentminded way.

It was a code that they had stumbled upon many years before. It meant that he would tell her at lunchtime, when the children were at school.

Ann always worried when he was out of the house in the middle of the night, but less so in recent years. When she woke in the morning and he still wasn't back, her concern mounted. They had a secure marriage, and she never seriously considered that there might be another woman. Still, she knew doctors who had affairs, so this three-hour house call wasn't something that she could shrug off easily. As bizarre as the story was, she felt a sense of relief when she heard about the baby.

2

Dr. Rory began practicing medicine in this small farm town after he mustered out of the service following the Second World War—thirteen years, next month. At first, he examined patients in a small storefront next to a seed company; and later he received them in his Main Street office–an addition to the center-chimney colonial that he and his wife, Ann, bought in 1949. The doctor was quite proud of his little office suite—two examining rooms, a consultation room, a small lavatory, and a large waiting room. His nurse, Marie Fortunato, did her paperwork in a nook just off the waiting room.

Dr. Dunleavy, in an effort to put people at ease, insisted that everyone call him Dr. Rory. Both the people of Wellesport and his patients gladly accepted this informal appellation.

Also, the doctor booked no appointments; office hours, yes—appointments, no. It was first come, first served. Other doctors laughed, but it was exactly as Dr. Rory wanted it. Happily, it was exactly as his patients wanted it too, for in a few short years, he had the largest practice in town.

There were two doctors in the area when Rory Dunleavy came to town at the suggestion of a surgeon friend. Old Dr. Packard snubbed him, while the other physician helped him in every way that he could. John Gale was a very secure man, also out of Harvard Med School. When the Dunleavy's twins were born, they named the boy John. Dr. Gale was flattered beyond words. Still, everyone called the boy Jack, while his twin sister, Elizabeth, picked up the nickname, Wibby, along the way.

In addition, the Dunleavys had an older boy, Rory Dunleavy, Jr., whom everyone called Zeke. Though they were Catholics and the church forbade birth control, common sense prevailed, and they had only the three children that they wanted.

Ordinarily, a house call during the night didn't slow Dr. Rory down at all. He could usually complete it in an hour, and go right back to bed. He had never required much sleep anyway, so working a full day after a night call was not something that tired him.

He was, however, grateful that the post office had finally raised the cost of the stamp to four cents at the beginning of August because, in turn, he felt more comfortable bumping up his office fee from six to seven dollars. It had long been the practice of doctors to raise their fees only after some conspicuous hike like that of the postage stamp. Such an increase made everyone cognizant that prices were rising.

Relaxing now in the kitchen, he removed his suit coat and draped it over the back of one of the wooden chairs. He exchanged the usual morning greetings with his children, and strode to the front hallway of the house.

Rory Dunleavy was a tall, sturdily built man, who had to duck his head under some of the doorways as he lumbered through the antique colonial. Floorboards creaked, as his two hundred pound frame tested each in its turn. He was more athletic than he looked, and he even swam the 100-yard butterfly on Trinity College's swim team, when he was doing his undergraduate work. He no longer completes, but still enjoys a quick swim when the opportunity presents itself.

Opening the front door, at first he couldn't find the newspaper. Michael Cooney was the paperboy and, by even the most charitable accounts, no one should have to start his day dealing with a Cooney.

The star-crossed Cooneys were the neighbors to the south— Veronica and Bill, and their thirteen kids in a ramshackle, old house on the very outside edge of reasonable, rational living.

After a short search, he found the newspaper in the farthest shrub from the front door, wet with the morning dew, and now practically unreadable. Dr. Rory understood a lot more about the Cooneys than others, and decided to say nothing about the boy's unusual delivery system. Besides, it didn't seem likely that Michael would have the paper route for more than a couple of weeks. How long would other people put up with his sloppy delivery habits?

Dr. Rory brought the paper to the kitchen table and tried to read the wet rag, while he waited for his coffee.

The headline of the paper was of particular interest to him. It screamed in seventy-two-point type, "CUTLER WAIVES APPEAL." Below, in smaller font, the headline continued, "TO DIE IN CHAIR." As the prison doctor, Dr. Rory knew Henry

Cutler, as he had attended to this murderer a number of times. Now it seemed that Henry Cutler had decided to stop trying to beat his sentence. There was a list of publicity-seeking lawyers a country mile long, who would trade their first born, for the chance to represent the killer on appeal. Apparently, Henry Cutler didn't like lawyers any more than the seven young girls he had so gruesomely butchered.

In a way, one couldn't blame the lawyers for wanting to represent a killer. Lawyers weren't allowed to advertise their services any more than Dr. Rory was. If they wanted to feed their families, they had to get their names before the public somehow.

The paper did not give the exact date of the execution, but it did leave the reader with the impression that it would not be a long wait.

As the doctor read the paper, another thought kept popping into his mind. His older boy, Zeke, was sixteen now and had his license to drive, which up to a point was just fine, except that he and Zeke were beginning to get on each other's nerves over the question of ownership with regard to the new Buick.

Possession being nine-tenths of the law, and what with Zeke simonizing the car daily, it was easy to see how the facts might get a little fuzzy. Zeke, sensing a losing battle aborning, had taken the offensive with a completely novel approach. He didn't want to skirmish over Dr. Rory's Buick any longer, and at the same time, he knew perfectly well that he would not be allowed to buy a car of his own. Accordingly, he proposed that he be allowed to build one from scratch.

Even Dr. Rory, who knew Zeke like the bones of the hand, was taken aback. Build a car? From scratch? Could Zeke do it? Even if he got help, he would be leaving for college in two years. Could he build a car in his spare time, with limited funds and insufficient knowledge, and still finish the thing in two years? Not likely. And what if he did? As the boy's father, would he dare let Zeke drive around in what would surely amount to a bucket of bolts held together with used electric wire and baling twine?

Dr. Rory's face grew solemn as he tried to envision the myriad of possibilities that lay ahead if he said yes.

He knew that as things stood now, it was only a question of time before Zeke simonized the paint off his Buick. Trying to build a car might be a good learning experience for Zeke. Dr. Rory, was proud of himself for practicing medicine, but he was only too aware that he was not doing any of life's creative work. As awful as it sounded, he was actually performing the ultimate maintenance function. He invented no new procedures or equipment; he simply applied the wisdom of others in straightening out the health problems of the people of Wellesport.

It was his hope that his children would get to work creatively, but this would never happen if he foreclosed on their early endeavors in that direction. He thought of Thomas Edison, whose parents must certainly have set the fences very wide. He didn't know if he could do as well, but he wanted to try. Besides, he knew several men in town who were building boats in their garages or cabin cruisers out behind their barns. One man was even building an airplane.

His biggest fear was that Zeke might actually do it. He had options though. If Zeke got close to finishing the automobile, his father could hurriedly start putting roadblocks in the boy's way. Zeke did his schoolwork, although he studied not at all and got A's. He worked his job at the drugstore, but that was only a few hours a week. Where would he get the money for parts? Could he do it?

At length, Dr. Rory decided to allow Zeke to build the car, but under three conditions: First, if Zeke's marks in school dropped at all, his father would lock the garage door and that would be the end of things until the next grading period. Secondly, if Zeke's household chores—taking out the trash and mowing the lawn—didn't get done, again the barn door would be locked. And lastly, if any of the parts for the car arrived from Midnight Auto Supply, or someone else dealing in stolen parts, then the project would end right then and there. Period.

Watching Dr. Rory and his son Zeke was like watching two great generals locked in a desperate battle. Dr. Rory was George Washington crossing the Delaware on Christmas Eve to surprise Lord Cornwallis' Hessians. Zeke was Cornwallis sending word to his Hessians to build nice big campfires for Washington, and then go into town and have some fun.

While Dr. Rory wrestled with the automobile question, his children finished their breakfast quickly and left for school by the back door. Dr. Rory decided that he would sit Zeke down in his consultation room that night after dinner and go over the finer points of this car building enterprise.

As for the rest of the day, he would go to the hospital in the city to see some patients, swing by the prison for a quick look, and be back home for his regular office hours by eleven o'clock. A fairly routine day.

3

Wellesport, by most accounts, was the oldest town in the state, although there was a surfeit of pretenders to the title. The problem stemmed from the early days of the republic, when the Pequot Indians still wandered the area in large numbers. There were trading posts up and down the Pompaucau River, and if every trading post were considered a town, Wellesport might easily be only the tenth oldest hamlet in the state. Clearly, though, trading posts were not towns; so Wellesport, with its present population of 7,000 souls, claimed the title for itself—no thanks to anyone for the right.

The prison employed the largest number of people followed by the farms and seed houses. Then, as with every other burg in the world, there were grocery stores, barber shops, garages, lawyer's offices and drugstores. The town was almost self-sufficient save for the generation of electricity, and it looked to the city for its telephone service, radio programs, and the images that appeared on television.

As with so many other towns, the roads were a nonsensical grid of crooked lines, where modern roads superimposed themselves over old cart paths and, even smaller, horse paths. The major streets were paved, while cinders and gravel serviced the side roads. Traffic moved slowly through the old village of necessity, for even a moderate rate of speed would shake a vehicle apart on the smaller roads, and probably cause an accident on the larger thoroughfares, what with all the farm equipment moving about.

Geographically, the town was really two towns, divided down the center by Route 5. The town fathers had employed the good sense to keep almost all of the businesses on this one road, thus preserving the quiet of the eastern and western parts of town. The old village was on the east side, wedged between this highway and the Pompaucau River. The west side of Wellesport, up until World War II, was hardly developed at all with just a few farm houses that had been there for almost three hundred years.

However, since the end of the war, this western side of town had been alive with the sounds of hammers and power saws as new houses sprung up like weeds in what had been cow pastures and corn fields. Still in all, there were perhaps twenty-five square miles of fields, which in the summertime, rustled with the stalks and shucks of the most delicious Golden Bantam sweet corn grown anywhere in the United States. The new part of town also had a golf club. By and large though, if you didn't farm, play golf or own one of the new houses, you had little interest in frequenting the west side of town. So it was that all of the public buildings—the town hall, the library, the police station and the schools—were right on Main Street in the old village.

Outsiders might assume that the townspeople were unhappy with the prison looming over the north end of the old town, but they would be wrong. The villagers felt no apprehension whatsoever, and because the prison was so quiet, it went almost completely unnoticed. About the only reminder was the presence of trustees in small groups around town doing all sorts of jobs, both for the prison and for the town.

Right and left of the prison, on River Road, were some houses owned by the state. On the west was Warden Stoner's house. It was a stately colonial, which had been built before the American Revolution, and was almost completely surrounded by rolling lawns and expansive gardens that sprouted every kind of flower imaginable. A rose trellis, covered the first hundred feet of a walkway from the house to the prison. It was all lovingly planted, pruned and cared for by the trustees.

On the east side of the prison were two smaller cottages for the chaplain and the deputy warden. These bungalows had lawns and gardens of their own, which were also tended by the trustees.

There was a small cemetery behind the prison for inmates who died without family or friends. It was enclosed by a picket fence with small and delicate white roses growing on it.

Apart from all this, there was a larger cemetery for the people of the town, which sat perpetually in the shadow of the immense steeple of the Congregational Church, smack in the center of the village. The trustees mowed and weeded around the hundreds of headstones and footstones, and they tended the flowers, flags and wreaths here too.

The trustees were assigned more than just the light work of flowers and grass clippings, sorry to say. River Road crossed Main Street and headed downhill, eventually winding up at the train station and barge docks by the river. These men, who had earned the right to spend their days outside the prison walls, also had to spend long hours in the winter at the train siding shoveling the coal needed to power the prison's heating plant. They dug drainage ditches and built up flood levies, doing anything and everything that the warden or his deputy could dream up. Still they didn't complain. The guards on trustee duty were the oldest of the guards and didn't care how long a job took. If they talked with the prisoners and the townspeople all day long, and wound up in the same spot the next day doing the exact same task, that was just fine with them.

The town had never bothered to buy a fire horn. That duty was simply given over to the prison. There was someone at the telephone and the air horn inside the prison twenty-four hours a day, seven days a week. The town had only two policemen with precious little to do, but they needed their sleep like everyone else.

The turnkey guard, inside the prison, usually answered the phone when a fire was called in, and blasted out a code on the horn. The hydrants all had numbers, so the guard located the fire on a map, and then blurted out the hydrant number on the air trumpet. Two blasts, then four—River and Main. One blast, then two—Elm and Broad. The volunteer firemen had codebooks, but most of them memorized the locations by dint of repetition. Upon hearing the horn, they jumped into their cars and headed for the coordinates. A simpler system never existed.

In the one hundred and thirty-one years that the prison had been in Wellesport, there had only been nine escape attempts in which convicts actually got beyond the walls. There had been no successful attempts since Benko Sadek was named deputy warden in 1944. Warden Stoner's acumen, when it came to hiring his deputy, had afforded him the softest of sinecures, and probably the best sleep of any grown man in Wellesport.

Of course, all of this might change now that Henry Cutler was on death row. There hadn't been an execution at the prison since Warden Stoner took the job. The last time the call been placed to the party line in Sumak Lake was in 1935. The deeply religious and mysterious master electrician, Mr. X, drove the six hours from high up in the Adirondack Mountains of New York State to Wellesport,

Connecticut to do his work efficiently and then quietly disappear into the high peaks region. Only the warden knew the man's name.

Warden Stoner was not surprised at Henry Cutler's decision not to appeal his conviction. Over the years, the warden had seen any number of ruses and delaying tactics by condemned men, particularly the more desperate ones. He issued strict orders to all of his personnel that they were forbidden to discuss anything to do with Henry Cutler or his impending execution. Violation of this order would be grounds for immediate dismissal. The warden had also taken the precaution of calling the governor. He had no intention of dealing in any significant way with any person or group who wanted to picket the prison on behalf of this twisted killer. Nor did he want to talk to the press.

Governor Belden backed Warden Stoner's decisions, but in an effort to distance himself from the execution, he told the warden that the sentence was to be carried out in the early hours of the morning, and a simple one-paragraph statement would suffice. The governor would compose the exact message that he wanted read to the press, and a state trooper would deliver it to Harvey Stoner within the week.

Warden Stoner knew that Henry Cutler could change his mind at any time. Thanks to well-placed sources, he was also aware of Cutler's deviousness and propensity to make trouble. Actually, that had been his very first thought when he heard about Cutler's decision. The commotion caused by the impending execution, along with the condition of the deteriorating prison, convinced him that Cutler saw the announcement as his best chance to pull off an escape.

Death row inmates spent only one hour a day outside of their cells, but the stream of visitors could be endless. Moreover, Harvey Stoner wasn't in a position to do much. If it was ever discovered that Cutler was being denied access to clergy, family or medical care, it could create serious difficulties for the warden. In that sense, Cutler had some leverage. Warden Stoner's best guess was that Henry Cutler intended to use that leverage for all it was worth. The warden had enormous faith in his deputy, Benko Sadek, but in this case, he would watch carefully too.

The people of the town would carry on their own speculation. Adults would talk about the 1935 execution, while young children would ask whether or not the lights in town would dim when the switch was thrown. (The lights would not actually dim because the death house had its own power source.) In an almost imperceptible way though, the mood of the town would change. There would still be the Grange Fair and holiday parades, the cows would be milked and the chickens would lay, but things would be different.

4

The early morning light streamed through an open bedroom window in Benko Sadek's small cottage, glinting off two gold-framed pictures on the dresser.

One of the pictures showed a young couple shortly after their marriage. The man had on the full dress uniform of the Marine Corps, and the woman was wearing a light summer dress of some indistinguishable pastel color. The man had his hat tipped far forward so that his eyes could not be made out clearly while the woman, who could be described as plain, had the eyes of a fawn in a forest fire.

The picture was taken in South Carolina, while Benko was a Drill Sergeant at Parris Island, during World War II. Sadly, that was in better times. Now, almost fifteen years later, with his fey southern belle in a state mental hospital, and Benko working as the deputy warden of a prison, things were very different.

The second picture was a faded image of a much older woman, ridiculously misdressed in a flowered frock set off by an oversized, gaudy hat, and festooned with necklaces and bracelets of cheap costume jewelry. This was Benko's mother, now ten years passed.

The room was sparsely decorated. Besides the dresser, which also supported a bottle of Rexall Bay Rum, the only furniture was a double bed and a night table. Competing with the morning chatter of the birds was the clamant ticking of a wind-up alarm clock. Despite the gentle breeze floating through the cottage, the bedroom still smelled like low tide in a fishing village. Benko, in many ways resembled his immigrant father, including his tendency toward bad personal hygiene.

During his time in the military, Benko had worked hard to overcome this flaw, but now he was backsliding at a frightening pace. The body odor he could sometimes mask with the Bay Rum, but his teeth were in need of work, and hard drinking had turned his eyes into ugly, jaundiced cesspools.

On the bed lying face down was the naked body of Benko Sadek—the carcass of a great ape. Wild shocks of salt and pepper hair covered his back and legs. What little skin could be seen was leathery and sallow. His right hand moved to whisk a fly away from the small of his back. The hand was huge but misshapen—the knuckles enlarged and the fingers misaligned.

He had to rise soon. The prisoners would be up shortly, and today there was a special piece of business that would not wait.

As he slowly roused himself from the bed, he reached over to the night table and poured some whiskey from a bottle of Fleischmann's into a water glass. Not too much today, for he would need all of his wits and most of his self-control. It would have to be just a small eye-opener.

Benko got to his feet, and shuffled to the bathroom to urinate and pass gas. He splashed some cold water on his face and wandered back into the bedroom where he opened the top dresser drawer and removed a fresh pair of underwear. He pulled these on and then went to the closet to find a pair of slacks, a shirt and a tie for the day.

He chose his clothes carefully. The shirt and tie were of little consequence, but the pants had to be black. Also, today he would wear black rubber soled shoes instead of the leather ones he usually wore. He put these items on, and walked through the kitchen. He'd eat at the prison later.

He grabbed his beat-up, brown fedora from the hook by the backdoor, placed it on his head—tipping it far forward to hide his eyes—and then shuffled out the back door of the cottage.

It was only a short walk to the front entrance of the prison. As he moved, he went through a mental checklist of the routine he would be required to perform in a short time. It was a dance of sorts, a *pas de deux*, choreographed personally by him. It was the final insult for prisoners who refused to fall into line.

A visit to Benko's office was preceded by long stretches in the hole—solitary confinement. Before that, there would be extra duties and loss of privileges. When all else failed, the errant prisoner was brought to Benko Sadek's office to be straightened out for good.

As for Benko, he felt that he had raised this whole ugly business of corporal punishment to a fine art. It actually gave him a sense of satisfaction that he had reduced the thing to a fairly rare ritual with positive and lasting results throughout the prison. At the same time, even he had to admit that he enjoyed savaging other human beings. He didn't dwell on it, but there it was.

Benko looked up at the thirty-foot high walls of the old brownstone prison. Not a single stone had been moved since 1827 when the prison was built. The ivy covering the walls made it look more like a college than a prison, but the foliage masked two unfortunate facts—the buildings were crumbling and the prison was overcrowded. In one short year, in the fall of 1959, the inmates would be moved to a new facility in another part of the state. The aged prison at Wellesport was scheduled for demolition.

Presently, Benko arrived at the front door of the prison. Except for the truck entrance built into the east wall, this was the only entrance or exit.

A night duty guard signaled the turnkey and the door opened for the Dep. As soon as he got inside the prison, he began his assessment.

"Any trouble last night?" he asked a stocky guard. Benko already knew the answer. On the night before a beating, there was an eerie silence in the cellblocks. Any one of the inmates could be going to the Dep's office in the morning.

"Quiet as a mouse fart," said the guard, trying not to sound too flip.

"Good. The trustees? Have they moved the furniture out of my office yet?" Again, Benko already knew the answer. This little drill had been worked out with precision, and no one would dare screw it up.

"Yes, sir. We had them up early."

"Good. When the others go to breakfast, have the men bring Schiarbo to my office." He said this with finality and then left in the direction of the stairs.

"Yes, sir," said the guard, setting off to make sure that everyone was ready. The others in the detail would be trustees with very little time left on their sentences and with no interest whatsoever in disobeying. Four trustees, together with two guards, comprised the dance committee.

In the early hours of the morning, they went to the Dep's office and removed all of the furnishings right down to the picture hooks on the walls. They stacked everything in the hall outside the office.

Next, they went to the kitchen where breakfast was being prepared and got sponges, cleansers, mops, and pails filled with boiling water and covered over with towels to keep them hot. These they brought upstairs and left in the hallway next to the furniture. Then, they waited.

At six-thirty, as the other inmates walked in single file to the dining hall, they brought the transgressor upstairs. They stripped him to the waist, frisked him, and pushed him into the Dep's office. Once the prisoner was inside, they closed the hasp on the outside of the door so that he couldn't get out. Finally, they got the stretcher ready.

On this day, things went like clockwork. The prisoner didn't even resist. He went so far as to claim that he had been looking forward to this day. At long last, people would see whom they were dealing with. On and on, he bragged. The guards just looked at one another, not knowing what to think. Maybe this guy belonged in the "bughouse." Who knew?

Abruptly, when he found himself inside the Dep's office, the crowing stopped. Even tough-talking Anthony Schiarbo was shocked by what he saw.

Benko Sadek stood in the center of the room, naked from the waist up—wearing only black pants and shoes. He stood six foot-four inches tall and was two hundred and fifty pounds of hard, heavily sculpted muscles. He had been doing some warm up exercises, so that the rippling flesh of his arms and stomach were glistening with a light sweat. His feet were spread apart and his fists rested defiantly on his hips. His ruddy face was devoid of emotion. Lastly, and unnervingly, his huge arms and massive barrel chest were as hairy as those of a zoo animal.

It began. In a slow and deep voice, Benko delivered a speech that he had practiced to perfection.

"Mr. Schiarbo, you have been brought to me because you have failed to obey the rules of this institution. Today, that will end. I want you to know, though, that this will be a fair fight. While you are in this room, I am no longer the deputy warden. You are to fight with everything that you have in you. I intend to do the same. Any questions?"

Schiarbo was no different than any of the others. He just stood there blinking at Benko, too frightened to remember his own name.

With the inmate's complete acquiescence, the fight started. Benko put one fist up in front of each breast, and began to circle the room. These first few minutes were important, and as the two circled the room, they actually resembled the combatants on the Friday Night Fights televised live from Madison Square Garden. This reinforced equality in the inmate's mind—more succinctly, that this would indeed be a fair fight.

Benko even took into account what he called the "grievance level" of the inmate. If the prisoner was level headed—rare, but not unheard of—then this dancing stage could be kept to a minimum. However, if the con was paranoid and likely to think that he was being given a raw deal, then the Dep would dance with him for as long as ten minutes with each party throwing desultory punches.

Either way, the charade inexorably moved to stage two. When he thought the prisoner was satisfied with himself and the fairness of it all, Benko feinted with a hard right to the prisoner's face. The man covered with his hands, at which time the Dep sent his left fist into the inmate's stomach with the power of a locomotive. For the rest of the fight, the prisoner never regained his breath. At present, Schiarbo was doubled over and gasping for air.

Benko quietly moved behind the inmate, and sent a thundering snap punch into the man's left kidney. Schiarbo let out an agonizing scream of pain as he straightened up like a fence post. The fight was bloodless so far, but this would change. As the story left the prison hospital, it was essential that the other rule-breaking punks got the message.

The Dep worked his way around to the inmate's front side again for his favorite punch. Schiarbo's face contorted with pain as his head tipped back in perfect position for the nose-breaking punch. Even if the prisoner could get a hand up, he would have no chance of stopping Benko's blow.

Leaning back for a longer delivery, Benko lashed out with a powerful left cross that crashed into the bridge of Schiarbo's nose. There was a loud cracking sound as blood spattered the walls. This punch had been a favorite of the Dep's for a long time, but not only for the sheer savagery of it. Its true beauty was the damage that it did to the orbits around the eyes. With this one blow, the Dep could keep Schiarbo in the prison hospital for a whole extra week, and the advertising value throughout the prison would be priceless.

The Dep knew that few of these tough-talking punks had ever been deep into a fight before. They were masters of the sucker punch and simple intimidation, like all bullies, but one look at their soft faces told the whole story. His job here was to create an impression on the prisoner's mind that would last him for the remainder of his stay at Wellesport. If the memory of this sickening little dance lasted him a lifetime, so much the better. Therefore, even though this fight was actually over, Benko still had work to do.

Schiarbo was on the floor now, curled up in a ball. Towering over the convict and with the adrenaline flowing, Benko fought a powerful urge to urinate on the punk. Instead, he talked gently to the lowly inmate, slowly coaxing him to his feet. The prisoner was covering his bloody face with both hands, so Benko spent the next few seconds breaking ribs. First on the prisoner's right side, and then with his right hand, he went for the three lower ribs on the opposite side.

It pleased him immensely that at fifty-two years old, he hadn't lost the snap in his right hand. He had spent a great deal of time in the Marine Corps bringing his right hand up in power, until it was every bit as good as his left.

After an assortment of jabs to dress up the inmate's body with contusions, and when Benko was sure that this little lesson had achieved some level of indelibility, then and only then, would he deliver the last punch. Squinting slightly and taking precise aim, he threw a left that knocked out Schiarbo's two front teeth. No matter. The prison dentist would make him a set of false ones, a lasting memento of his days at the Connecticut State Prison at Wellesport.

As the prisoner's body crumpled to the floor for the last time, barely conscious and whimpering involuntarily, the Dep whispered under his breath, "Pantywaist."

The Dep was barely breathing hard when he was done with Anthony Schiarbo. He had turned out to be more hot air than even the Dep had imagined. All the same, his days as a troublemaker were over.

As a final humiliation, Benko might have moved him from the print shop to the hennery or the piggery. Unfortunately for Schiarbo, it was September and the weather was too nice. If it had been January, this punk would be shoveling manure in the cold as soon as he could walk. However, a loser like Schiarbo would never get an outdoor job in September.

The Dep knocked four times on the door to let the trustees know that his business was concluded. Into the office they carried the water buckets and the stretcher. The pails of water were set on the windowsill for Benko to use first. While he was giving himself a quick sponge bath, they moved the limp body of Anthony Schiarbo onto the stretcher and left for the prison hospital. Two of the trustees acted as litter bearers while one of the guards walked alongside. The last guard would watch as the other two trustees used the same water Benko had washed up with to clean his office, and then they'd replace the furniture.

"Any problems?" the guard asked the Dep.

"Pantywaist," replied Benko.

"He sure could talk tough," offered the guard.

"Bring me all the tough talkers," said Benko dismissively.

The guard handed the Dep his shirt and tie. Benko dressed quickly. It would be yardout for the prisoners shortly, and he wanted to be up on the wall. It was important for the inmates to see him on the wall, walking from tower to tower, talking with the guards, clearly unscathed by his meeting with Anthony Schiarbo.

The Dep left his office and exited the administration building at the first floor level. He walked across an open courtyard, and then climbed the spiral stairs inside the cove guard tower. This watchtower sat in the center of the back wall of the prison, thirty feet in the air. It was the only tower that could be accessed from the ground.

From this central point on the wall, Benko started for the northwest tower that was about three hundred feet away. As he walked, it was clear that he was slightly bowlegged, and there was something unusual about the way his upper torso moved. As his long arms swung stiffly, the palms of his hands faced the rear.

As Benko moved along the top of the wall, his mind was free enough to notice the beautiful weather. He looked outside the wall to the north and could feel the cool September breeze on his face. Just outside the prison walls was the hennery, the piggery, and then about twenty acres of corn, beets, carrots, beans, and other vegetables. Just beyond these fields lay the Wellesport Cove, a bulbous body of water connected to the Pompaucau River by a small channel.

From his elevated position, Benko could even make out part of Hidden Island, tucked as it was behind an arm of land on the northernmost part of the cove. He loved the gentle breeze that scooted off Wellesport Cove in all sorts of weather. It reminded him of South Carolina, where he had been a young Marine and a newlywed, where his future seemed so bright, and where he had been happy.

In a few minutes, he was at the northwest corner of the wall, where a beefy guard named LaVasseur was standing just outside the tower. Cradled in his arms was the Winchester Model 94 rifle that all the guards rocked during yardout. Lanyards around their necks clipped to the stocks of the rifles and prevented the weapons from ever falling down into the yard. (When neighboring boys saw the guards up on the walls at yardout, they recognized the rifles immediately as the same ones the cowboys used on TV.) Other guards, armed only with fifteen-inch oak "blackjacks," stood with their backs against the walls inside the exercise yard with the prisoners. In a strange irony, the prisoners in the carpentry shop made these truncheons.

The morning and afternoon yardouts each lasted for one hour. Under the original Auburn system, there was only one yardout for an hour before the evening meal. However, the prison had become so badly overcrowded that a second yardout was added to placate the prisoners until they could be moved to the new facility. On Sunday afternoons, yardout lasted for four hours—clearly the highpoint of the inmates' week.

The Connecticut State Prison at Wellesport was one of only a handful of penitentiaries in the country that still adhered strictly to the silence rule of the famous "Auburn System." Even when the prisoners worked in the shops, they remained silent all day long.

Each shop had its own peculiar set of hand signals for an inmate to request more wood, cloth, leather, paper or whatever was needed. (The Dep allowed inmates to use transistor radios in their cells at night, but only with earplugs.)

Benko talked briefly with LaVasseur and then strode to the next tower. When he was half way there, and standing atop the west wall of the exercise yard, he stopped. Turning slowly toward the prisoners below, he spread his legs slightly, put his fists on his hips, and glowered down at his charges.

The prisoners stole only quick glances of the massive form of Benko Sadek illuminated brightly by the morning sun against the backdrop of a cobalt blue sky. With his fedora pulled down hard over his forehead, they could not see his eyes. They cowered before him, nauseatingly aware that he was Thor, their own personal god of thunder. He had the power to give and he had the power to take. The strongest among them felt craven before him and turned away.

He held this pose for only a few brief minutes, all the while thinking: "Here. Take a good look, you wankers. Look at your keeper, your God. Go ahead. Break my rules and we'll see who's boss around here. Worthless pantywaists."

By the time yardout was completed, Benko had circled the whole prison and checked in with four more guards.

Benko walked back to his office. As he strode, he made a mental note to check on Henry Cutler in the death row complex as soon as he finished some paperwork. He had learned to smell a slippery prisoner and Henry Cutler smelled bad. The Dep made it a point to pay him a visit several times a day and always at different times. Cutler had tortured, killed and mutilated seven young girls and, in addition, had a history as a troublemaker going back to grammar school. Benko was determined to watch him carefully.

Other than that, it promised to be one more day pretty much like yesterday, and every bit the prototype for tomorrow.

5

When Benko Sadek was six years old, he watched his father break his mother's leg with a piece of iron pipe. Alcohol and violence were the suckling milk of his youth in Philadelphia.

Never was there an apology of any kind from his father either. "She had it coming" was his only comment.

Tadeusz Sadek worked in a mill running a lathe and was frequently laid off as the economy went through its periodic downturns. Benko was sixteen when the recession of 1922 put his father out of work for the umpteenth time and joining the Marines seemed like a good way to ease the lean times at the tenement where he lived with his folks. He was big for his age so, with a few lies and the signatures of both parents, he was off to Parris Island, South Carolina for basic training.

From the start, Benko loved the Marine Corps: the spit and polish, the strict regimen, the *esprit de corps*. His life, for the first time, had order and meaning. He also loved the sense of brotherhood, of being an important part of something much bigger than himself—all for one, one for all. He soaked it up like sunshine.

His size made him a natural on the boxing team—undefeated as it turned out. Benko considered a technical knockout an affront to his manhood. When he got into the ring, the genes of all his ancestors in the animal kingdom came bubbling to the surface as he mercilessly disemboweled his opponents. He finished his career with twenty-six knockouts and only one TKO.

He also became one of the best shots at Parris Island. Twenty-ten vision and the sturdy frame of a perfect mesomorph made him a finalist in every competition.

He worked his way up through the ranks, finally becoming a first rate Drill Instructor. Benko had to work diligently to keep the vicious and sadistic side of his personality at bay, but he accomplished even this as he flowered in the Corps.

Actually, it turned out to be much harder to make sergeant than Benko had thought. He spent long nights studying in the latrine with a flashlight to get through the written tests, but it was time well spent. He became a Drill Sergeant in 1930 and got married eight years later.

Polly Graham was twelve years younger than Benko when she married him right out of junior college. Shy and quiet, she was at first good for Benko, imposing a quiet manner on an otherwise wild animal. Time would alter this situation terribly, but at the outset it was grand. Polly's parents were scared to death of Benko, for no reason that they could say—his size and manner just scared everyone. In time, however, they came to accept him. Not in a loving way, but still they tolerated him as he was.

When the war finally started for the Americans, Benko was a thirty-five year old Drill Sergeant. A year and a half of fighting in the South Pacific and, in 1944, he landed stateside in his old job at Parris Island.

He felt that he was a good Drill Instructor. Maybe he was tougher than the others, but fair. And he got good results. No Christmas cards, but good results.

Then toward the end of the war, when the caliber of the draftees had fallen to a level Benko deplored, the bad side of his personality, day by day, came to the fore. The recruits were soft and fat, and couldn't get out of their own way, much less march in step. Benko took a personal interest in shaping up these loathsome wastrels.

Physically, Benko was at the peak of his powers. He stood six foot-four and was a rock hard two hundred and thirty pounds.

He could have been on a Marine recruiting poster—proud and tough.

Sadly, all that changed when one of his charges had the gall to die in the swamps one night while out on a training mission. He was particularly disgusted with this one fat ass and he was riding him harder than he had ever ridden anyone before. Now this clown had the inexcusable bad manners to die in the swamps.

Benko's contempt knew no bounds. At the same time though, he knew that his military career was over.

The Marines knew how to get rid of an embarrassment like Benko Sadek and get rid of him they did. Because it was wartime, he received a lightning fast court-martial, a general discharge at the rank of private and was hustled off the base in record time.

In a matter of weeks, his life had been turned upside down. One day, he was a respected and feared Drill Sergeant and, three weeks later, he was a nobody. He drank before but in keeping with the

Marine tough guy image and always in the company of others. Now he drank all day every day and always alone.

Money was getting tighter. No Marine can save much even in the best of times and, in this regard, he was no different from anyone else at Parris Island. Like so many women during the war years, his wife Polly was a volunteer. He had to find work.

Unbeknownst to Benko at the time, his size, naturally violent personality, and military training had prepared him singularly for the job of deputy warden of a penitentiary. Also, unknown to him was the fact that at the very same instant that the fat draftee had drowned like a rat in the South Carolina swamps, the deputy warden of the Connecticut State Prison at Wellesport had suffered a fatal heart attack. The job would have to be filled quickly and, with the wartime manpower shortages, the competition would be slim to none.

Benko had arranged for his one true friend in the Corps to buy his groceries at the PX in an effort to make his meager savings last a little longer and it was through this friend that he heard about the deputy warden job.

He had to drive all night long to make the interview, but it was a profitable trip. Not only did he get the job but also free housing in a small cottage on the grounds of the prison.

The warden of the prison was a man named Harvey Stoner. Warden Stoner had worked his way up through the prison system in New York State before coming to the attention of Democratic Governor William Prentis of Connecticut. The governor appointed him the new warden shortly before the Japanese bombed Pearl Harbor and, although Prentis was not reelected in 1942, the new Republican Governor Richard Woodford kept him on.

Unlike the typical political appointee, Warden Stoner knew his job inside and out. He had worked at Elmira and Auburn, where the famous "Auburn System" originated in the early 1800's. As a result of his own experience, he knew exactly the kind of man he wanted for his deputy warden.

When Benko Sadek was ushered into his office, he knew his search was over. There had been the usual grumbling from the guards who felt the new deputy warden should come from within the ranks, but it was not to be.

Warden Stoner knew that in order for his own job to be secure, the prison had to be completely invisible. If the governor, the newspapers and the public never gave a single waking thought to the prison and its unique population, and as long as there were no riots or escapes, he could have the job for as long as he wanted it. He could attend the Governor's Ball, the Prison Board luncheons, play golf at the local country club and generally enjoy life. He could do all this for as long as he liked if, and only if, he had "walking fear" running the prison.

In the end, Warden Stoner cared little about the fat draftee who died in the South Carolina swamps just so long as it didn't happen again in Wellesport. As a matter of fact, he felt that it might actually work to his advantage. Eventually, the inmates would hear the story of the Marine dying at the hands of Benko Sadek and they would give him a wide berth. The vast majority of the inmates were nickel and dime punks—they would cower in the face of a real killer.

So it was. Benko Sadek had a new franchise and Warden Stoner had his "walking fear." It was a partnership forged in the hottest spot in hell and destined to last until Harvey Stoner retired. The deputy would do all the work of running the prison and the warden would shuffle the papers and take the credit, just like any other well-oiled bureaucracy. Now, Benko Sadek and Harvey Stoner were blessed with the care and demise of Connecticut's current spectacular prisoner, Henry Cutler.

6

Henry Cutler's life could not have begun in a worse way. When his prostitute mother found out that she was pregnant, she went to a quack doctor for an abortion.

The state had relieved this man of his medical license many years before for narcotics violations, and now he was reduced to reading Tolstoy, dreaming the dreams of the disinherited and doing illegal abortions on working girls. Unfortunately for skinny, little Pearl Cutler, the state had been very wise to lift this doctor's license, for he turned out to be every bit as inept as officialdom surmised. There was plenty of blood and pain, but the fetus miraculously did not abort. Unfortunately, Pearl didn't know that the baby had survived and in a very short time was earning her living again from the touch of men. Only later, when even a quack wouldn't try the abortion, did she find out that she was still with child.

Wracked with guilt for trying to abort the fetus the first time, she decided to keep the baby and settled in for the remainder of her gestation period.

In the winter of 1928, with Hartford's temperature in the single digits and snow shutting down the world, she gave birth to a puny five-pound baby boy. She named him Henry after one of her tricks—a politician. When the pol found out, he quickly took his business to a hooker with more discretion and less memory.

For a little while, Pearl tried to be a good mother, but in truth she had no mothering skills at all. Her idea of motherhood could be compressed into the one event in science she was able to remember from an otherwise pitiful education. She recalled the moment when the mother robin pushes the baby robins out of the nest. She couldn't remember that some fledglings weren't able to fly. It completely escaped her that some fell hard, becoming the foodstuffs of feral cats and raccoons.

It mattered little though. With the pressure to earn a living, she was on her back before the stretch marks faded and Henry was left in the care of anyone who would watch him.

Henry had a strong native intelligence, but was slow to walk and talk. When he did finally get to school age, he was desperately behind the other kids and destined to fall further behind. And, at six years old, Henry still wet the bed. Not every night, but often enough that Pearl had completely lost patience with him. Convinced that he was doing it on purpose, she began to beat him with a metal dustpan. Mornings began with a terrible beating, then out the door to school, both dirty and hungry, with not a hope of learning a thing.

Henry was held back in first grade in a well-meaning attempt to give him a better start in his schooling, but it didn't help. Without a parent who cared, it was hopeless. The teachers, of course, knew all too well what was going on, but with thirty-five and forty children per class, there was no time for the individual attention the boy needed.

Besides, Henry did not exactly endear himself to his teachers. He constantly upset the class with inappropriate behavior and quickly became every teacher's nemesis. The idea of holding him back a grade now was unthinkable because none of the teachers wanted him for a second year.

This situation played itself out dismally through the fifth grade, when he was caught torturing neighborhood cats. To the complete befuddlement of the educators, Pearl showed no concern at all. To her credit though, she allowed Henry to receive counseling at the school.

In a sad commentary on bad roots, at the tender young age of eleven it was already too late for Henry Cutler. He became increasingly belligerent and progressed rapidly into more varied forms of antisocial behavior. Sometimes alone and sometimes with newfound friends who the caprice of chance brought him into contact with, Henry created trouble wherever he went.

He began to pal around with another dead-end kid, Rollie Leduc. After school they would go to a wooded area outside of the city, smoke cigarettes and make evil little plans. The chemistry between these two produced a geometric effect on their mayhem. It wasn't long before they were starting fires all over the city.

The first fire was an innocent little thing in an abandoned rubbish barrel down by the docks, but they progressed in short order to a warehouse loaded to the rafters with dry goods. The owners of A. Lehman & Sons were not pleased. Neither was Henry when he discovered that this arson, together with his earlier run-ins with the police, made him exhibit "A" at the Alfred Manning Home For Boys.

Reform school turned out to be only a minor adjustment for Henry. Stigma was his middle name and what was this but more of the same? Pearl visited almost never, and life was as normal as it was ever going to get.

Actually, from Henry's point of view, reform school was a necessary turning point. Eventually, he would have to fend for himself and one thing the Manning School produced was great auto mechanics. So Henry—though it must be noted that he was not given the choice—became a first rate grease monkey. By the time he got out, he could strip a Ford V-8 engine down to nuts and bolts and have the whole thing back in the car and running in three eight-hour shifts. For the first time in his life, he excelled at something. He had the good hands.

At the reformatory, he messed around with the engines of old clunkers the school had and, during the final years of World War II, he even worked on government vehicles.

Another talent, which Henry discovered at reform school, came as a complete surprise. From the simple doodling all people do from time to time, Henry graduated to some rather sophisticated drawings of cars and landscapes. He even tried his hand at portraiture with more than the usual number of compliments from others. What he would do with this new skill was anybody's guess. While he was open, even proud of his new skills with cars and drawing, he kept another world completely to himself.

Henry, almost without realizing it, remembered all of the construction details from the tenement houses that practically fell down around him when he was living with Pearl. So it was no great trial to find a loose two-by-four firestop at the first floor level above the chapel basement. By removing this block of wood, he was able to stuff his pornography stash up inside the wall cavity between the studs.

Not only the teachers, but also his fellow students to a person, would have dropped dead to see the pictures to which he masturbated. Henry liked to see pictures of women in pain—ropes and gags, whips and chains, and the like. He particularly liked it if the women's faces were contorted in terror.

He fantasized endlessly about kidnapping women and taking them to some remote wooded area where he could submit them to his will. As he masturbated, he closed his eyes and pictured a naked woman, bound and gagged, with flowing blond hair, and milky white skin . . . her nipples pert and pink . . . and himself using a bowie knife on her.

In time the fantasies got more and more elaborate. Still, no matter what the fantasy, they always ended with him slipping the blade of his bowie knife up under the sternums of his victims and twisting it into their hearts. During the last few flashes of this fantasy, he would ejaculate wildly all over the stone walls of the chapel's basement.

Night after night, he considered the logistics of his fantasies. All ropes, gags, disguises, and other necessities must be stolen. He must scout the woods carefully to find a spot that would ensure maximum privacy. The bodies could be simply hidden in the brush. They wouldn't be found for months and a couple of good rainstorms would ruin any evidence.

He'd also need to find a way to get the women to the woods, which meant a car of some sort. The war had put a huge premium on automobiles, but if he looked long enough, he would find one. And it would be a nondescript car with no dents or other markings on it. Stolen tags. Ordinary Goodyear tires.

That was about as far as his plan had developed. Until he was let out of reform school and could get a job as a mechanic someplace, it would remain a fantasy.

If he could blend into the woodwork, Pearl might let him stay with her for a while—that would help with money. This was Henry Cutler's idea of a plan in the spring of 1947.

***

Eleven years later, in the fall of 1958, Henry Cutler lay on his bunk in the death row building of the Connecticut State Prison at Wellesport. Seven grisly murders had brought him to this end—a quiet cell, surrounded by the silent cells of two other condemned men, with nothing but time on his hands. He firmly believed that he could escape, and he had already begun the planning that it would take to achieve that end. In the meantime, he tracked the movements of the guards and mapped every inch of the prison in his head.

He had been arrested shortly after the Ruthie Sorensen murder, but there had been six schoolgirls who left this world at his hands before Ruthie. Each girl begged and pleaded for her life as he reveled in this newfound power. Never for an instant did he think of letting any of them go.

He had had a great deal of trouble in his first futile attempt at getting the girl into his car. It unnerved him badly. For days afterwards, he read the newspapers morning and night for any mention of his bungled attempt at abducting the girl, but there were only small pieces in the papers—nothing to cause him any real trouble.

He would have to come up with a better method of getting these girls into his car and this little dilemma kept him inactive for almost a year. He cruised around in his car and observed the behavior of the girls who might be his victims. Since it seemed that in those days the whole teenage population was cruising around in their own cars or those of their father's, it gave him great cover. They tootled while he hunted—a wolf looking for a weakling. Finally, when he felt he had come up with some foolproof techniques for getting his victims into his car, and after he had pinched the necessary props, he tried again.

She was another thin, blonde teenager. This time Cutler dressed as a firefighter on his way to work in the city, and the girl was happy to accept a ride home. But she never got home. He chloroformed the girl and drove her to Meshome State Forest where he pulled aside a wooden barrier and slowly motored down an old logging road.

He gagged her, tied her frail body to a tree, and unhurriedly sliced off her clothes. Then he raped her and butchered her like a hog. He left her body deep in a thicket where it wouldn't be found for months.

Again he read the newspapers for days looking for some mention of the girl, but there was only a small story some time later about her disappearance. The newspaper referred to her as a runaway.

Cutler figured correctly that they would not find the body for months. He was also right when he surmised that the police wouldn't have a clue as to what was happening.

Henry had polished his routine a great deal in the months after his first botch-up. He had to accept the fact that he really did not have the social skills to talk a girl into his car on the pretext of going to a party or some such thing. Instead, he developed a series of deceptions where the girl would automatically trust the person offering the ride. In another sleight, the girl would think she was helping a stranger find a place of business or some other landmark.

He was stunned at how well these tricks worked. Once the girls were in the car, he would simply whack them in the face with a tire iron or, if he could find some chloroform, use that to render the girls temporarily unconscious. He preferred the chloroform, but it was hard to come by and required some diluting or the fun would be lost. After the girls were immobilized, he would cover them with a dark blanket and head for the woods.

Now distanced from the tangibility of his played out fantasies, his mind drifted from one victim to the next until he got to his freshest kill.

It was the middle of September, two years earlier, and Ruthie Sorensen had just turned sixteen. She was petite and had pale Scandinavian good looks, but she was extremely self-conscious of her lazy eye. She was a junior at Long Ledge High School, just south of Wellesport, where she was an almost straight "A" student, struggling as she did her whole life with mathematics.

She was a cheerleader for the Long Ledge Wildcats and she was also in a number of clubs that met after school. Her genuine willingness to help others and her quiet temperament made her a popular member of her class.

She dressed fashionably preferring white blouses with Peter Pan collars, bell-shaped skirts, and black and white saddle shoes. She wore her medium-long light blonde hair in a high ponytail. Though she fancied her dress as special, it was practically the school uniform of the juniors at Long Ledge High.

The Sorensen family had lived in Long Ledge for generations, with Ruthie's father tending the same land that her great-grandfather had farmed at the time of the Civil War. Her family was considered a fixture in the community, seemingly involved in everything, and sitting in the fifteenth row of Saint Peter's Lutheran Church every Sunday. Ruthie was looking forward to getting her driver's license soon. She had been up on a tractor since she was six, so it didn't seem likely she'd have any trouble with the family's Ford station wagon. She was excited, but would have to sit through the school's Driver's Education program, a new state requirement. With a little patience, she would be an accredited driver by Christmas.

And so it was that on a gorgeous September day, Ruthie left Pauline Stackmiller's house and was walking home when a stranger drove up and asked her if she knew where the Sorensen place was. A package with a farm implements company logo sat on the back seat. The young man seemed pleasant enough as he talked about being lost and squinted at a clipboard. He tipped the clipboard toward her and she could see her father's name and address—

> Mr. Lars Sorensen
> Broad Brook Farm
> 100 Broad Brook Rd.
> Long Ledge 7, Connecticut

"That's my father. That's our farm," she said without thinking. "It's right around this bend. I'll show you."

She could have no way of knowing Henry Cutler had painted the big decal on the box in the back seat as well as the logo on the invoice. The rest of the information he got from the Sorensen's trash.

She disappeared in that September's breeze and her distraught and confused family never saw her again. One neighbor thought he had seen a Ford sedan of some neutral color—maybe gray, maybe tan—in the area that day, but nothing more.

Hunters found her scattered body parts a long month later.

7

At the extreme south end of Main Street in Wellesport, there was a rusty metal sign about the size of a serving tray that read: S.B. Doyle & Son. Beneath that was the lettered declaration: Welders and Mechanics. The name board hung by a set of rusty chains from a sign gallows and a replacement a few years earlier would have been in the nick of time.

```
+-----------------------------------------+
|                                         |
|   S. B. DOYLE & SON                     |
|      WELDERS & MECHANICS                |
|                                         |
+-----------------------------------------+
```

A half-mile down a dirt road toward the river, sat the home and shop of Soapy Doyle. Soapy and Henry Cutler shared one or two talents and interests, but in actuality they couldn't be more different. Soapy was actually the "Son" on the sign, having inherited the home and the business, when his father died some twelve years back.

In school, the younger Doyle's friends sarcastically nicknamed him Soapy when it became clear to them that he never used any. The name stuck in an assortment of variations. Grammy Dunleavy called him "the soap grease man," referring to the horse-and-wagon peddlers of her childhood who trundled through the streets of Boston collecting cooking grease and selling chunks of soap. Much like the farms of the plains states, Soapy's home was small, more like a squat shack, while the business building was an enormous barn. This red-shingled affair was almost completely surrounded by the remnants of cars, tractors, small buses, trucks, cement mixers and other pieces of machinery and scrap metal. The center of this huge barn functioned as the hub of Soapy's thriving business.

In this cavernous central room, the short, fat and profane Soapy worked on all types of motors and machinery. When Soapy tuned and timed engines, words like "worked" and "labored" fell short of the mark. It was like saying that Beethoven "worked" at music, for Soapy was the best in ten counties—body and soul by Quaker State.

He had the touch, the magic fingers, the imagination and the creativity to truly understand mechanical things. When an engine made a disagreeable noise, he was likely to place one end of a broomstick on the motor, and the other up against his own ear to find the trouble. Like a doctor using a stethoscope, Soapy moved the broomstick lovingly over the different surfaces of the engine, while his brain computed the unfathomable. As tenacious as a bloodhound, he never quit until he found the problem.

In this immense middle bay of the barn, Soapy had decorated the walls and ceiling with the centerfolds of a new magazine called Playboy. He had even gone the extra step of subscribing to this scandalous publication, so that he wouldn't miss a single issue. Thanks to his own diligence, Soapy now had the best working environment in Wellesport. A whole firmament of half-naked, corn-fed, Iowa farm girls smiling down on him while he restored form and function to all things mechanical.

There sat a gold-painted 55-gallon drum in the center of the back wall that Soapy tried to use for a spittoon. The wall surfaces surrounding this cuspidor were mottled with the brown spittle of ten thousand misses, while the inside was as clean as an operating theater.

On busy days, with customers milling about, Soapy caused quite a bit of anxiety with his sloppy delivery and general lack of aim. Soapy paused cussing. The room fell silent. A low guttural sound emitted from his innards, working its way slowly to a roar, with the commingling of phlegm, tobacco, molasses and spit. With his arms half raised for balance, Soapy planted his left foot forward and arched his shoulders back. Those in his company took a long, prudent step backwards just as their mechanical friend launched this earth-colored, rolling, tumbling, showering meteorite of spittle in the direction of the cuspidor. At this point, the spectators meekly assumed their original places in life and waited for history to be made.

With its perfect parabolic trajectory and fabulous end-over-end form, this gob of immiscible juices excited the crowd, right up to the point where it touched down on the milky white kneecap of Miss February, tacked five feet to the right of the spittoon.

The assemblage groaned. Their disappointment was the heartfelt anguish of people who truly believed in Soapy and, more to the point, selfishly wanted to be there when the golden spittoon finally lost its virginity.

Some said that Soapy was the exception to the rule, while others liked to say that he was the exception that proved the rule. Perhaps it was best stated that even though he broke all the rules, he was universally loved. Vulgar and profane, ugly, fat and greasy, he was the least likely person to be loved, but for some inexplicable reason, people just loved Soapy. Wellesport would be just another mark on a map without him.

Quite apart from being able to reassemble mechanical things in the right configuration, Soapy could cuss a part off a car better than any ten blasphemous, godless sailors. It was his special gift. He would say, "If you can't cuss a part off a car, you can't be a godamn mechanic." When you heard this, the proof stood before you.

One bright September day, into Soapy's world walked Zeke Dunleavy with three friends. Soapy said that he'd be right with them, after he cussed the starter motor off the Pontiac on which he was working. To a symphony of the worst and most ill-connected profanities they had ever heard, the boys wandered around the shop dreamily admiring the gatefolds of Playboy; a veritable pastiche of pleasure—more square footage of feminine intrigue than they were likely to enjoy in a lifetime—and without the slightest chance of being caught. Their mothers wouldn't dare venture into the place, for Soapy's world was a man's world—no women allowed.

While his schoolmates wandered about, Zeke's attention was suddenly captivated by something even more engrossing than breasts and beguiling smiles. In the corner of Soapy's shop, dangling from the links of one shiny set of chain falls, hung a sight so pretty as to take his breath away. Freshly painted in gloss black paint with sparkling aqua valve covers was his every daydream condensed to steel and wire.

Drawing the attention of no one, Zeke spasmed through the grotesque lament of "never was and never will be" until a powerful linkage engaged his brain. He realized that he could forget about all the math, English and history he knew—now was the time for some applied brainpower. No sooner had the imperative jolted his brain than an idea of considerable possibility materialized. A plan. A plan hatched of desperation and covetousness, with not a chance in a lifetime of working without some powerfully persuasive missives from Zeke.

Now to convince Soapy that this sparkling, shining, gleaming substitute for 135 Belgian draft horses belonged in only one place in all the world, and that one place was the first model ever of the Dunleavy SSK Drophead Coupe.

Soapy slid out from under the Pontiac, and nodded hello to the boys as he percolated a revolting lunger of spittle. As quickly as snapping a lug bolt, he planted his left foot, and all present intelligently took a giant step backward, except Zeke. He had steeled himself to walk through fire to acquire the Olds V-8 engine dangling from the chain falls, so he couldn't let Soapy see him cower in the face of a little spittle? No sir. He was here to do business and Soapy might as well know it right off.

"So how's the godamn football team this year, boys?" asked Soapy, eyeing Zeke carefully.

"They're lookin' real good, Soapy," offered Zeke. He had to think quickly. Would Soapy resent a sixteen-year-old high school junior calling him by his nickname? Hell, nobody in town used his Christian name. What was it anyway? Besides, Soapy brought his aches and pains to Dr. Rory, so maybe, even if he erred, he would be forgiven.

Waste of thought, he concluded. Soapy's own children called him by his nickname so how could Zeke offend him by doing the same?

Zeke's plan flowered from what he sensed was a short circuit in the way people bargained for things, and his reasoning was simplicity itself. Most people negotiating to buy something tried to denigrate the item to the point where the seller might legitimately ask, "If you feel that it's such a piece of crap, why would you want it at any price?"

Zeke reasoned, "What if he built the motor up to the point were Soapy couldn't bear to let just anybody have the thing? What if he could convince Soapy that this motor represented a prized example of a 'Rocket' Oldsmobile V-8 and that it rightfully belonged in a museum? What if he could actually give this motor a pedigree, a status among engines so regal that Soapy couldn't let it go to anyone who wasn't willing to wipe it down with a chiffon rag morning and night?

"Who," he would ask Soapy "would be responsible enough to change the oil, and all of the filters religiously every thousand miles?"

"And who would change the belts once a year whether they needed it or not?"

"And who would change the plugs every five thousand miles?"

In short, "Who would love this priceless colossus?"

Who indeed?

***

On Saturday, September 20th, all over the town of Wellesport, high school juniors were eating bowls of Sugar Pops and Wheaties fortifying for the type of work generally done by experienced riggers. As it happened, this was the day Zeke Dunleavy, together with an unruly band of believers, would descend on Soapy Doyle's place of business with fifty dollars in cold cash and lay claim to Zeke's 'Rocket' Oldsmobile V-8 engine. With some stout means of transport and a little help—such as it was—Zeke would haul this marvel of internal combustion back to the barn behind the Dunleavy's place on Main Street. Just one short week out of the starting blocks and Dunleavy Motors would have the power plant for its first ever SSK Drophead Coupe.

He had already found a 1949 Olds chassis rusting away behind Artie Wheeler's barn. It had been in a rollover. The body wasn't good for anything. The motor and transmission had been sold, but he could have what remained for ten dollars. By putting the bite on Grammy Dunleavy for an early birthday present, he had his chassis.

While eating cereal, Zeke read the paper. To the right hand side of the front page, was a small article that was captioned: "GOV ACCEPTS CUTLER'S DECISION." The article went on to say that the governor would issue no reprieves of any kind for a man who tortured and killed seven young girls. End of story. It was good politics. The year after Governor Belden's election, 1955, there were fewer homicides in the United States than at any other time since 1910. Someone was doing something right.

On the sports page, he noticed that in the revival of the America's Cup off Newport, Rhode Island, the American entry *Columbia* was beating the stuffings out of the British entry, *Sceptre*. He mused, "Why does it always seem so right for us to be beating the British? Was it only the logical historical follow-up to the Revolution?"

Zeke was too excited, however, to read much of the paper. He had to prepare the transportation for his newest purchase. As he ate, he pondered his good luck. Who would have guessed that Soapy Doyle would take fifty dollars for an engine worth ten times that much? He knew people were always trying to do things for their doctors—and by extension the doctor's family—but still, this was quite a gesture. Then again, there might have been another dimension to the deal that he believed had moved Soapy in his direction. It was exactly the kind of thing Soapy admired; a young guy with a dream, against all odds, trying to do something a whole army of college-trained engineers in Detroit couldn't do right. Soapy probably didn't know the word "bravura," but it didn't stop him from understanding the emotion behind the word.

Also, Zeke felt Soapy might actually value the engine—together with his own workmanship—so much he really fancied the idea of the engine resting lovingly in the Dunleavy SSK Drophead Coupe.

Or, perhaps it was a case where the whole was bigger than the sum of the parts. Taken together, all of the little arguments formed one big argument almost as powerful as a certain V-8 engine.

Whatever the reason, Zeke didn't take his good fortune for granted. Moreover, he perceived rightly, that to ask Dr. Rory for help in getting the engine home would violate the unwritten rules of their little compact. Zeke had heard Dr. Rory quote from Teddy Roosevelt's *In The Arena* more times than he cared to remember. He took it to mean that if you wanted to be an eagle, you had to soar alone.

Shortly after breakfast, Zeke's posse gathered for the trek to Soapy's shop. They went around Dr. Rory's office and out to the barn, where they noticed for the first time a new sign over the doorway of the last bay. It announced:

The "Safety Fast" part of the sign Zeke had culled from *Great Motorcars Of The World.* In truth, it had been the motto of some long-forgotten automobile company that was sued into bankruptcy as a result of an accident. Still, he found it laudatory no one ever sued them for building cars that were too slow. It should be noted also that Zeke, ever alert to the signals of trouble in his little kingdom, perceived his mother's uneasiness with Detroit on the Pompaucau. In order to mollify her, he decided to incorporate the word "safety" into the company's *raison d'etre.* It, at least so far, was working.

Inside the bay, Zeke was cutting up 2 x 4's with a handsaw, and lashing them together with clothesline rope in a more or less square configuration. The very picture of high excitement and distended nerves, Zeke cut and lashed to the sound of The Elegants blaring from a small transistor radio on the workbench. At the end of the song, he chimed in discordantly for the final refrain ". . . where are you little sta-a-a-r?"

A 1949 Oldsmobile V-8 internal combustion engine—with transmission—tipped the scales at slightly over nine hundred pounds and, of course, it was cumbersome. Even with limited planning, a novice rigger knew it would take a transport of some considerable grit and growl to move this beast the two miles from Soapy's place to Dunleavy Motors. So Zeke Dunleavy, tops in his class and probable future valedictorian of Wellesport High School, not to be disgraced or shamed in any way, gave the matter considerable thought. Only after studying every conceivable option, did he settle on the one method of transport that would guarantee success—he chose his sister Wibby's red wagon for the job.

So it happened that this puny, hapless, vermilion metal contrivance, the serving platform of ten thousand glasses of lemonade, delivered lovingly into the gullets of traveling salesmen by Wibby Dunleavy, would be called upon for yeoman duty one last time. It stood in the center of the bay, dwarfed by the large barn, its white wheels catching the morning twilight and showing a thin layer of hard black rubber around their circumferences.

On the top of this wagon, Zeke placed the two-by-four framework and, with just a few pieces of rope and an ocean of high hopes, Zeke and his friends were on their way. The wagon, laden with the wooden superstructure, took on a heft that disguised its utter incompatibility with the task at hand.

The group assembled included Zeke, his brother Jack and eight other friends from school. With the high spirits of a Mardi Gras crowd, they marched along Main Street taking turns pulling the little red wagon. Because Zeke was the smartest and most charismatic of the bunch, it never occurred to anyone to ask about the weight of the engine or the specific capabilities of the wagon. Besides, who would want to be ostracized for bringing up such troublesome questions?

Just before 8 A.M., they reached the left hand turn to Soapy Doyle's place. They rounded the corner without even slowing down, finishing the walk in short order. When they got to the big, center bay of Soapy's barn, Soapy was sitting inside drinking coffee from a cardboard cup.

"Hell of a nice morning for it. How you doing, boys?" Soapy said cheerily.

Each of the boys answered the question in a different way, with one of the boys even saying "Fine, Mr. Soapy," at which point everyone started laughing.

"Come to take home my beautiful sumbitchin' Olds V-8, huh?" said Soapy as he got up and eyed the little red wagon suspiciously. As he walked around, great sewer noises began to percolate in his esophagus, and just like that he planted his left foot. Everyone stepped back except Zeke, and he let a morning monster chaw fly through the air. Majestic and otherworldly in its lazy flight, it disappointed quickly when it spattered on the big toe of Miss January, a good eight feet from the shiny spittoon. Soapy just shook his head the way a father does when he's disappointed in his son.

Soapy and Zeke went off to a desk to conduct their business while the rest of the boys stared in awe at the centerfolds, wandering from one to the next, bumping into each other, hormones red-lined, understanding nothing, comprehending everything, wondering everything, saying nothing. Most of them had never been to Soapy's before, and some of them had never seen Playboy much less the Sistine Chapel of gatefold art. They were mesmerized, excited and spellbound by nature's best argument.

"Let's go you guys," said Zeke, trying to break them from the powerful spell of erotica at least long enough to give him a hand.

"Whenever you're ready," said one, his eyes never leaving the ceiling.

"Back the wagon in under the motor," commanded Zeke.

What appeared to be one of the strongest of the bunch helped Zeke maneuver the wagon so that it was directly under the motor, which still hung from the chain falls. Just this small bit of activity caused the engine to spin gently in the air, giving the impression of lightness.

Now Soapy began to pull on the chains, and the motor headed for the wagon in slow motion. Because of the mechanical advantage of a set of chain falls, Soapy seemed to be working like crazy to accomplish what gravity could accomplish in a split second, given the chance. However, it was going to be very important to settle the engine down slowly if the wagon was going to have any chance at all of bearing the load.

"Down . . . Down . . . Looking nice," Zeke was giving the cadence to Soapy as this behemoth settled gently on the little red wagon. Except that after it settled, it didn't stop settling. It settled some more and still more, as all eyes were on Zeke. He was down on all fours checking the clearance from the bottom of the wagon to the concrete floor, and he kept saying "Down . . . Down . . . Down." The wagon groaned, suffering all the indignities of catastrophic metal fatigue, while Zeke kept saying, "Down . . . Down . . . Down . . ."

Finally the engine stopped moving. The clearance between the bottom of the metal wagon and the concrete floor was exactly zero and its four little white wheels pointed their centers toward the sky like as many wildflowers growing out from under a rock.

All the same, Zeke seemed pleased. The engine sat nicely on the frame of two-by-fours, and except for the fact that the wagon was crushed like a beer can, things couldn't have looked better.

After studying the engine for a bit and then studying Zeke for a while, Soapy spoke.

"Maybe it would be better if I was to deliver the sumbitch to your place with my godamn wrecker," he said hopefully.

"I was sure that the wagon could do it," said Zeke absentmindedly.

"What are we supposed to tell Wibby?" whispered his brother Jack.

"I don't know. I guess if she really wants me to, I can get her another one," Zeke said, still studying the flattened red metal under his new engine.

"I could deliver it to your house with my godamn wrecker. Even drop it into your damn chassis. No charge," said Soapy trying to headoff the gathering gloom. He hadn't planned on delivering the engine, much less helping to install it in the old chassis, but if it wouldn't get done any other way, he would do it.

Zeke snapped out of his cloud as soon as he heard the magic words "no charge."

"You would do that?" asked Zeke.

"I can't see no other way the godamn thing's going to get done," said Soapy. At this point, he began making those guttural sounds, planted his left foot, and everyone except Zeke pulled back. He let a fiery comet of molasses-soaked, tobacco sputum sail toward the cuspidor. As a whole universe of semi-clothed, toothsome centerfolds looked down lovingly on Soapy, he recorded his closest volley in years, missing by a scant six inches. Soapy smiled proudly.

"If you're serious, I accept," said Zeke.

"When do you want the sumbitch? Are the damn motor mounts on the chassis good?" asked Soapy, thinking ahead.

"Yes. The motor mounts are solid, but we have to get the chassis to our barn. We can do that today. Do you want to deliver it, say, Monday?"

"Fine by me," said Soapy.

"We get out of school at two-thirty."

"How about if I deliver the sumbitch at three?" asked Soapy.

"That'd be perfect," said Zeke.

With that, the boys took a last, longing look at Soapy's gatefold girls and started back for the Dunleavy house, taking turns dragging the crumpled red wagon, now smaller than ever. Wibby's poor, little red wagon had shown heart, but was no match for the laws of physics.

8

While Zeke called in a short lifetime of favors to speed along the production of the world's first Dunleavy Coupe, his brother, Jack, was completely wrapped up in Boy Scouts and the sport of the season, football.

The Scouts held meetings on Wednesday nights from six-thirty to eight, which worked out well, since there was nothing of value on the television, until *Ozzie and Harriet* came on at eight. If the meeting got out on time, and his parents didn't object, Jack got to see most of the show.

Jack knew his sister would agree to do every bit of housework, including any carpentry, masonry and even plumbing, if she could just watch Ricky Nelson sing his current hit at the end of the show. Though his latest song had been number one on the record charts six weeks earlier, he hadn't sung "Poor Little Fool" at the end of the show for almost two months now, so he sang it again.

Wibby never took her eyes off Ricky Nelson. Jack opened his mouth to say something in the middle of the song and practically got "shushed" to death. Wibby's world stopped cold on its axis when Ricky Nelson sang.

As with every other family across the country, the Dunleavys had more than a few battles centering on two opposing forces— homework and television. It would appear there were only a handful of options as each family tailored some form of peace treaty with this "salesman in the home."

Some people allowed their children to do their homework in the afternoon, so that they could watch their favorite shows in the evening. For others, television was completely out on school nights. To judge by the network offerings during the week, apparently most parents in America allowed their children to watch at least some television on school nights.

Father Knows Best, Wyatt Earp, Broken Arrow, Leave It To Beaver, The Real McCoys, and *Dragnet* were all shown on weeknights, not to mention *Lassie* and *Maverick* on Sunday nights.

The television created another problem that was a cinch to predict. Whose favorite show was the whole family going to watch? With three channels, conflicts were inevitable. Even before color television, many homes had more than one set.

In the Dunleavy home, it wasn't quite the problem that it was in other homes for two big reasons. First of all, Dr. Rory would much rather read and listen to an opera or a symphony in the front parlor than watch television, with two notable exceptions—he cheered lustily during the Friday Night Fights, and usually dozed through most of the baseball or football games on Sunday afternoons.

The second reason was Ann Dunleavy, who found just as much enjoyment in *Ozzie and Harriet* as her children, with a twist. Ann watched Zeke, Jack and Wibby watch television. The show mattered not at all to her.

A small diversion would be a good way to describe television for the Dunleavy boys. Jack, at twelve, was a Star Scout, and working on his ninth merit badge enroute to Life Scout. He was consumed with the idea of becoming an Eagle Scout, but particularly enjoyed the outdoor life—the hiking and camping, the jamborees. Everything about Scouting fascinated him and every summer he spent two weeks at Scout camp.

He did not know it then, but he would learn more in Scouting that he would use the rest of his life, than in any other endeavor except for his formal schooling. Knowledge and wisdom poured into his head without recognition from him at all. Scouting was a perfect combination of fun and learning that, unfortunately, has been lost or never existed in the standard educational systems.

Most Wednesday nights, Jack Dunleavy tied knots, learned Morse Code and made fires with bow and spindle and flint and steel. Sometimes, he even used matches.

All the while, the Scouts were tutored by men in the community, who gave generously of their time so that the next generation might have what someone else had given to them many decades earlier.

Jack's role models were not among his teachers at Wellesport Elementary School, but were instead the scoutmasters and assistant scoutmasters. With their help, he worked diligently to get the final two merit badges that would get him to Life Scout—Citizenship in the Community and First Aid.

He succumbed to the natural human tendency to save the two hardest ones until last, but barring the unforeseen, they would be added to his sash this autumn. He would be a Life Scout by Christmas. In the spring and summer, he planned to allow more time for camping and hiking.

Like most of his buddies, he played whichever sport was in season, and since it was fall, the game was football. He and his friends would race home after school, change their clothes, and gather in the Dunleavy's big backyard to play an acutely truncated game of football.

In their version of the game, a lone ball carrier would run up to the far back end of the Dunleavy's property, with only the railroad tracks and the Pompaucau River behind him. Then, with head down and ball tucked securely in his ribs, he would match his broken field running against the tackling skills of eight or ten defenders.

One by one, they tried to break free of the tacklers to score a touchdown, but it never happened. Actually, they could consider themselves lucky if they were brought down on the south side of the property, where it was grassy and dry.

Each runner started out toward the south property line, but more often than not, acting in rugby scrum fashion, the tacklers would bulldog the runner toward the apple trees on the north, where he would be unceremoniously ground into a pile of wormy, fetid windfalls. If you protested too much, you were called a sissy, or worse.

Jack and his friends spent long autumn afternoons, ripping the sweatshirts off one another and tearing the grass-stained knees out of innumerable pairs of chinos. The smallest runners had the largest apple stains. The most powerful runners could wear the same clothes two days in a row.

Then one breezy day, while they were running the green right out of the grass, a lone ball carrier heard a noise in the distance, and all of the players stopped and look at each other for an instant before running to the back of the property. With all heads turned to the south, they would squint to make out in the distance a familiar sight—the gandy dancers.

They always came from the south, and always in the autumn, wiggling and squirming as they straightened the tracks. First, a little to the east. The next section, a little to the west. It was a crew of six or eight men in raggedy clothes, carrying six foot long steel bars.

The Gandy Manufacturing Company of Chicago made the bars, and when these ragamuffins tucked these tools under the rails, they would give a series of herky-jerky upward motions in unison. Sometimes, they would have to do this a half dozen times in the same spot, to get the tracks back where they belonged. From a distance, with their arms and legs all akimbo and their torsos rising up and down, their writhing and jiggling resembled some kind of a dance. Thus, the name gandy dancers.

Also, they sang rhythmic chants as they worked. From a distance, they sounded like African spirituals. But up close, it was quickly evident that at least some of them had a ribald quality. In any event, the gandy dancers sang constantly as they worked.

The Connecticut Valley Railroad went bankrupt nine times in its one hundred ten year history, because it was a poorly conceived idea from the start. Unlike the other highly successful railroads in the country, the CVRR did not connect two great industrial centers. Instead, it connected Hartford, in the center of the state, with the very sparsely populated summer resort town of Old Saybrook, at the southern end of its run. Providing a breathtaking ride in the summer and fall months, it was nobody's idea of fun the rest of the year. So it went belly up, over and over again.

The great mystery was that it never wanted for entrepreneurs eager to revive the old road, only to sink into bankruptcy a few years later.

Now, on an average day, only one train went through town with no more than two cars and a caboose engaged, while Wellesport waited patiently for the CVRR to breathe its last. To keep costs down, the gandy dancers were reduced to one trip a year.

As they got closer, Jack ran back to the house. Opening the back door, he yelled to his mother, "Ma, gandy dancers are comin'."

His mother appeared, and looked out to the back of the property, where the football players were lined up across the yard.

"I'll fix something cold for them. Come inside," she said.

Ann Dunleavy reached in a cabinet and took out a bright yellow Bakelite pitcher, and a bottle of Zar-X bug juice. She mixed it quickly, and added a few ice cubes. She gave Jack some paper cups, some fig newtons and the bug juice.

Jack balanced everything against his chest, and waddled back to the tracks just in time to meet the gandy dancers as they worked their way north toward the roundhouse in the city.

The gandy dancers accepted the Zar-X with gratitude, and politely answered a bunch of foolish questions from the footballers. Just before they resumed their work, the foreman thanked Jack, told him to thank his mother, and then said, "We might not be seein' y'all again. Dis may be it."

"Whatcha mean?" asked the boys in unison.

"We ben hearin' somfin' bad wid da comp'ny. Dunno wad it means?" said the man. He gave a kind of a shrug with his shoulders and put a strange grin on his face. Jack could see that one of his front teeth was gold. He stood over six feet tall, and was a physically strong man, and he seemed unconcerned by the possible loss of his job.

The gandy dancers went back to work, chanting about their travails, as they bobbed and lowed their way up the tracks.

Jack and his friends returned to their football game, paying little or no attention to the information passed on by the man. Except to hop rides on the train, which they did from time to time, the CVRR meant little to them.

They were at that wonderful age where daily they were bathed in the naiveté of youth—the only time in one's life when everything makes perfect sense. A time, of course, before you find out that the human race isn't one big team with everyone pulling together. Before you figure out that some people are playing by a completely different set of rules. And sadly, it is long before the realization that you are not going to be immune from some of life's ugliness.

***

So while Zeke finagled assorted car parts and Jack marched toward Life Scout, twelve-year-old Wibby, together with her large circle of friends, spent her leisure time listening to the latest records. In addition, they talked about boys, experimented with their hair and danced "The Bop."

Wibby alone had a considerable collection of forty-fives, bought with her allowance. Now that she could baby-sit, it was only a question of time before she had the largest collection in town. If she bought the records at a discount store, like Kresge's, a single hour of baby-sitting would pay for one forty-five.

Her tastes ran mostly to the Everly Brothers and Ricky Nelson but she had "Tammy" by Debbie Reynolds, "To Know Him Is To Love Him" by The Teddy Bears, "Who's Sorry Now" by Connie Francis, "Twilight Time" by The Platters, and at least one record by every other top ten recording artist. Naturally, she had Elvis in spades; "Your Cheatin' Heart," "Love Me Tender," "A Fool Such As I" and more.

Her friends brought over their records as well. They made a special effort not to buy the same records and, by shopping together, were able to accomplish this fairly easily. Wibby's friend from next door, Laurie Cooney, was the least of her problems when it came to repeats. While everyone else was in love with Ricky Nelson, she would buy records like "Purple People Eater" by Sheb Wooley or "Witch Doctor" by David Saville. You couldn't even dance to the records that Laurie Cooney bought.

Friends and manners being what they were, Wibby felt obliged to play one of her records now and then, just to keep the peace.

Everyone in the group felt a little sorry for Laurie Cooney. Here was the prettiest girl in town, who dressed like a rag doll, bit her nails, and didn't know the first thing about make-up, or anything else that should be of interest to a young girl. She mostly said nothing, staring out the window, floating through life, always a million miles away.

Her father "Big Bill" Cooney was a self-centered martinet. It was no secret that he drank constantly and had more different jobs in his forty years than Dr. Rory had tongue depressors. He was six foot three inches of starch and shine, red-faced blarney and violence. The Dunleavys, more than once, watched in horror as an enraged Big Bill kicked his sons down the back stairs with his heavy Irish brogues.

Birth control was one of those things that people rarely talked about. The Catholic Church—"Holy Mother the Church"—in a simple and loathsome effort to win the battle of the cradle would not allow the flock to practice birth control. Millions upon millions of families had more children than they could financially or emotionally support.

In a cruel refinement of the torture, The Church told the blessed congregants that they could practice "the rhythm method." A woman would monitor her cycle and then only have sex during the safest times of the month. The method worked for a scant few, with some wealthier women seeking abortions under procedural pseudonyms, and poorer women finding themselves with one more mouth to feed.

The Pope and his people in Rome must certainly have had access to at least as many medical experts as other organizations of comparable size, and therefore, knew that "the rhythm method" was a sham. It didn't matter. They sold it like corn flakes.

Thus Big Bill Cooney came home, night after night, three sheets to the wind, and horny. The end result—thirteen kids and counting. Veronica Cooney spent what little free time she had in Saint Michael's Church making novenas, while Big Bill occupied himself with life in saloons. When they finally got together, it was to grind out more papists in the deep swale of their four poster—the best Catholics in Wellesport.

The townspeople, both high and low, had a not so deeply hidden contempt for Veronica and Bill Cooney. People just couldn't understand their utter stupidity and lack of common sense, but one and all, felt a deep sadness for the children. Everyone sensed that no good would come out of such an ill-assorted collection of humanity. A drunken father coupled with a religious zealot for a mother, often managing neither enough food nor clothing. Into this mix, combine the quiet despair, anger and violence that are the inevitable by-products of such madness.

At least presently, Big Bill had a job selling Yellow Pages advertising and the family had enough to eat. The paint would peel off the house, and the kids would go to school with holes in their clothes, but at least their bellies would be full.

To add just a touch of hope, the oldest son would graduate from the high school this year, and join the Navy. The craziness would continue, but it would only be 12/13ths as bad.

While the townspeople did feel sadness for the Cooney children, their classmates couldn't help but pick on them for their odd family size, and their messy appearances. One of the farm kids had a pig, which he named Veronica, and when her time came, he named all the little piglets after the Cooney kids.

There were others though who befriended the Cooney children, particularly the girls. The mothers of Wellesport would sneak a little sampler of toilet water into the pockets of the Cooney girls' coats, when they came to visit their own daughters. Or they might plan a trip to the store, to coincide with a visit by one of the Cooney girls. They couldn't just sit by and do nothing, while they had the wherewithal to help in some way, however small.

9

After having breakfast with his wife and kids, Dr. Rory went into his office to call his answering service and to retrieve his black medical bag. Every morning before he went to the hospital he would call his answering service to see which of his patients were in the hospital and for what reason. Some of the admittances he knew about, because he had authorized them. Others were emergencies, which he knew nothing about. The call to his answering service eliminated surprises.

He pulled apart the two top sections of his leather medical bag and checked the different compartments to make sure there were plenty of bandages, gauze, finger cots, syringes and drugs.

After replenishing his supplies as needed, he closed up the small compartments, pulled the two halves of the top of the bag together and turned the clasp to lock it.

After thirteen years, he had grown tired of lugging around this cumbrous medical bag, but whenever he was given to such feelings, he would remember his fellow resident, Ed "Monty" Montgomery, who brought the house down one day when he observed that, "A good actor never forgets his props." Dr. Rory smiled gently at the memory and darted back into the house. On the way he grabbed a small pile of manila envelopes and folders of x-rays and charts.

Enroute to the kitchen, he stopped at the hall closet to select the appropriate suit coat and hat. On the way to the back door, he leaned down and kissed his wife, Ann, who was sitting at the kitchen table and mumbled something about seeing her later in the day.

He then pushed the button in the mudroom, which activated the electric overhead door opener out at the barn. Ann Dunleavy had bought him the opener as a Christmas present, two years earlier. It was a Delco Automatic Overhead Garage Door Opener, and the very first one in town. She claimed to have nightmares of him suffering a heart attack while pulling open the heavy garage door. So, she had bought him the opener.

Dr. Rory wasn't really a person for frills, but had learned to love the electric opener. Not that he had much choice, but he'd bought

Ann one the following Mother's Day, and had it installed in the bay where she kept her station wagon.

His Buick Special was kept behind the barn's first door where, two hundred years earlier, the original owners of the property, kept their horses. Ann Dunleavy kept her new Mercury Voyager station wagon in the second bay. The third bay had been a catchall for lawn and garden equipment, but now doubled as the home of Dunleavy Motors. There had been no need to dress up this third bay, so it still had the rickety, swinging doors on it.

Dr. Rory had a few minutes before leaving for the hospital, so he walked the extra thirty feet, and pulled aside one of the barn doors to inspect Zeke's car-building experiment.

He could hardly believe his eyes. Only one week into the production, and his oldest child had managed to assemble a complete chassis with four wheels, gas tank, radiator, engine, transmission and drive shaft. He even had the steering wheel set up.

Of course, once the skin had been torn off of the old chassis and the motor installed, most of the heavier work had been completed. All the same, it was quite a shock to realize that if Zeke were of a mind, he could probably take the bare bones machine out for a ride that very day.

Dr. Rory made a mental note to talk to Zeke about not using the car until it was completed. He walked back to his own car still shaking his head. He put his bag on the floor behind the front seat, started the engine, and left for the city.

As he drove, he lit a Camel, and absentmindedly listened to the patter of Wellesport's most famous citizen, Dick Bolt, the radio announcer for WCT-AM. His surname was a long hard-to-pronounce Polish name, so he simply changed it. He was just clever enough to convince his audience that he was really a dullard—always picking the loser in a race, a fight or a ball game. He even had his friends throw lavish dinners, where he was awarded trophies for picking the most losers in a single year. In this way, he could tell corny jokes, dumb stories, and use nauseating puns with impunity. People, regardless of their mental acumen, could listen to him secure in the knowledge that they were smarter than he was, which generally was not true. But it worked all the same.

Bolt's only rule, which was perfectly evident yet never scrutinized, had to do with his material. He used only that which was completely wholesome. Adults listened to his show in the tens of thousands throughout the capitol region of the state, but children could listen too. And did.

The first order of business after the news at 5 A.M. was the reading of the hog prices. Following them, he read the prices of corn, wheat, barley, soybeans and even eggs.

Dick Bolt had tailored his show like a journeyman corsetiere, catering at each different hour to a distinct segment of the population. As a result, he was successful beyond measure. On the air, he was avuncular to a fault.

Dr. Rory would see him sometimes at 5 A.M. on a Sunday morning, riding his bicycle around the streets of the old village on the one day he wasn't on the air, and the man wouldn't even lift his head to say hello. One day, just to get a laugh, Dr. Rory said to him, "Hey, I know you . . ." and just when Dick Bolt looked undone with discomfort, he said, "You're Jack Paar." Dick Bolt never even cracked a smile. He just continued his cycling.

Despite this little defrocking, Dr. Rory listened like everyone else to the reassuring baritone voice of Dick Bolt.

Zeke's progress with the automobile was gnawing at his father though. At the rate he was going, he'd have it completed by spring, maybe sooner. As Dr. Rory obsessed on the problem, almost as if by magic, the face of one of his patients flashed up in front of his eyes, just as lifelike as if the man were really there—Salvatore Rucci.

A few years after he had set up his practice, a man came to him with back trouble. Fortunately for the man, it proved to be only a muscular problem. His job as head of inspections for the Motor Vehicle Department, required him to spend a little too much time bent over the hoods of automobiles, and this had caused his back trouble. Nonetheless, with orders from Dr. Rory to lose some weight, coupled with some exercises to be done every morning, the back trouble subsided. Naturally, the man was grateful. He swore by Dr. Rory, and sent his wife and kids to see him at the very hint of illness.

Dr. Rory decided that he would call Salvatore Rucci and make sure once and for all that even if Zeke's car emerged with the engineering of a Mercedes and the élan of a Rolls Royce, it would fail inspection like a ruptured Fiat. While Zeke papered his walls with inspection failure papers, Dr. Rory would be right there to commiserate with him. Irrespective of the shameful duplicity of his plan, at least it would keep Zeke off the streets of Wellesport with "that thing," as he began to think of it, and alive until he got to college.

He arrived at Saint Joan d'Arc Hospital, and drove directly to the doctor's parking lot. It was the closest lot to the building, and if some errant motorist should park there without the blue sticker on his windshield, his car would be towed away faster than you could say "AHHH." The doctors were, of course, the royalty at Joan d'Arc, but it wasn't unearned.

In addition to the long years of study and dedication that it took to become a doctor, and a lifetime of carrying around other people's problems of the most intimate sort, whenever the little sisters of Saint Joan d'Arc initiated a new building drive, they shook-down the doctors unmercifully for a large chunk of the construction money. The little sisters weren't a bit shy about it either.

So the doctors who roamed the halls at Joan d'Arc had a real sense of ownership as everyone in the place said, "Yes, Doctor," "No, Doctor," "Can I help you, Doctor?" Over the years, some of the more cynical nurses at Joan d'Arc would joke about which doctor had the worst case of "white coat psychosis." Dr. Rory liked to think that he had not a trace of this "white coat psychosis," but in some people, it just manifested itself a little later.

He went to the doctor's lounge, put his hat on the rack, exchanged some pleasantries with the other men in the room and then departed to begin his rounds.

As he walked, he opened the folder for Billy Anderson, an eleven-year-old whom he had actually delivered back in 1947, when he had barely begun his practice. Billy's father had been the mailman, delivering all sorts of letters and packages to his tiny office next to the seed store, in the days after the war. Ted Anderson took a great liking to Dr. Rory and asked if he would attend his wife, when their new baby announced its pleasure. Dr. Rory had delivered a number of babies as an intern, and therefore, agreed immediately. Even as he accepted the honor, he knew delivering babies would not be possible if and when his waiting room got full. A doctor couldn't rush off in the middle of the day for a long and irksome delivery, when there were a dozen patients waiting to see him. Except for Shelly Oleski's nocturnal surprise, Billy Anderson had also been his last. Now, Billy had fallen out of a tree, and suffered a compound fracture of his right tibia. An orthopedist, Dr. Ennio Patrissi, had reasembled the mess with some stainless steel screws, and put Billy's leg in a full cast, which was now slightly elevated to ease the pain.

In the lower right corner of the chart, in his almost illegible handwriting, were three cryptic lines—

> Ted and Helen.
> Billy, pitcher
> NY Giants, Gifford

Dr. Rory turned the corner into Billy Anderson's room, put on a big smile and joked, "You're never going to get the Cy Young Award like this. You'll be pitching for the Altoona Beavers."

Billy Anderson looked at Dr. Rory, and smiled broadly. It was the first time he had smiled since he fell out of the tree.

Dr. Rory grabbed the chart hanging on the end of the bed, commandeered a straight back chair, pulled it up next to his young patient and sat down.

He now took on a more solicitous tone when he asked, "So how're you feeling, champ?"

"I'm feeling good," said Billy. "Leg kinda hurts."

"The first day after surgery is the toughest. Lots of bone and tissue trying to repair itself."

As he looked at the chart, Dr. Rory feigned seriousness and said, "Well, Billy, looks like you created quite a problem for Dr. Patrissi. You used up all of his stainless steel screws. He's probably at the hardware store right now buying more."

Billy smiled again, but then changed his tone and asked, "Dr. Rory, how long will I have this cast on?"

"Well, it usually takes about eight weeks with a compound fracture. When someone's young and strong like you though, it often takes less. Look on the bright side—at least you won't miss any Giants games on television. You can watch Frank Gifford try to earn his nine thousand bucks."

Billy happily understood that his doctor knew all about his likes and loyalties.

"Are your mother and father still around?" asked the Doctor.

"They went home, but they're coming back this afternoon," said his young patient.

"Well, I'll talk to them later then. Is there anything that you need?"

When his young patient said no, Dr. Rory rose and replaced the chair and the chart. "I'll make sure that you get the prettiest nurses and I'll look in on you tomorrow," he said with a grin.

"Thank you, Dr. Rory," said the boy. And just like that, the good doctor was off to see his next patient.

As he sauntered down the hall of the hospital, Dr. Rory smiled gently and considered what a great time it was to be practicing medicine. Billy Anderson's leg had been set by Ennio Patrissi, the best orthopedic surgeon in the capitol area. The most caring and professional nurses that money could buy would watch over the boy twenty-four hours a day and his parents would hover over their son like horseflies in a stable, satisfying his simpler needs. He was completely unnecessary to the recovery of this little boy and yet the insurance company would pay the entire tab for him to look in on his little patient each day, for as long as he was in the hospital. The family would be grateful to God they had a doctor who cared so much, and blessing of blessings, he never had to mention money to the family. His services wouldn't cost them a dime.

He reflected back on his own childhood, when a kid had to actually be in the throws of a death rattle, before the family would break down and take him to the doctor. No one had health insurance and doctors of all specialties frequently got paid in chickens, apples or whatever the family could scare up. Many bills went uncollected for years, but still it was considered extremely bad form for a doctor to put a lien on someone's home. It simply wasn't done.

Now, thanks to World War II, he got a first-class medical education and his patients got health insurance through their employers. A man who owned a factory couldn't raise wages during the war, so in order to keep workers from defecting to other companies, he plied them with benefits—paid vacations, sick days, extra holidays and health insurance.

He took the elevator up two flights to visit an old Italian patient of his, a woman who was suffering from congestive heart failure. Breezing off the elevator, he opened her file, and peered at the lower right hand corner. It read—

Rosie and Carmine
Red peppers-cellar, knitting
Carmine, mechanic
Tony, Angie, Paulie.

He closed the file and rounded the corner into her room.

"Buon giorno, ragazzina. Come stai?" Over the years, he had learned how to carry on a limited conversation in about ten different languages, in an effort to put his patients more at ease. The romance languages were the easiest, because so many English words were derived from the original Latin. However, German and some of the Slavic languages had been tougher. All the same, he prided himself on the effort.

As a further stimulus to learn a little of these languages, he recalled the experience of another general practitioner, many years his senior. This physician had a Spanish-speaking patient who left him after twenty-five years. The reason? She said, in all that time, he had not learned to speak Spanish! Lesson learned.

He didn't feel he had to know anything more than "Hello," "Good-bye" and "Where does it hurt?" but the value of these few phrases was incalculable. Even small children smiled and accepted him openly, after they heard this big bear of a man speak in their native tongue.

He grabbed the chart and a wooden chair, and pulled them up to the bed, where he began to talk more intimately with the old woman. They had conversed for a while, when into the room walked her husband, a little man in workman's clothes with a jeff cap in his hands.

Dr. Rory rose and held out his hand.

"Buon giorno, Carmine. Come stai?"

"Buon giorno, Dottore Dunleavy," the man said reverentially, as they shook hands. He was one of a handful of patients, who simply refused to call him Dr. Rory. It actually humbled the doctor that this man would address him with such dignity. The man even gave a slight bow, as he shook the doctor's hand.

"Carmine, si accomoda, per favore," said the doctor.

With this, the man pulled the other wooden chair over to the bed and the three of them began a conversation—in English this time. Dr. Rory produced a pen and a pad of paper with the Pfizer pharmaceutical logo in the upper left hand corner and began to draw. At the center of this paper, he drew a frontal view of the human heart, even taking the time to shade in some of the contours, as he talked. In the simplest of language, he gave them a lesson in cardiology, patiently answering all of their questions, as he drew.

Using his naturally gentle manner, he explained to them that, unfortunately, there was very little that medical science could do for Rosie. Her heart was slowly losing its ability to pump blood, in the exact same way that any pump loses its ability to move fluids, as it begins to wear out. That was why her hands and feet were cold, why she had trouble breathing, and why she was becoming forgetful. The blood simply wasn't getting to all the organs in the quantities needed to make them function properly. Everything would be done to keep Rosie comfortable, but once she got home, she would not be able to do much of anything. The work of running the house would fall to Carmine and his three children, if they could help. Dr. Rory knew that all the children were married now, and had families of their own, but they would simply have to pitch in.

He finished with his examination of Rosie, merely listening to the faint sounds of her heart with his stethoscope. He kidded with her about her hot peppers, which she hung to dry on strings in her basement. He told her that he liked hot peppers too, but that he got tired of closing the bathroom window the next morning, so that the neighbors wouldn't hear him screaming. Then he turned to leave.

Carmine and Rosie grinned at the doctor's humor. It was the thing that Dr. Rory had come to admire the most about his Italian patients. He called it their "noble earthiness." Another Italian patient had told him when he first started his practice that the Italians had an old expression, which loosely translated meant "There's nothing new in the world. It has all happened before. ."

As he left her room, in her thick accent, Rosie said, "Thanka you, Fathera Dunleavy. Thanka you so much, Fathera."

Many of his elderly Catholic patients mistakenly called him Father Dunleavy. He didn't even bother to correct them anymore.

Dr. Rory was aware that Carmine was following him into the hall, and indicating with a gesture that he wanted to talk with the doctor privately.

When they were sufficiently alone, the man asked Dr. Rory if it would be too much on Rosie's heart if he married her. For a moment, the men just stared at one another.

"You mean exchange vows again?" Dr. Rory said.

Carmine lowered his head and said, "No." He went on to explain that when he and Rosie got to America, they had the clothes on their backs and nothing else. They both went to work immediately. Two, sometimes three jobs just to make it in America. They assured each other that they would get married, albeit at some later date. Despite the best intentions, they never did get married. Once the kids came along, it would have proved too big an embarrassment. Now, after sixty years together, they wanted to get married.

What could he say? Dr. Rory told him that he thought it was a great idea, and by all means, to do it. He did, however, warned him, that if they had a simple ceremony right there at the hospital, it would be much easier on Rosie's heart, than a church service.

Carmine thanked the doctor profusely for his approval, and turned to re-enter his soon-to-be bride's room.

Having seen the only two patients he had in the hospital, Dr. Rory strolled to the doctor's lounge, where he fetched his hat and retraced his steps to Wellesport.

10

As he guided his two-tone, powder blue and white Buick into Wellesport, Dr. Rory Dunleavy couldn't help but notice the difference in the streets, yards and houses. Where the city could support only the rudiments of foliage, Wellesport fairly exploded with towering oak, maple and elm trees. The lawns were all mowed beautifully, with plantings of every sort completely surrounding the houses, barns and outbuildings—ivy, pachysandra, forsythia, trailing arbutus, bougainvillea, rhododendron and the state flower, mountain laurel, to name just a few. The city was black and white and Wellesport was Technicolor.

Women hung out their wash, as they did in the city, but instead of three clothes lines atop one another pyramiding thirty feet into the air, the lines were tucked with great delicacy behind trellises and hedgerows. Ladies even hung their lingerie behind the protective cover of sheets, and other bedding. It was considered courteous to be mindful of the sensibilities of others.

The last mile of his drive, which brought him up to the prison, was a joy—a daily confirmation of his decision to start his practice and raise his family in this beautiful river town.

As he motored down City Line Avenue to the west of the prison, he could see two trustees working in the fields. A Canuck named Frenchie and a voluminous dark-skinned man named Ruppert were using scuffle hoes to keep down the weeds, until the last of the squash and pumpkins could be harvested. The trustees planted acorn, zucchini, and summer squash. They also grew two different types of pumpkins—sugar pumpkins to make pies for their own dining tables, and Connecticut field pumpkins, which they wholesaled to the town's farmers, who in turn, sold them to the locals for jack-o'-lanterns.

The prison industries program had deals with outsiders all over the state, which kept the prison operating only slightly at a loss. People unfamiliar with the prison system were always surprised to learn that from 1827 until the Civil War, the prison actually turned a substantial profit each year.

Dr. Rory had attended Frenchie about a month ago, after he had taken a clubbing from Benko Sadek. One of the local kids, with an afternoon newspaper route, had been giving his extra papers to Frenchie in exchange for baseballs, which had been hit over the walls into the garden. Prisoners were not allowed to have uncensored newspapers or magazines, so Frenchie had taken a few blows on the head from the Dep.

Feelings for Frenchie ran high in the prison though, so Benko had decided that after two days in the hospital and one week in the hole, he would return him to his chores in the garden.

Frenchie and Ruppert were considered as harmless as little idiot kids, when in fact they had both killed their wives. In each instance, it was a case of wild passion coupled with temporary insanity. They would do long years in prison, but the likelihood of either of them reoffending was not even to be considered.

The Frenchman was dealt about the cruelest blow that a married man can receive. He had a job bulling around the huge rolls of newsprint at the *Enterprise*, the morning paper, which went to press at midnight. His shift ran from eleven at night until seven the following morning.

During the course of the shift, a couple of wise guys were spreading the word that they had found a housewife who would take on all comers for two bucks a head. When the ugliest and simplest dope in the place started bragging about his experiences, Frenchie just couldn't believe it. The moron, not to be dismissed so easily, offered to take Frenchie to the place. The next night, this idiot walked Frenchie right up to the front door of his own apartment!

Frenchie, unfortunately, kept a gun at home, and with little in the way of discussion, shot his wife stone cold dead.

Turning his car east on River Road in front of the prison, Dr. Rory pulled into the main entrance, and past the well-tended flowerbeds, until he reached a small cul-de-sac at the main door.

Ordinarily, this front driveway was used exclusively by the state police, who were either dropping off prisoners or taking others out for court dates. Still, there were a few parking places against the curb; one for Dr. Rory, one for the part-time prison dentist, Dr. Feldman, and one for a general surgeon, Dr. Belanger, also on the staff of Joan d'Arc, who worked for the prison system on an as-needed basis.

There were a few extra spaces for visiting dignitaries like the governor, should he ever decide to visit. With Governor Belden, it seemed most likely that he would show up when the next riot was completely under control, but before the local television cameras stopped rolling.

Dr. Rory shut off the engine, grabbed his bag and strode to the front door of the prison.

The ivy on the brownstone walls rustled in the brisk fall breeze, as he pushed the bell. In an instant, a turnkey named Charley opened the door for him. He was escorted to the next set of gates, which would get him to the corridor that led to the hospital. He still, however, had not entered the cellblocks, which were behind a third set of gates.

As he walked down the corridor, he passed all of the different administrative offices, the chapel, the library, the commissary and a number of other rooms. The hospital and bughouse were in the same building, which stood on the far west end of the administration building and fronted the large exercise yard.

If a prisoner hit a foul ball near left field, it would hit the hospital and bughouse. The hospital occupied the lower level, while the bughouse took up the whole upper floor.

Despite its depressing surroundings, the hospital was actually set up for a variety of situations. It had its own x-ray equipment, a small lab to do simple tests, electrocardiogram and electroencephalogram machines and thirty beds. The nurses—only male for obvious reasons—provided pretty good care.

As Dr. Rory entered the large ward, he removed his hat and exchanged greetings with the hospital superintendent, a man named Foley. Then, he turned immediately to check on what he considered his most serious case, Anthony Schiarbo.

A week before, when Dr. Rory had seen the beat up inmate for the first time, he didn't think that he would be able to control his anger. After attending to Schiarbo's wounds, the doctor demanded to speak to the warden right away. Before even looking at his other incarcerated patients, Dr. Rory stormed back to Warden Stoner's office at the center of the administration building and raged for the better part of an hour. He talked about the immorality of beating prisoners half to death, the unconscionable inhumanity of this type of treatment and the complete lack of necessity for this brutality as a form of punishment.

This was not the first time he attempted this conversation with Harvey Stoner. Dr. Rory had attended to four others beaten almost as badly as Schiarbo in the three years since he had been the prison doctor. Still, he had never seen anyone as badly broken as Schiarbo.

Unfortunately, Dr. Rory's ranting didn't affect the warden at all. Harvey Stoner, in the very same soothing tones that Dr. Rory used on his patients, explained the system of rewards and punishments, which had proven effective over a very long period of time. He empathized with the doctor's position, but had no intention of changing anything. As far as Warden Stoner was concerned, Schiarbo got exactly what he deserved. As a matter of fact, he was grateful to the inmate for practically volunteering to be the poster boy for bad behavior. He had played the part of the miscreant beautifully and the prison had been quiet as a monastery ever since.

Warden Stoner sensed that the outrage the doctor felt might cause him to try to contact the governor or the prison board, so he disabused him of that possibility while he had the chance. He explained to Dr. Rory that the governor would not even discuss the issue as long as the prison was quiet, and the prison board served at the pleasure of the governor. Case closed.

Dr. Rory Dunleavy stalked back to the prison hospital with a sense of impotence that he just could not abide. He cursed Benko Sadek for the sadistic animal he was and Harvey Stoner for the spineless bureaucrat he had become. Laterally, however, his steps slowed and he regained his composure.

He knew there was nothing he could do that day and he had patients to see. He went back into the hospital, just as today, and did the job that he was trained to do.

Nonetheless, it stuck in his craw. He had to find a way to put an end to the senseless beatings and he made up his mind to do just that.

Anthony Schiarbo's injuries had begun to heal nicely, and left no apparent problems except for the change in his dentition. Still, that did little to change the way Dr. Rory felt about the situation.

Today, he attended to the dozen or so prisoners in the hospital without any difficulty. There was nothing more serious than an old lifer with emphysema. He was already on oxygen and cortisone and there was little anyone could do for the man. He would die soon and, having no family, he would exit the brownstone walls in a pine box, to be laid to rest in the prison cemetery not fifty yards from where Frenchie and Ruppert tended their garden. There would be a small service, with a prayer from the chaplain, but no headstone.

Dr. Rory also examined two new prisoners who were undergoing their two weeks of mandatory quarantine.

Then he made a quick trip to the solitary confinement cells, far removed from the regular cellblocks and below ground. An inmate in solitary sat on the floor of a five-by-twelve cell for anywhere from five to thirty days. He got bread and water twice a day and a full meal every fifth day. State law required that a doctor examine him every day.

Finally Dr. Rory returned to the prison hospital, gathering up his hat and bag, and left for the front entrance. It was eleven o'clock now. He was running late as usual.

By driving east on River Road and south on Main, he turned left into his own driveway just a few minutes later, guiding the car slowly up the gravel drive on the south side of his office.

Ann Dunleavy's car was gone. She was food shopping, getting her hair done or running any of a hundred other errands that kept the Dunleavy household going.

It was his upbringing not to waste electricity or cause machinery to wear out before its time, so he left the garage door up for now and tramped to the back door of the house.

Entering the kitchen, he walked to the front hall, placed his hat on the rack and proceeded through the front parlor. Just before entering his office, he stopped at a mirror. Pulling a comb from a case in his pocket, where he also kept pens, a thermometer and a penlight, he ran it quickly through his prematurely graying hair. That done, he opened the door, put his bag on the small table in his consultation room and sat at his desk to sort through a pile of messages from his nurse, Marie Fortunato.

It was the usual pile of requests for prescription renewals, business cards from the detail men who the drug companies sent, requests for consults from families, and on and on.

A small inanity popped into his head. The makers of every sort of elixir and potion, from the ridiculous to the sublime, told the public in their television ads to "consult with their family physician," as if he had all the time in the world. His waiting room was quiet, but he knew it was full.

There was a light knock at the door. Marie Fortunato poked her head in. They caught up on a few things, and then she said, "Mrs. Gravely is in 'two.'" His real day was about to begin. He would shuttle from one examining room to the other until about six o'clock, when Marie would lock the door, after hanging a little sign on the outside explaining that the doctor was gone for the day. He cleared up some paperwork, said goodnight and walked back into the house.

He snuck back into the house at about one-thirty to grab a sandwich and, later in the day, he called his wife on the telephone just before going in to see his last patient. He did this each day, just to let her know when to expect him for dinner. On nights when he was extremely busy, he would tell her to start without him. To the extent that he had any control over this though, he tried to keep it to a minimum. The vast majority of men in the country were able to enjoy dinner with their families, and he wanted no less for himself.

Marie Fortunato would lock up the office, just as she would be the one to open it the following morning. She lived with her husband, Joe, only about five blocks away on Church Street, and she walked both ways. She liked the walk, and felt that it helped to keep her weight under control.

Marie had gone to the nursing school at Joan d'Arc, but couldn't adjust to the rotating shifts at the hospital. After suffering through her third cold in a year, she jumped at the chance to go to work for Dr. Rory, when he first started practicing. They got along famously, with him doing the examining, and her doing everything else. She was the soul of discretion, empathetic and caring to the patients, while at the same time, she could throw a detail man out of the office with such diplomacy that he thought leaving was his idea.

Dr. Rory paid her higher than any other nurse working in a doctor's office, although he couldn't keep up with hospital pay. For Marie Fortunato, though, a lower wage presented no problem. She loved her job.

¶¶

On the last day of September, a Tuesday, Zeke Dunleavy sat in his second period English class, waiting to read his latest composition.

Their first assignment of the year had been to describe life inside of a ping-pong ball. Prior to this exercise, the class had complained bitterly to their new composition teacher, Mr. Gilpin, for his bleak imagination, so he pulled out all the stops to try and excite his band of semi-illiterates. The second assignment was to describe what life was like in the Japanese city of Hiroshima immediately after the atomic bomb was dropped.

Most of the essays were predictable in their descriptions of the mayhem, pain and suffering, droning on and on.

With Mr. Gilpin convinced that they would have been better off with more ping-pong stories, he called on Zeke.

"Mr. Dunleavy, if there is a merciful God, he will allow you to end this torment posthaste. Please, thrill us with your vast and colorful imagination."

"Yes, sir," said Zeke as he made his way to the front of the room. If Zeke had been listening carefully as he walked, he might have heard the sound of Dunleavy Motors hitting the scrap heap along with Auburn, Duesenberg, Packard and a whole parking lot of other automotive losers. His little essay was about to seriously imperil the viability of the Dunleavy Coupe.

Unfortunately, Zeke heard nothing, save the sound of his own voice, as he introduced his classmates to his Japanese wife, Yoshi, and his two little Japanese children, Mamiko and Miyumi. He then took them on a guided tour of his, now completely flattened, paper house on the outskirts of Hiroshima, and somberly into a rapidly descending tale of woe about his life, and dim prospects for the future.

The essay began to resemble those of his classmates, and Mr. Gilpin had begun to squirm in his seat, as Zeke delivered the final paragraph.

Ever the optimist, Zeke and Yoshi with their two kids, Mamiko and Miyumi, had decided that they were lucky to be alive, and that with a little perseverance they could build a new—and maybe even better—life. With the help of Buddha, they would pull themselves up by their sandal straps, and start the rebuilding process. This very day, they would pack up what few possessions they could salvage, and move in with his wife's sister in the beautiful seaside city of Nagasaki.

When Zeke finished, the class laughed for the better part of fifteen minutes. Everyone, that is, except Mr. Gilpin. He asked to see Zeke after school.

By the end of the day, the story was all over the building, with Zeke elevated to mythic status among the would-be school wits. The ruling class at Wellesport High, unfortunately, took a different view of the incident.

These things are almost impossible to calculate, but apparently by their lights, thirteen years was an insufficient period of elapsed time between the deaths of two hundred thousand human beings, and the piercing wit of one Rory Dunleavy, Jr.

They saw no option, but to call a parent-teacher conference to adjust Zeke's sensibilities.

Naturally, Zeke thought that they were making "a federal case out of it." Nonetheless, the principal, Mr. Guilmet, made a call to the Dunleavy house, and out of respect for the doctor, made an appointment for eight o'clock that evening in his office at the school.

***

Dr. Rory and his wife, Ann, arrived at the school, and went to the principal's office. Zeke had already pled his case to his father, so that there would be no surprises.

They listened quietly, as Mr. Guilmet did indeed "make a federal case out of it." He was the most difficult man with which to have a conversation, for he twitched around in his seat, as if he was sitting on carpet tacks.

Dr. Rory had been in the Army, and knew all about mindless bureaucrats. He also knew that, to mix a metaphor, "Nobody ever won an argument with a bureaucrat." Therefore, he and his wife listened quietly, asked what seemed to be serious questions, and shook their heads soberly as this fool discussed their son.

The meeting lasted for about a half hour, at which time the Dunleavys walked back to their car, closed the doors, and roared with laughter.

If for no other reason than to save themselves from Act II, they asked Zeke to send any future efforts at black humor to Mad Magazine, and give the reactionaries at Wellesport High something a little more serious.

In the end, Dunleavy Motors was never in the balance.

***

The following day, Dr. Rory was in the middle of office hours, when Marie Fortunato pulled him aside between patients, and handed him a telephone slip. He read it quickly, and then assumed a pained expression.

Slipping into his consultation room, he dialed CHapel 9-5741, which he had memorized by this time. A golden-voiced hostess answered the phone, "Ucello's Oyster House."

The doctor responded, "Yes. This is Dr. Rory Dunleavy in Wellesport. Can I please speak with Vito Ucello?"

"Yes, of course, Doctor. One moment, please." The woman had that knowing sound in her voice.

Presently Vito Ucello said, *"Buon giorno, Doctore. Come stai?"*

"Bene. Bene," said Dr. Rory. Then he told Vito of his last trip to his restaurant, and how much his wife had enjoyed the fried clams.

"Alla da way froma Nova Scotia," boasted Vito in his thick accent. "Everya day," he added.

"Well, Ann just couldn't stop talking about them, and my swordfish was excellent too."

The two men talked on and on about food and the restaurant business, the way men do when they are not anxious to get to the real point of the call. Finally, the doctor realized that he had patients to see, and his task wasn't getting any easier. At last he said, "Has my mother been in for lunch with her girlfriends lately?"

"Yes, Doctore. She wasa here today. She hada da scallops. I prepara them myself. *Molto delizioso.*"

"Tell me," said the doctor delicately, "Was she a little . . . ahh . . . short on her bill."

"Ah, yes. Unfortunat-a-ly, she was shorta abouta tena dolla."

"Well . . . How about if I send you a check right now, and we don't tell the old girl. Would that be all right with you, my friend?"

"Thata be justa fine. Youa gooda son," said the restaurateur.

"Thank you," said Dr. Rory. *"Buon giorno."*

It had been a family secret forever, unwillingly shared by Vito Ucello, that Bridgett Dunleavy occasionally had light fingers. Selectively would be a better word, for she never stole a thing in a department store or drugstore—not even a lipstick. However, when she went to lunch with her girlfriends or would take Ann or Wibby out on their birthdays, she just couldn't help herself. She had begun with just the condiments, then a saltshaker here and a peppershaker there. Lately, after the meal, she would slide everything that wasn't nailed down into her oversized handbag.

She had furnished her home with Ucello's flatware, plates, glasses, sugar bowls, and spice shakers—even the ice cream sundae stemware.

Her luncheons had become embarrassing little crime waves — "take Willie Sutton to lunch day." At seventy-five years old, it wasn't likely that she was going to change, so Dr. Rory devised a plan that had worked reasonably well over the years. First, he enlisted the help of Vito Ucello in squaring the books without any fuss; and second, whenever he talked to his mother, he would mention some new restaurant, which was getting good press.

The second half of his plan was enormously successful on two counts. To begin with, he knew that his mother was a stickler for matching place settings, and she liked Ucello's food, so poor Vito was destined to be the target of this geriatric scofflaw. Secondly, he knew his mother to be as recalcitrant as a bad case of hemorrhoids, so all he had to do was mention another restaurant in passing, and she would keep going to Ucello's forever or until they ran out of tableware, whichever came first.

By his own calculation, he had sent Vito a king's ransom over the years, in dribs and drabs, not to mention the money he and Ann spent in the place, just to keep this little charade going.

The one thing he wouldn't do, though, was confront his mother. He loved her too much to humiliate her, and at her age, that was the only thing that would be accomplished. This farce would be kept up until she was a hundred, just so long as she never found out that he knew. Sometimes, it even seemed funny, just so long as his mother didn't decide, one fine day, to try another restaurant. He would worry about that, if and when, it happened.

12

Benko Sadek sat at his desk, looking at a sunrise and sunset timetable in the Farmer's Almanac. It was the beginning of October, and he was thinking about the change back to Eastern Standard Time. Morning yardout could remain the same, but the afternoon exercise period would have to be moved up a bit.

After morning mess, the inmates were brought back to their cells for the second count. There was a count at sunrise and then a count back at their cells after every meal—four counts a day. After this second count, the morning yardout could proceed as usual, since official sunrise was never any later than 7:20 A.M. After yardout, the prisoners went directly to the shops.

As the deputy warden, he had to have finely tuned antennae. The mess hall was the worst place of all, with most riots beginning there, and almost always on the hottest day of the year. August was the month to really pay attention. They had even tried a system, where the prisoners would eat in shifts during heat waves. It hadn't helped. Without any sort of air conditioning anywhere in the building, tempers were short, even among the staff.

As he studied the Almanac more closely, he could see that the change back to Eastern Standard Time would be 2 a.m. Sunday, October 26th, two weeks hence. Time would turn back an hour. The inmates would have to leave the shops at three o'clock, to finish yardout by four-thirty P.M. The prisoners' total work time on winter days dropped to a scant four and a half hours.

It seemed to him like some recurring nightmare, that just as he solved one problem, another appeared. In this case, the full moon was only two days after the clock change, and again, the guards would have to be told to be on the alert. It sounded like an old wives' tale, but on the nights of the full moons, the prisoners were unusually restless, and thus, prone to trouble—and not just on that night, but the day before and the day after as well.

One prisoner acted so badly three days before the full moon, he invariably landed in solitary. It took Benko a number of months before he finally saw the pattern, and took the steps necessary to help everyone out of the situation. In this case, the prisoner voluntarily went to the hole for the day.

It was the nature of the job. Each prisoner was a special case, which might at some point require an unusual bit of attention. Most, as might be expected, had problems, directly or indirectly, related to spending long periods of time in a cage. Each of them dealt with the problem differently. In truth, about sixty percent of the prisoners had serious psychiatric problems, which society chose to ignore. So, the Dep's job could be doubly hard, especially when dealing with a psychotic troublemaker, as he feared was the case with Henry Cutler.

Just the thought of this butcher made the Dep decide to go check on him. He folded a pile of notes that he was working on, put them in his shirt pocket, grabbed his fedora, and headed for the hall. He would inspect the shops while he was out on his rounds.

Walking from his office, he came to a stairwell that led to the first floor near the main entrance. By going through the east cell block and the laundry, he would arrive at death row—ten lonesome cells, five on each side, with a sixteen-foot wide corridor between them. The lone jailer on duty sat at a desk near the end of this corridor, doing nothing.

As soon as Benko entered the chamber, the guard rose to his feet, and he and the Dep talked quietly for a few minutes.

Benko walked over to Cutler's cell, asked him how the accommodations were, and if he needed anything.

Henry Cutler thought for a minute and said, "Love to have some paintin' materials."

"Against the rules," said the Dep. Benko took great pleasure in depriving a sadistic killer like Cutler of something as meaningless as art supplies. Besides the clothing on his back, the only thing that a condemned man was allowed to have was a Bible, a toilet kit, and letter writing materials. Still, just as with the other prisoners, he was only allowed two letters a week.

"No problem. I've done without before," he said as he smiled at Benko.

"Are you going to be one of those pantywaists who changes his mind at the last minute and decides to appeal his sentence?" asked Benko mockingly.

"Nope," said Cutler bravely. "I'm in it 'til the end."

The Dep couldn't help but admire his stoic stance. Still, he didn't believe that Cutler would hold up. He'd seen this jailhouse valor before, and he'd seen it disappear like a morning mist at the first light of day. He would wait and watch, with a strong emphasis on the word watch.

He knew, in his heart that Cutler would find a way to squeeze through a keyhole given the opportunity, but he still couldn't figure out how Henry Cutler expected to escape from death row.

Even if Cutler had friends on the outside, storming the prison had never been tried, because of all the gates at the two entrances. Going over the wall, during his one-hour solitary yardouts, seemed just as implausible. It was a straight up, thirty-foot climb, with an armed guard watching every second. No hope there.

Every time he visited death row, he tried to put himself in Cutler's place. Not accepting the free appeals work of Connecticut's smoothest-talking lawyers was either madness or part of a plan. He had learned to distrust prisoners' decisions that seemed to be against their own interests.

From death row, he walked out into the small, attached exercise yard. It could fit inside the infield of the regulation baseball diamond, at the other end of the prison. The ground was just dirt, but even if time were not a factor, it would take a week to tunnel under the walls, which went ten feet into the ground.

The Dep wondered if Cutler knew that the walls went so deep into the ground. Perhaps, it would be wise if he had one of the guards casually mention it to him, during his yardout.

The walls, indeed, went well into the ground, and flared to a width of six feet at the bottom. The face of the walls was as smooth as brownstone and mortar could get, and as straight vertically as a plumb line. It was a beautiful, professional job done entirely by prisoners in 1827.

There were no windows, and only one door leading to the exercise yard—the one that he had just walked through. In addition, the inside of the walls were clean—no down spouts, no vines to grab onto. There was ivy on the outside, but he couldn't see how that would be of any help to Cutler. Benko just shook his head, and went back into the death row cellblock.

The Dep's last stop would have been the cells set aside for female prisoners—only ten cells, just south of the death chamber—but these inmates were transferred to the new Niantic Women's Prison in 1930. When the women were there, pink curtains hung inside the bars, and the women were allowed to close them for their private business. It was in these cells that Connecticut's infamous arsenic ladies spent the bulk of their lives.

Amy Archer-Gilligan, the inspiration for the comic play *Arsenic and Old Lace,* poisoned about twenty boarders at her Windsor nursing home before she was tried and sentenced to prison for the rest of her days. It is thought that her total body count approached thirty, counting the patients she poisoned at her first nursing home in Newington. Her last few years were spent at the Middletown Hospital for the Criminally Insane. She died in 1962 at age eighty-nine.

"Arsenic Annie" Monahan of New Haven killed three husbands and a niece before she was sentenced to prison in 1919 for the remainder of her natural life. "Arsenic Annie" was transferred to the new Niantic Women's prison in 1930 and died there just after she turned ninety.

Easily the most attractive murderess to do time at the Wellesport prison was Lydia Sherman of Derby. Newspapers called her "beautiful and vicious." In all, she poisoned three husbands and ten children. Sherman actually escaped from the prison in May 1877, but was soon recaptured at a boarding house in Providence, living under an assumed name. Lydia Sherman eventually died of old age, and without anyone to claim her remains, she was laid to rest in the tiny prison cemetery near the warden's house.

Seven other murderesses, Lucina Coleman, Lorena Alexander, Kate Cobb, Catherine Dunn, Bessie Wakefield, Lillian Manson and Hannah Donovan—most of whom preferred arsenic—did long stretches at Wellesport prison, each with the blood of a single victim on their hands.

All these women were lucky. Since 1663, when two women, Rebecca Greensmith and Mary Barnes, were convicted of witchcraft and hanged from an elm tree on the Albany turnpike, no women have been executed by the state. For whatever reason, capital punishment in Connecticut has been strictly reserved for men.

Walking back through the laundry, Benko stopped to talk to the guard on duty. A snitch had informed Benko that new prisoners were bribing the inmates on laundry detail to bleach their clothing, so that they wouldn't look so obviously like the new guys on the cellblock. He wanted this cigarettes-for-bleach trading to stop.

Ordinarily, Benko wasn't opposed to these little side industries, because it kept the prisoners occupied. In spite of this, and because of their proximity to Henry Cutler, he wanted to keep the laundry crew on a short leash. Shirts, pants, and sheets all made perfectly adequate ropes in a pinch, so everything was counted and double counted as never before.

From the laundry, Benko went back through the east cellblock, and the cell room, which everyone called "Grand Central Station" because it was the confluence of the east and north cellblocks and the administration and hospital wing, on the west.

He turned to his right, and strolled the entire length of the north cellblock, and back again. It was still early, and the prisoners were in the exercise yard. He could hear a low din through the west windows, but beyond that, the three tiers of cells on each side were eerily quiet.

He went back to Grand Central, and headed to the west. The first person he met was the chaplain, whom he did not get along with particularly well. Chaplain Noel Eggars was nature's opposite of Benko Sadek—small, frail, ascetic, and prone to neurotic twitches.

The Dep always felt like he needed a drink after spending any time at all in the company of the chaplain.

He'd had run-ins with this meddling little turd many times over his treatment of the prisoners. Serious arguments ensued after Anthony Schiarbo received a dose of his wrath, back in September. Finally in exasperation, Benko had lowered his ruddy, contorted face over the chaplain's upturned, feminine features, and barked at him, "You take care of their fuckin' souls, and I'll take care of their fuckin' bodies." The good cleric had scurried off, in a trembling, stuttering rage.

Now Reverend Eggars wanted to tell the Dep that a prisoner's mother was on her deathbed, and this inmate wanted special permission to attend her funeral when the time came. The Dep knew the prisoner well. He was a long timer, but had adjusted to prison life fairly well, giving little trouble. Still, such a request could only be granted by the warden, which was a good thing. If the warden decided to let the prisoner attend the funeral, it would be a situation fraught with problems. Obviously, the prisoner would not be wearing handcuffs at the service or the gravesite. It would also tie up two guards in plainclothes for the day. And last, but not least, what about all the other prisoners whose mothers died, while they were behind bars? Should they allow any and all prisoners to attend their mother's funerals?

"Tell the prisoner to make a formal request to see the warden," Benko told the Chaplain. "It'll be Harvey's call."

Actually, any prisoner could see the warden with a grievance or request at any time, by simply informing the head guard on his cellblock. The requests didn't even go to the Dep. They went directly to the warden. And this warden maintained an open door policy, whereby he would meet any request for an audience—no exceptions.

This prisoner was smarter than the average inmate, though. In order not to offend Benko Sadek, he funneled his request up through channels, rather than go over the Dep's head. Usually Warden Stoner gave an inmate a mountain of lip service and nothing else. Who knew how he would handle this one?

By the time the Dep finished talking to Reverand Eggars, yardout had ended, and the prisoners shuffled off to their respective shops. Benko watched as prisoners marched past him for the print shop. He followed the guards into the shop, where he took a quick look at the place, and then spoke to the head guard. They had to raise their voices over the clang of the letterpress printing presses, which had begun their day's labors. They were small presses, which could print only one page at a time, but the prisoners managed to do all of the printing for a dozen state agencies, all of the forms and handbooks for the prison, as well as the prison newspaper, the *Cardinal*. It was a weekly paper, just four pages, but it gave prisoners all the information they needed about the past week, and the menu for the week ahead—a small sense of normalcy in a sea of isolation.

When Benko left the print shop, he exited a side door into an outside courtyard, which led to the shirt factory. Except for the cellblocks and the administration building, it was the biggest structure inside the prison. This factory employed one hundred prisoners, who worked six days a week, turning out the clothing, kitchen, and bedding needs for the entire prison. All new prisoners started in the shirt shop.

Besides the prison's needs, the inmates in the shirt shop made clothes for outside jobbers who paid the state for their services. The state paid the prisoners—fifteen cents a day. Just as in any garment factory, there were cutters, sewers, pressers and boxers. The whole third floor, a space the size of a basketball court, was dedicated exclusively to the making of buttonholes. The Dep loved this building. It teamed with energy as piles of useful, rugged clothing were turned out in complete vocal silence. The inmates, with the use of elaborate hand signals "asked" other prisoners for more fabric, thread, buttons or whatever they needed. The efficiency of the shop fascinated and pleased the Dep.

He dawdled for a while inspecting a shirt here, a pair of pants there. "Beautiful work," he said almost inaudibly.

Unfortunately, there were no garment factories in the central Connecticut area. Upon release, how many of these cons would drift into New York, where they could put their newfound skills to productive use? Probably very few. Unlike the trustees working in the kitchen—who could later get a job at any diner in the country— these prisoners were learning a dead-end skill. What would happen to these men? The prison authorities knew only too well.

Benko had been in the shirt shop long enough. It was time to get moving. He walked back into the courtyard, and sauntered farther to the north, near the wall, where there was a small cluster of buildings. The bathhouse and the storehouse would be empty, but he had to check on things in the solitary confinement building.

One guard, seated at a table in a dark, airless room below grade, greeted him in a whisper. Each cell in solitary was sealed off from the world by two plate steel doors, so the three prisoners in the cells didn't even hear him enter the building.

All three of the prisoners had pulled two weeks for fighting, so the Dep looked in the guard's logbook to make sure that Dr. Rory was checking them each day. He also wanted to make sure that no one was sneaking them any food.

Benko continued on his rounds, circling the north cellblock, which came to within twenty-five feet of the wall. He then entered the carpentry shop, another place he loved. The never-ending whir of heavy machinery excited him. The inmates assigned to this shop produced a respectable catalog of beautiful products, and the added bonus of transferable skills gained, was icing on the cake.

He walked up to a middle-aged man, totally engrossed in his work at a wood lathe. The inmate was making one of the oak blackjacks, that the guards used to club the prisoners, when necessary.

The inmate noticed the Dep, and Benko pointed to the embryonic blackjack, and then at himself. The prisoner smiled a big smile, and waived both his hands in an exaggerated sign for "No." Benko gave the inmate a slight, twisted grin, and moved down the line.

At the center of the carpentry shop, a prisoner was assembling the most intricate little jewelry box that Benko had ever seen. It was a solid cherry item, half the size of a shoebox, with twelve delicate drawers, their insides covered with stuffed pink satin. The drawers could be pulled open with tiny brass and tortoiseshell handles. He stared in wonderment. It was like finding a Swiss watch in a pile of pig shit. He made a circle with his index finger and thumb indicating the A-OK sign, but the man just stared back blankly as if the Dep were an intruder.

It reminded Benko of a hard fact of prison life. All of his charges had many different sides to them, as indeed every human being does, but very few people on the outside have been to the raw places that these men have. Get sentimental in here, and you put your life in danger.

He could complete his morning tour with just one last stop at the prison kitchen, a little to the southeast of the carpentry shop. He walked slowly soaking up the warm October sunshine.

Benko entered the kitchen as some of the prisoners were still washing breakfast trays in a massive, hand-operated dishwasher. A larger contingent of inmates was engaged in the business of preparing lunch. Today, it would be potato soup and tuna fish sandwiches. Milk or coffee—they pick.

Typically, the kitchen baked three hundred loaves of bread a day, and cooked two hundred twenty-five pounds of beef and ten bushels of potatoes for a single evening meal. Beyond that, they canned fruits and vegetables grown in the fields around the Wellesport facility and the prison farm in the northern part of the state—mostly apples, tomatoes, peaches, squash, carrots, and spinach. Altogether they put up one hundred eighty-five thousand #10 cans of produce annually, enough to fill thirty railroad cars.

He spent a great deal of time with the guards on kitchen duty, because the dining room was the heart and soul of the whole prison. It fed the nine hundred odd prisoners as well as the guards, and any of the administrative staff that cared to eat. It was a mammoth operation, with plenty of temptation for shady deals and the stealing of food, spoons, cups, and even metal trays.

Every deputy warden in the country knew that the first item on any "list of complaints" during a riot was more and better food. And, as stated, that riot would have started right here in the dining room.

When the prisoners were eating, ten guards manned the catwalks which completely encircled the big room up above, while another twenty guards stood with their backs to the walls, blackjacks at the ready, on the dining level.

It just wasn't possible to overemphasize the importance of this one room in the prison.

Finally, Benko said his good-byes, and strolled back to his office. There would be a pile of paperwork to attend to before lunch.

13

It seemed that a kid named Gino Finelli loomed everywhere, at least as far as the Dunleavys were concerned. He and Zeke Dunleavy had toddled around in diapers together, and been the best of friends ever since. Gino was never the intellectual peer of Zeke, but he more than made up for it in charm and humor. Particularly humor.

It was standard procedure, when Dr. Rory and his wife, Ann, went away for any reason, Zeke would stay at the Finelli's house. Of course, the reverse held true as well.

It was during these overnight forays that Zeke noticed a mammoth difference between the Dunleavys and the Finellis.

One Saturday night, when Zeke and Gino were in the eighth grade, Zeke was "sleepin' over" at the Finelli's place, while his parents were at a medical seminar in Chicago. Mrs. Finelli always prepared sumptuous meals, with unheard of names like Stuffed Peppers alla Turka, Risotto Paesano and Ossabuco Milanese. Zeke stuffed himself like a visiting sultan. After dinner, the whole family watched television much the same as Zeke did at home, finally retiring at eleven o'clock.

No sooner were they all tucked in, when Mr. Finelli let out a thunderous detonation of a fart. It shook the plaster walls, and coaxed small giggles from the room where Gino's two sisters slept.

In due course, Gino answered his father with the flatus of a ruptured wind tunnel—a blast to render an eiderdown quilt worthless.

Just when Zeke thought that the last volley of the night had been spent, Gino's sisters started in with the small, dainty offerings of young girls. In short order, these were drowned out by Mr. Finelli's absolute last and final comment on the matter—an deafening explosion that tested to the limit the frangibility of the fenestration.

Zeke buried his head under the covers in laughter. It was as if a southbound gaggle of Canadian geese had nested in the rafters for the night.

The following morning, he dreaded going down to breakfast, envisioning recriminations of every sort. But when he entered the kitchen, everyone was busy reading the Sunday papers, and silently eating sausage and eggs. The girls were making some comment about the Dodgers, their favorite baseball team, while Mrs. Finelli stood at the stove cooking more eggs.

She said good morning to the two boys, told them that everyone was going to the nine o'clock mass, and then continued with the cooking.

The only remark concerning the geese in the rafters was when Mrs. Finelli said that she thought she was on Omaha Beach the night before. Everyone laughed, and then simply continued what they were doing.

Zeke was amazed. Here was a group of people who considered the human body, and all its shortcomings, just some joke by the Almighty. Human beings had these fabulous brains that could dream and construct everything from airplanes to antibiotics. Indeed, it seemed that almost every day another secret of the universe was solved. Even now, all the talk was about putting a man into outer space. And yet, humans were trapped in bodies that functioned little better than those of barnyard animals.

In the Dunleavy household, it had all been disguised to the point of denial, whereas the Finellis treated it all as humorous. It didn't take Wellesport High's future valedictorian long to realize which deference to decorum made him more comfortable.

Mr. Finelli never got past the fifth grade, but what he lacked in book learning, he more than made up for in affability and common sense. He wasn't about to spend his whole life worrying about such small things.

He, together with his brother Rocko, owned an auto junkyard in the city. They had acres and acres of wrecked cars, which they cannibalized daily to meet the public's need for used parts. Their land was along the Pompaucau River in the low-lying meadows, for which they paid almost no taxes, because it had a tendency to flood. Actually, the land had not flooded since 1938, but it was still considered enough of a threat to keep the taxman at bay. The Finellis also had a company policy, whereby they would never pay for a vehicle. They would steer their wrecker to almost any state in the Northeast to get a wreck or an abandoned automobile, but would not fork over one thin dime in compensation. So with low taxes, and a free inventory of parts, they did very well.

Gino Finelli had worked at his father's junkyard since the fifth grade. It would be a mistake, however, to assume that he was the coffee boy. He actually donned a green shirt that said "Gino" over the pocket, and worked hard removing car parts and waiting on customers.

Occasionally during the summers, when Zeke wasn't working at Zemel's drugstore, caddying at the country club or mowing lawns, he would visit his friend at the junkyard. The two would bounce along the long dirt roads between the rusted skeletons as Gino removed a wiper motor here or a radiator there. It was actually great fun, bombing along in a 1943 Plymouth with no doors, no hood and no trunk—just a front seat, a drive train and four wheels.

Gino drove like a madman, as they splashed through the deep puddles that never seemed to dry up, and once in a while, ricocheted off some wreck positioned too close to the road.

It was during these rides from the Pontiac section to the Cadillac section that Zeke first got the idea to build a car using— what else?—the parts from countless skeletons of other cars. One day, while Gino was getting a brake drum from a 1949 Cadillac, Zeke noticed two other Cadillacs almost side by side. There was a 1946 Coupe de Ville, with its whole back end completely crushed, and a little further along the row, another 1946 Coupe de Ville, with its front end demolished. A little knowledge, some labor and paint, and presto, a whole new car would be born.

Slowly over the years though, Zeke altered his original concept, and decided that if he ever did build a car, the body of the car had to look like the 1929 Mercedes SSK—the most beautiful car ever built. As long as you were going to put in the effort, why not have the finished product resemble the best? The idea for the fiberglass body came with Chevrolet's contribution to the sports car class— the Corvette.

Released in 1954, the Corvette was the very first fiberglass car. It had a steel frame, and the usual amount of chrome and glass, but the skin was all fiberglass. The best part, as far as Zeke was concerned, was that fiberglass could be had for a fraction of what steel would cost. It was difficult to work with, but at least it wouldn't break the bank.

Now at sixteen, Zeke and Gino were still as close as ever, and thank God, because Zeke was going to need Gino's encyclopedic knowledge of cars to chase down all of the parts necessary to build his dream.

Having assembled the major components of the chassis and drive train, it suddenly dawned on Zeke one unusually chilly morning, that fiberglass could not be fabricated in cold weather. As his next task, he had planned to run the miles of wires that even the most rudimentary car had, but realized that he had better get the skin on the car before it got too cold. If he didn't move quickly, he'd have to wait until spring.

This was especially true in Zeke's case, because the method that he was going to use to create his body parts had never been tried before, and probably never would be again. He would mold the parts by placing a rubber sheet and then some fiberglass fabric on the fenders and running boards of another Mercedes. By slobbering the whole mess with fiberglass resin, he could mold each part in about fifteen minutes.

His only problem was finding another old Mercedes. This was harder than one might imagine in an agricultural town like Wellesport. Even when farmers took their wives to the store, they used pick-up trucks. Their family cars weren't always a step up.

That said, when the state bought Benko Sadek's property decades ago, an old rusty Mercedes—up on blocks in a small garage at the back of the property—came with the deal. The cottage had belonged to a seed salesman who inherited the motorcar and planned to restore it one day. Sadly, the man ran out of days and the restoration never took place. It wasn't a 1929 Drophead coupe, but an earlier Mercedes with similar fenders and running boards. With some imagination and hard work, Zeke could make these parts work.

The families living near the prison would have seen Zeke darting into the garage during the daylight hours, so he had to execute his plan under the cover of darkness. By sneaking out of the house after supper, when he was supposed to be doing his homework, he could zip into Benko Sadek's garage without being seen. By the beam of a small flashlight, he could mold the necessary body parts, wait the prescribed minutes and scoot. He set to work.

Benko Sadek would be well on his way to a drunken stupor and probably half asleep by the time Zeke arrived. The plan worked to perfection . . . for a time. Through the spaces in the wooden doors on the front of the garage, Zeke regularly stole quick glances at the back of Benko Sadek's cottage. All went well.

Then one night as Zeke was busily smearing the fiberglass resin on one of the running boards, he heard Benko's back door slam. He doused his flashlight and froze, with his heart racing. Heavy footsteps followed. They got louder and louder as Zeke cowered in fear. Zeke had heard stories about the Dep's violent streak and was paralyzed by the thought of Benko's fists. Had Benko seen Zeke's light? Had he heard something? What would he do to Zeke?

After one, two, three . . . five agonizing minutes, Zeke heard the familiar sound of household trash crashing into a galvanized steel barrel on the west side of the garage—only three feet from where he was crouched! Except for the thin wooden wall of the garage, Benko could reach out and grab Zeke. A few minutes later, the Dep's footfall could be heard again as he made his way back to the cottage. Finally the door slammed again. Zeke took a full breath for the first time in ten minutes.

 Back at Dunleavy Motors, in the weeks ahead, Zeke used tongue depressors, wire and glue, to cobble the parts together in much the same fashion as a crew of paleontologists would hold together the remains of a dinosaur on exhibit in a museum. Lastly, all he had to do was fill in the empty spaces with more cloth and resin, and the auto's body would be ready for sanding.

It sounded very simple, but the whole process took more than six weeks. For Zeke though, the riskiest part was done.

One item puzzled him. He wanted a wooden dashboard for his car, but a nice piece of mahogany or walnut, custom cut, drilled, and varnished would cost a fortune. Ordinarily, that is. In Wellesport, there was a resource that most towns lacked. There was the carpentry shop at the prison with expert woodworkers and time an irrelevancy. Zeke bought a couple of packs of cigarettes and approached Frenchie, while the latter was winterizing the warden's house. He showed him the drawing of the dashboard that he wanted, complete with ten coats of varnish, sanded lightly between coats.

Frenchie studied the plan, simply said, "I know a guy," and took the cigarettes.

***

At the intersection of Church and Main Streets, about an eighth of a mile to the south of the Dunleavy's place, stood a small block of stores. Next to Lundi's five and dime was a small food store called Wellesport Grocery. On the north corner of this block, and closest to Church Street, Wellesport Drug Company conducted business.

The store was owned by Saul and Meyer Zemel. Veronica Cooney called them the "most Christian Jews" she ever met. They had come to Wellesport after the war, and bought the store from a man named Courtney. From the very beginning, it promised to be a bigger success than it had already been, because the first things that the brothers did was lengthen the hours, expand the soda fountain, and offer free delivery of prescriptions. The decision to expand hours was rather fortuitous.

One morning, Meyer's wife had a stomach pain nonpareil, and she prevailed upon her husband to run down to the store at five-thirty in the morning, and get her a palliative. When he got to the store, Meyer was surprised to see a man named Charley McGinnis, standing outside the place.

As a result of the war, Charley McGinnis couldn't sleep worth a damn, and wound up walking the streets from first light every day. After walking for a time, he would wind up at the Wellesport Drug counter for coffee and donuts.

Charley worked at an insurance company in the city, and aside from his insomnia, was as reliable as the noon air horn from the prison. Sensing a golden opportunity, Meyer asked him if he would like to have a key. He could open the door at five-thirty, or whatever time he got there, and have all the free coffee and donuts he wanted, if he would just wait on the few customers who might show up at that hour. Charley agreed, and by offering a similar deal at night to Charley's friend, Curly O'Connell, Wellesport Drug Company was open from five-thirty in the morning until eleven o'clock at night, seven days a week. The Zemels would work as the druggists and managers, from eight in the morning until eight at night, splitting the hours between them as best they could.

Because their drugstore, with its inviting soda fountain, was now open almost eighteen hours a day, it became a huge gathering spot, and the revenues rose accordingly. Still, the drugs, the perfume, the cigarettes and the whiskey alone couldn't make the store a gathering place. A great lunch counter, with lots of fresh coffee, roast beef and pastrami could. And did.

As soon as he turned sixteen, Zeke had walked into the Wellesport Drug Company, and asked Saul and Meyer for a job. The place was completely full of workers of every description, from the girls who worked the perfume and gift counter, to the old-timer who drove the delivery car. There were soda jerks, cooks, cashiers and bookkeepers. That didn't even count Charley and Curly, the two war vets who opened and closed the store. All the same, when Zeke asked for a job, the two brothers took a fast look at one another, and said, "Sure, we've got something for you." Two smart druggists weren't about to turn down the son of the doctor with the biggest practice in town, now were they?

With his newly printed social security card, and a clean shirt, Zeke took his first real job as a soda jerk for seventy-five cents an hour. The Zemels, being extremely sharp businessmen, told Zeke Dunleavy the same thing they told every new soda jerk. Employees got their food at half price, but they could have all the free coke they wanted.

Each of the soda fountain apparatuses delivered a different flavor of syrup, so the first thing any new soda jerk did was make a cherry coke, and then a strawberry coke. Next, a butterscotch coke and a vanilla coke. And finally, high on the wild side, a chocolate coke.

The average soda jerk was in the bathroom retching his guts out within two hours of starting the job, with Saul and Meyer feigning sympathy. They were, however, happy in the knowledge that their new soda jerk wouldn't be consuming any of the profits for the better part of a year.

Zeke actually caused the Zemels some real concern, for near the end of his first day, he was still swilling down chocolate cokes like a circus performer. As the clock inched toward six, with only ten minutes to go in his shift, and whole hours ahead of the previous record holder, Zeke stopped what he was doing, turned white as his apron, and dashed for the bathroom. The Zemels slept well that night.

Zeke eventually became the utility infielder of Wellesport Drug. He checked in the orders from the distributors, stocked shelves, ran the cash register, swept the floors, and drove the delivery car. For sheer variety, it was a great job, and Zeke loved it. In addition to the money, on any given day, he got to see about five percent of the normal people in town, and one hundred percent of the characters.

14

In the second week of October, Pope Pius XII died, and Veronica Cooney put on a display of lunacy fit for an asylum. She draped black crepe over her front door, and dressed all of her girls in black. It actually became a subject for betting, as to how long the crepe would remain draped over her front entrance.

The people of Wellesport did not wear their religions on their sleeves, and distrusted people who did. With thirteen children, Veronica Cooney was already suspect.

She didn't even know how long she was going to keep the black crepe flying, but when the smoke from the chimney in Rome came out white, two and a half weeks later, she took advantage of the opportunity to remove the mourning cloth. Angelo Giuseppi Roncalli became Pope John XXIII, and Veronica Cooney was delighted that such a humble and holy man had ascended to St. Peter's chair. How she knew he was humble and holy was anybody's guess.

Just to get her mind off the suspense in Vatican City, Veronica took Wibby Dunleavy and some of her girls, in her run-down station wagon, to Havens Farm to get some pumpkins for the front steps. They would carve them just before Halloween, so that they wouldn't rot. While they were there, Wibby bought some apple cider for her family. Her father particularly liked the sweet taste of the pressed apples. He would have a glass or two as he watched the football game on Sunday afternoon.

In the month of October, one of the never-ending chores seemed to be the raking of leaves. The Dunleavys set up a conga line, and raked the leaves up the backyard toward the river. At the very top of the yard, was a rubbish barrel with holes punched in it. Leaves were systematically fed into the flaming barrel, and fall clean-up's smoke signals billowed out to the Pompaucau.

Every weekend in the fall, some absentminded homeowner would leave his fire unattended just long enough for a spark to get loose, and burn his whole backyard, or a nearby field. The peaceful autumn afternoons were interminably punctuated by the sound of the fire horn from the prison. Then, almost simultaneously, fifty of Wellesport's volunteer firefighters would come screeching up to the fire, pop open their trunk lids, pull out their orange coats, and put out the blaze. They were a dedicated bunch, who saved the town enormous sums of money over the years, by relieving Wellesport of the responsibility of hiring a full time fire company.

Each time there was a fire, Speckie Deagan's filling station all but closed down as his mechanics jumped into their cars, and sped down Route 5 toward the trouble. Customers, no doubt, wondered what became of their bills, if their cars happened to be on the racks when the horn went off. It was a tribute to their undying good sense, that no one ever mentioned the matter. If, in the course of a year, their bills were ten dollars higher than they should have been, it was a small fraction of an investment in a full time fire company.

The people of the town continuously walked about, but in the fall, spending time outdoors was a gift from the Almighty. Ah, to breathe in the crisp air and smell the reassuring aroma of burning leaves. It was euphoria itself to witness first hand the spectacular alizarin crimsons together with the cadmium yellows and oranges, all blended majestically with the sap green holdouts, as Mother Nature had her orgasm.

Autumn always seemed like a time of great excitement, as men climbed ancient wooden ladders to clean gutters, and to change the wooden screens over to glass storm windows for the winter. Outside faucets were shut off so as not to freeze, and some people put bales of hay around chicken houses and barns, in an effort to keep their livestock from freezing to death. Areas prone to drifting sprouted snow fences, and some of the residents even built little teepees out of two-by-fours and burlap, to shield a favorite bush or shrub. Even though this beautiful season was the harbinger of tough time to come, the residents of Wellesport were in high spirits.

The town encouraged competition for the best front lawn Halloween decoration. It began, as many of these things do, with one neighbor simply trying to outdo the other. They were, undoubtedly, shamed into full battle mode by their children.

Sensing the need for order, Wellesport's annual Halloween contest was taken over by the local Grange, which insisted that for an entry to be considered, it had to cost, in toto, less than three dollars. This was the price of a couple of pumpkins, and three or four bales of hay. Still, the entries were awe inspiring, and if the participants didn't cross the line on the budget, they certainly nudged it severely. Mostly on Main Street, the displays gravitated towards the sublime, ranging from the characters of popular movies to mythical animals, like Pegasus the Pumpkin and the Headless Horseman of Sleepy Hollow. This last entry turned out to be the winner, and it won hands down.

It stood in the middle of the front lawn at the Prendergast's house—a huge, straw stallion and rider, with an enormous pumpkin held up as if ready to be thrown at Ichabod Crane. Racing *à cheval* is the cowardly Ichabod. His mount is at the side yard, with only its upkicked derriere to the viewer. Very clever.

***

Jack Dunleavy's scouting troop declared a tradition that the last camping trip of the year would be held the third weekend in October. Across town, Troop 85 used to have a winter camping trip in January, until it began to resemble the ignominy of the Valley Forge experience around 1777. A couple of the more level-headed fathers got together, and put a stop to it. There were no merit badges for frostbite.

Jack eagerly looked forward to this October expedition. He sharpened all his knives and his hatchet, polished his hiking boots, and even covered them with a water repellent just in case of foul weather. He checked his tent and sleeping bag. It seemed to him that every thing was in tiptop shape.

The scouts in Troop 33 were divided into five patrols of six boys each. Each patrol would choose a separate campsite, dig their own latrine, and cook all their own meals. So naturally, each patrol would have to have a complete set of kitchen utensils, pots and pans, and so forth.

It was agreed that on Thursday night before the big weekend, all the members of Jack's patrol would meet at Walter Knight's house to fill the backpacks, and make the final plans. Wally Knight lived on Standish Street, which was a side street off of Main, and only a stone's throw from the Dunleavy's place, but because Jack had all the cooking gear, tents, and shovels, he asked his mother to give him a ride.

Ann Dunleavy was happy to oblige. She would have liked to be a part of the Boy Scout experience, but it was for men and boys only. She would have to be content with lending a hand to her daughter, Wibby, and her Girl Scout Troop. In her mind though, the Girl Scouts' activities were scaled back considerably from the boys and she would have preferred to be with the boys.

Ann Dunleavy had been raised on a farm in New Hampshire, the only girl with five older brothers. By the time she reached her full stature, she could outwork any of them, and very often did. Much has been written about tomboys, often implying that the feminine side of a particular subject was small to nonexistent. This was not the case with Ann Dunn Detweiller. She was one hundred percent of both. Her father saw to that. He used to say to her, "We can always use a good hand, but remember, I've already got five sons."

While her brothers went off to agricultural schools, her father convinced her to go into nursing. "Better future," he said. Taking his advise, she packed off to Massachusetts General Hospital School of Nursing, where she got good grades, and Dr. Rory Dunleavy. She was four years younger than him, but the years on the farm, coupled with four years of nursing school, had turned her into a woman mature beyond her years. In many ways, she was more mature than Dr. Rory, but she was smart enough not to let on.

She helped Jack load her Mercury station wagon with what appeared to be enough camping gear for an army, and they headed for the Knight's home.

"Are you boys going to be able to carry all this stuff?" she asked.

"Sure, we'll just divide it up evenly among the six of us," her son replied, almost by rote.

Whenever he went on a camping trip, she asked him the same questions, but in a slightly different form. She already knew all the answers, but it was a time-honored form of communication between parent and child, the subtext of which was, "I care about you."

So on the short drive to the Knight's, she continued with her gentle questions, finally saying, "If you'll see me before you go, I'll give you a little container of Dr. Rory's samples, just in case."

It was an oddity with her loosely tailored farm background and seventeen years of marriage, that she still referred to her husband as Dr. Rory, even to her own children. However, it was something she never thought about. It felt right, so she just did it.

The "samples" that she was referring to, when she offered them to Jack, were the little packets of drugs that the detail men left with her husband. Three or four tablets to a little plastic wrapper, they would sometimes leave several hundred doses of their latest drugs, or even one of their old standbys, if a doctor were to request it. Quite a few doctors would ask the detail men for large quantities of antacids, even though they were among the oldest of the drugs that a salesman might carry.

Pretty much, the detail men would do anything they could to get a doctor to try their company's drugs. There would be pens, pencils, notepads, calendars, custom trout flies, tie clips. The gifts ran the gamut, right up to dinners and seminar trips—anything. Ninety percent of the time, the doctor would be too busy to even see the detail men, and contriving to limit that possibility, they gave gifts to the doctors' receptionists and nurses as well. Not a few times, a detail man would get so close to a doctor's receptionist, that he wound up marrying the girl. But that happened in all businesses, so why should a doctor's office be any different?

The standard Boy Scout first aid kit had gauze, tape, some bandages, burn cream, and snakebite necessities. This was all well and good, except there are only two types of poisonous snakes in Connecticut, the Timber Rattler and the Northern Copperhead. Both of these snakes are referred to as "risk avoiders," which means simply that, even if one hid right in the basement of Jack's house and he walked down there, the snake wouldn't bite him. These snakes slither away as soon as they sense a human approaching.

What the Boy Scout first aid kit didn't contain was antacids, aspirin, anti-diarrheals, and sunburn lotion—in short, all of the things that a doctor's wife could get for you, along with a pretty fair explanation of the use thereof. Jack used bandages from the official first aid kit a couple of times, and his mother's first aid essentials on almost every camping trip. Be prepared.

When, with the help of the others, the boys got all the gear into Walter Knight's basement, they set out to build six piles, each of which would weigh no more than forty-five pounds. The way it usually worked out was that, the boy who had to carry the mess kit in his backpack, had someone else carrying half of his clothes. It was a jumble sorting things out in camp, but the system usually worked pretty well.

With everything packed except the food, they quit for the night. They would pack the food first thing Saturday morning and be off. This last trip of the year was always to Camp Winonee in the northwest corner of the state—four thousand acres encircling a thousand acre lake, in the middle of nowhere. Because of the elevation, autumn was about two weeks further advanced at Camp Winonee, so the trees would be almost bare. Still, the trip was a source of great anticipation.

***

On Saturday, the weather looked bad—overcast and threatening rain. Mr. Steere, the scoutmaster, huddled with the two fathers who had been railroaded into helping. A decision would have to be made, because the weather reports were worsening by the minute.

All the same, these grown men, some veterans of wartime combat were loath to cancel, as if someone might still question their manhood. And because no one had anything else planned for the weekend, it was a go.

The food was packed, the cars filled, and Troop 33 was on its way to Camp Winonee.

As they left town, everyone talked at once about what a great time they were going to have, and several wondered out loud if anybody thought it would rain at the camp. Nobody knew, or better stated, nobody was saying. There was an eerie silence after the discussion of the rain, as each scout, undoubtedly, considered his own preparations for such an event. Did the silence mean that some were concerned?

After a drive of about an hour, the caravan passed a matched set of thirty-foot tall totem poles. Each one was emblazoned with a dozen individual totems, representing the sun god, the hunting god, the moon god, and any other god, real or imagined, by the wood carver. Cheery, colorful totem poles, they anointed all who entered with the spirit of adventure, and the promise of mystery and excitement in the woods.

The cars pulled up to an administration building, where Troop 33 was registered, and thirty little bladders were emptied. Back in the cars, it was announced that they would have the north side of a mountain, at the most distant section of the Winonee Reservation, all to themselves. The boys also noticed on the windshields, that it had started to sprinkle. They drove in silence on a rutted, dirt road for what seemed like another hour, when at last the cars came to a halt, side by side, in a small parking area at a trail sign, which read—

- Wilderness Area -
All Scouts Must First Check In At
The Ranger Station.

The cars were unloaded, as it started to drizzle a little harder. Everyone shouldered his pack, and set out on the trail up the mountain.

After fifteen minutes of hiking, the scouts stopped to put ponchos on over their bodies and packs. Another fifteen minutes, and they would be at their destination.

At last, they got to the sloping woodlands that would be their home for the next two days, the different patrols spreading out, with Jack's group getting a choice site near a small stream. It was strongly suggested by Mr. Steere that the tents be put up immediately. Without any prodding, two of the six Scouts started pitching tents, while two others went downhill a bit to dig a latrine. The last two began building a fire.

The tents went up without a problem, and for the moment they were watertight. The two boys digging the latrine immediately hit ledge, and had to settle for a beautiful bunch of saplings, lashed together to resemble a crude throne, but resting over a waste hole only six inches deep.

The fire wasn't much better. Jack and his companion were supposed to use flint and steel with a thrush's nest, or some such thing, to catch the spark. Given the rain, they went directly for the matches, and still they wound up with a piddling fire, which did nothing more than fill the whole campsite with smoke.

As the boys were about to begin cooking lunch, the rain started in earnest. Everyone took refuge in the tents. The downpour saturated the ground, which was only six inches of topsoil over ledge, and water rolled down the hill until the tents first flooded, and then collapsed altogether.

Cooking was dicey, and sleeping was worse, so the Scouts wound up standing under an oak tree in their ponchos eating Hershey bars.

When they got back to Wellesport on Sunday night, everyone was tired, hungry and constipated. Welcome to the great outdoors.

15

Jack Dunleavy walked home from school with his best friend Ed Nadeau, who lived two doors away. While they ambled along, they made plans for Halloween. There wasn't much to discuss. They would go as hobos, as they had every year in memory, and they would start at five o'clock. Thanks to Daylight Saving Time, it would be dark by then, and wouldn't necessarily look like they had jumped the gun.

Unfortunately, Jack's mind was elsewhere. His teacher handed back his math test with a fat red "D" penciled darkly across the top. His mother and father were sticklers on achievement in school. Education was the lodestar of Dr. Rory's life, and now his son had to show him a nearly-flunking grade. Jack wasn't looking forward to it. Scouting may have to be put on a back burner until his math scores came up.

At what seemed to be the exact same moment, Jack and Ed spotted out at the curb in front of Mrs. Petabella's house, what appeared to be an executioner's "electric chair."

It wasn't actually an electric chair. It was an immense, oak, straight back chair of the Empire style, in an accelerated state of disrepair, but damned if it didn't look exactly like the pictures of "Old Sparky," which they had seen in the Sunday *Enterprise*. When Henry Cutler had chosen not to appeal his death sentence, the *Enterprise* had run a lurid piece in the Sunday paper, chronicling all of the executions at the State Prison at Wellesport. There had been a total of seventy-two men put to death, including a couple of double hangings.

Hanging had been the preferred method from 1827 to 1935, when the first, and so far the only, execution was performed with electricity. Old Sparky had been sitting idle for twenty-three years. Henry Cutler would be number seventy-three, and with the prison scheduled for demolition late in 1959, might very well be the second and last one in Old Sparky.

The two boys looked at each other, and at last Jack said, "This would make a perfect electric chair for us out at Hidden Island. We can stage mock executions."

"Great idea," said Ed excitedly, "but how do we get it there?"

"Simple. We borrow the Pheiffer's dory, and we row it out there this afternoon as soon as it gets dark," said Jack.

"Perfect," said Ed. "The Pheiffers won't mind. They let anybody use that old boat. I'm not sure they even own it."

"We'll go home, change our clothes, and then meet back here. We better be quick about it, before the rubbish men show up," said Jack.

The two boys raced off for their homes, dumped their schoolbooks, changed clothes, and got back to Mrs. Petabella's place in a matter of minutes. They each took one end of the chair, and started wandering unsteadily toward the Wellesport Cove. It was about a half mile to the cove, past dozens of houses, past River Road, and then past the prison. At the end of their hike, they would come upon a small boat-launching ramp, and a wobbly dock with half a dozen rowboats of questionable seaworthiness. As they stumbled along with the chair, they had to rest in front of every house. At their first stop, Jack noticed all the people who were out raking leaves, so he said under his breath to Ed, "If anyone asks, we're going to break the chair up into firewood for Mrs. Pheiffer. He figured that if Mrs. Pheiffer ever asked about the firewood that she never got, they could say that the chair was too heavy, and they'd changed their minds, leaving it for the rubbish men.

They began again to wrestle with the chair. A man named Livesy, asked the boys where they were going with the chair, and just as cool as could be, the two lied through their teeth. But Mr. Livesy bought it. Jack and Ed weren't raised to be liars, but even at twelve they realized that, if the real answer to the question was, "none of your business," then a lie would be advisable.

After an eternity of fits and starts, the boys were at the dock. It wouldn't be dark for an hour yet, and neither of them wanted to row across Wellesport Cove until that time, so they hid the chair in the bushes, and went back home for some football.

An hour later, with sufficient darkness to mask their activities, they returned to the dock at the cove. Jack had found an old light fixture, which looked like half of a silver basketball with an electrical cord coming out of the middle of the convex surface. It looked eerily like the apparatus that was placed over the condemned man's head, during an execution.

Ed Nadeau took one look at the reflector light, and smiled broadly.

"Fantastic," he said. "Where did you get that?"

"It was in the barn," said Jack, and then added airily, "It won't be missed."

The two boys needed to bail out the Pheiffer's rowboat first, and so for the next half hour they took turns using an old Maxwell House can to scoop water out of the bilge. At last, they were able to load the chair into the boat and proceed. Owing to its size and weight, the chair simply had to go in the middle of the boat, with the boys taking up positions in the bow and stern. This negated the use of the rowlocks, and they were reduced to using the oars like paddles. It was much slower, but worked all the same.

They shoved off from the dock, and the boat rocked unnervingly, as they floated out into the cove. They paddled steadily as a wind from the north impeded their progress. They gamely paddled on toward the spit of land that protected Hidden Island.

When they reached the halfway point, they stopped to stretch, and with no attention given to coordination of movement, they inadvertently sent the boat on a rocking episode, from which it just couldn't recover. It tipped over with an enormous slosh, as the three occupants hit the water. "Old Sparky's" twin brother made a commanding, water-parting, splash, but miracle of miracles, it floated.

While they were slogging around in the water, a powerful searchlight, from the cove guard tower at the prison, beamed on them.

Neither one of the two had considered floating the chair out to Hidden Island, which would have been a lot easier. Oddly enough, that's exactly how the boys, the prize and the boat made it the rest of the way. The floodlight from the prison followed them the whole way, but didn't concern them. The guards were the only ones who could see them, and although the boys were embarrassed to be bobbing before witnesses, they knew that the guards weren't likely to give the episode a second thought, so long as their next count came out right.

The boys hid the chair and the electric fixture in the bushes on the spit of land in front of Hidden Island, figuring that they could retrieve them later. They turned the rowboat over to empty out the water, and departed for the dock with teeth chattering and upper bodies clenched up in knots. Since they were able to row on the way back, they beached the borrowed boat in good time, and hightailed it for home and a change of clothes. It was agreed that they would meet tomorrow at the same time, and bring the chair to the campsite that they used on Hidden Island. Finally, they parted.

When Jack got home, his mother was busy cooking dinner, so he was able to sneak by the kitchen, and ascend the stairs without having to explain his wet clothes. Zeke was in the barn working on his car, while Wibby watched the *Mickey Mouse Club*. She was getting a little old for the Mouseketeers, but there was nothing else on. Jack tiptoed up the back stairs to his room, and changed into dry duds.

When Jack got back downstairs, his mother asked where he'd been, and he told her that he and Ed had taken a walk to the cove. She said, "Oh, that's nice dear." He let out the breath stored inside his puffed cheeks.

***

Dr. Rory was late getting out of the office that night, and so the rest of the Dunleavys ate dinner without him. Pork chops.

While they were having dinner, they talked about teachers at school, upcoming activities and Halloween. For Zeke, that meant the Harvest Dance at the high school. Dates would have excluded half of the upper classes, so the faculty decided that it would be more of a "hop," with everyone coming stag. It was common knowledge that Zeke was sweet on Susie O'Rourke, but nothing was said to embarrass him.

The year before, Zeke set a cow loose in the middle of the sock hop. What seemed like a great gag, turned a little ugly, when the cow defecated in the middle of the dance floor. It was to be expected—her first sock hop, and the excitement was a little too much.

Laterally, fingers were pointed. Zeke fessed up and was given five detentions, back to back. He didn't mind, for he drew pictures of cars and suffered little.

This year things would be different. After Dr. Rory had given his son permission to build the automobile, Zeke was a changed man. Now he was very circumspect in activities that might not otherwise bear close scrutiny—a model citizen of sorts. He would probably spend this whole dance with Susie O'Rourke.

As for Jack, he was quiet at the table. He knew that he was going to have to get his father's signature on the math test after dinner, and he wasn't looking forward to it. Dr. Rory never hit anyone, but he could give you a look that made you feel smaller than one of the germs under the microscope in his office.

Jack would have to wait until later in the evening, after Dr. Rory returned home and finished his dinner.

About nine o'clock, Jack went into the front parlor, where Dr. Rory was listening to an opera, "Suor Angelica," on the hi-fi, and he asked if he could speak to him. His father smiled, turned the volume of the record down low, and sat forward in his chair.

"So what's up, champ?"

"Well . . . I did . . . kinda badly on a . . . umm . . . math test, and I need your . . . umm . . . signature on it," Jack said slowly.

Dr. Rory took the paper from his son and looked at it. He turned to his son, and asked him to have a seat. Jack took the seat next to his father.

"Tell me, Jack," began his father, "Did you study for this exam?"

Jack said that he did, but not enough.

"I guess what I'm getting at is whether or not you are understanding the material, or whether you just aren't trying. These are two entirely different things, and only you know the answer."

Jack hedged. He thought that sometimes he would rather get hit than to have to go through the third degree, but it wasn't his choice.

Dr. Rory thought for a moment. Then, he started slowly.

"Jack, just think of the gandy dancers who come by here straightening the railroad tracks each year. They work like dogs in the hot sun all day long, with precious little to show for it. They make the same hourly wage as your brother Zeke does at the drugstore, and they have no job security at all. Now Jack, someone's got to do that job, but I don't want that someone to be you. The only way to a good job is with a solid education. Do you understand?"

Jack nodded his agreement.

Finally Dr. Rory said, "If there is something here that you need extra help with, then we will see that you get the help, but it's up to you to let your mother and me know. Can you do that?" he asked gently.

"Yes, sir," said Jack.

Dr. Rory signed the paper. He had watched his son get good marks throughout all of the earlier grades, and he knew perfectly well that Jack simply hadn't studied for this test. He also knew that, as long as Jack knew that he knew, there would be no repeat of this for a while.

Jack returned to the small desk in his bedroom and began to study.

Halloween came and went with the usual number of soaped windows, and splattered eggs. Pretty much everyone under age sixteen went door-to-door, trick-or-treating since the war ended, and the Dunleavy children participated in the fairly new Trick-or-Treat for UNICEF program too. The adults would try to guess what the costumes were—the older boys were often disguised as bums or Elvis Presley, while the girls pretended to be good witches or brides—before dropping candy into the sacks and coins into the boxes.

***

Dinner at the prison on Halloween wasn't really anything out of the ordinary—beef stew—but thanks to the efforts of Frenchie and Ruppert, the tables looked a little nicer. Each one had a centerpiece of a small pumpkin or gourd.

In prison, a little thing can mean a great deal—just some small thing to break up the monotony—maybe remind some of the inmates of better times. Who knew? But it was a welcome sight, and the other prisoners appreciated it.

Frenchie and Ruppert had to get permission from the warden himself to put out the pumpkins and gourds, but Warden Stoner understood the value of these little things, and agreed at once.

When the trays were brought to the prisoners on death row, even the condemned men had a small gourd given to them.

Henry Cutler accepted his with a grin, and sat down to eat his meal. As he ate his food, he was mulling over the different parts of his plan that must fall together with clock-like precision for his escape to work. Nonetheless, he was convinced that it was possible.

His attorney had told him, that even though Henry himself was waiving his right to an appeal, the lawyer was going to file some motions with the courts to try to have his sentence commuted.

The lawyer had no interest in Henry Cutler at all. He felt badly for the families of Cutler's victims, and even had a teenage daughter of his own, but since lawyers were not allowed to advertise, he would file some motions just to get his own name in the paper. His colleagues knew the score, and wouldn't be troubled by his motions at all. Each and every one of them would do the same. He might even get to tell his story on television. In addition to the network shows, there were local shows on all sorts of topics, which enjoyed larger and larger audiences every year.

Henry Cutler told his lawyer that he didn't object. As a matter of fact he told the man, that if he had a year to make his peace with God, it would be helpful. His lawyer, salivating at a year's free advertising, agreed to help him get the time he needed.

Henry, for his part, knew that it would take him a year to break out of Wellesport. The plan, any plan, was going to take time. He also knew that, if he couldn't do it in a year, then it probably couldn't be done.

He finished his meal, and slid the tray on the floor until it was outside his cell, next to his shoes. In a short while, someone from the kitchen staff would pick up the tray.

He lay down on his cot, and waited for lights out.

At nine-thirty sharp, all the lights went off in the cells. Death row was quiet.

Henry waited until the guard sat down at his desk to the west of the cells. This particular guard, Ryan, was hard of hearing, and Henry knew it. Thankfully though, the guard could not see into Henry's cell from his desk.

Cutler used the time while Ryan was on duty to do his exercises. He had strung a small piece of wire, which he bought through the usual prison scroungers, from the light fixture, which was anchored in concrete. He would wrap his hands in socks and then pull himself up and down on the wire for the better part of an hour, to strengthen his upper body. He did this, night after night, until he could do it continuously in five-minute segments. He had been born small, but the work on cars, coupled with some weight lifting, had developed his upper body strength enormously.

He still felt, however, that if the deputy warden learned that he spent his nights building upper body strength, it wouldn't take the Dep long to figure out what he had in mind. It was information that Cutler did not want Benko Sadek to have.

16

As Zeke Dunleavy's automobile actually began to resemble the Mercedes Benz SSK Drophead Coupe that he considered the prototype of his car, a funny thing happened. One by one, people from around the town began to visit Dunleavy Motors to inspect the progress and talk to Zeke about automobiles in general.

They would shyly walk into the barn, pretending that they were just out for a walk, and were overcome with the urge to stop by to offer a little encouragement. Slyly, they would compare the picture of the original SSK with what Zeke had accomplished so far, and suddenly realize that it was indeed going to happen. Zeke was actually going to do it.

Someone once said that "success has a thousand fathers," and so it was going to be, with something as small as the dream of a high school junior. None of these latecomers had the foresight or the raw generosity of Soapy Doyle, but now they all wanted to be a part of the endeavor.

So, one man would ask if Zeke had located the headlights yet, and when he said no, the man would tell Zeke about a friend of a friend, who had that exact set of headlights in his barn. If Zeke wanted, he would talk to this friend of a friend about purchasing the headlights. Of course, when the man laid out the case to the friend of a friend, he would keep pounding away at the fact that this young man was his doctor's son, and really didn't have the money to finish the car without some special help. He would also highlight the fact that the lights weren't doing anybody any good where they were, and last but not least, with the change in the design of the new cars every year, the lights were not going to fit anything that Detroit was likely to produce any time soon. So the lights would be Zeke's for a pittance, or maybe just for a guided tour of the embryonic SSK, and a half hour of car talk.

It went this way all the time that Zeke was molding the skin for the automobile. Headlights here, bumpers there, a set of mirrors, a set of air horns and, finally, an oversized chrome radiator cover paraded into the bay of Dunleavy Motors.

Gino Finelli was a steady supplier of chrome and glass. By the time Zeke was ready to move on to the next stage of fitting out the

SSK with all of the accessories, he didn't have to look any further than his own barn.

Because of the change in the weather, he would have to wait until spring to paint the car, so he wiled away the winter months wiring the inside of the machine, and attaching ornamentation.

Frenchie, at the prison, had come through with a magnificent walnut dashboard, which was probably nicer than the one on the original Mercedes SSK. When Zeke peered into the finish, it was like Narcissus gazing into the pond. A man could shave using Zeke's new dashboard for a mirror. What couldn't a couple of packs of Pall Malls buy?

Once in a while, Ann Dunleavy would stop by the motorcar company to see how Zeke was doing. She would ask him questions like: "Is it going to have seat belts?" Or her stubborn favorite: "Just exactly how fast will this thing go?" Zeke put on the charm to quiet his mother's fears, knowing that she could kill the project with just a word to Dr. Rory. Time and again, he was able to send her away mollified, and the work continued.

In the end, Zeke ran overtime working on the skin, finally finishing it up just before the holiday.

***

Thanksgiving, that most peculiar of the American holidays, was going to be on November 27th this year. Barring some freak early season snowstorm, the Dunleavy's were expecting a full house.

In addition to Grammy Dunleavy, who lived right around the corner on Chestnut Street, there would be Ann Dunleavy's parents, Horst and Heidi Detweiller, and a goodly collection of siblings and cousins, some anticipated more than others.

They would arrive on Thursday morning, with pies and vegetable dishes, and they would stay until Sunday night, leaving in a long blaze of heartfelt good-byes. For the Dunleavy children, it would be the only time during the whole year when they would see their cousins, and that was exactly as it should be. After all, a friend can only be a friend if they can contribute to your life. The cousins, being from New Hampshire and Vermont, were not in a geographical position to contribute to the lives of anyone in

Connecticut, and so just as in every other family, the Dunleavys' cousins were strangers who were related to them. No more, no less. They saw each other once a year, enjoyed the visit enormously, and then returned to their lives.

Ann Dunleavy had planned well for the big weekend. All of the Dunleavy children would give up their rooms to their aunts and uncles, while the complete collection of cousins would spend the nights downstairs, in sleeping bags on the floor. The male cousins would sleep in the basement, while their sisters would sleep in the front parlor, where Dr. Rory usually listened to his music.

School would run a half day on the Wednesday before Thanksgiving, and would not reconvene until the following Monday, December 1st.

Wibby would help Ann Dunleavy with the preparations in the house, while Zeke and Jack would take the station wagon to Folding Hills to get the turkey. It was a drive of about twenty miles, into a part of the state that made Wellesport seem like Paris, by comparison. The miles and miles between farmhouses, gave Folding Hills a lonely quality. A turkey farm produced an awful stink, so they had a tendency to be out in the middle of nowhere.

A.T. Rule & Sons had been forced to move their live poultry operation before. Once homeowners, who wore white collars to work, outnumbered them they were quickly squeezed out of town.

From the Rule's point of view, even though Folding Hills was as rural as rural gets, their days were numbered there as well.

On Wednesday afternoon, Zeke and Jack rolled up to A.T. Rule & Sons to pick up the turkey, which their mother had ordered months before. When Zeke gave the family name, the clerk at the counter disappeared into the back room, and returned a few minutes later with a cardboard box the size of an orange crate. In it was a thirty-pound tom turkey, plucked, beheaded, and ready for the oven. The sweetbreads were wrapped separately and placed in the box too.

Zeke paid for the bird, and he and Jack each took one end of the box, and put it in the back of the station wagon. Their mother would be up at five the following morning to start roasting.

As they drove back to Wellesport, they talked about cars. Jack was only twelve and had his own pastimes, but getting one's drivers license had long ago supplanted any other rite of passage to adulthood for young boys. The automobile had transformed life forever, from simple transport to heavy dating, it was now of primary concern to teenage boys.

Jack had his own friends and interests, but he couldn't help but idolize his brother.

Zeke was Wellesport's own sun child, blessed with brains and good looks; he gave off heat and warmth wherever he went. He made the young dream the impossible, and he made the old folks suddenly remember life's potential. He was the pied piper, who unknowingly led the slow, the dimwitted, and the fearful to places where they could not go by themselves. Watching this morning star rise, gave others great strength. People everywhere gravitated toward these children of the sun, and in Wellesport, it was no different. Zeke was the sun child and everyone knew it, including his brother Jack.

They got back to Wellesport near dark. The days were getting impossibly short, and with the trees bare now and the crops all in, Wellesport had the feeling of a bird that couldn't sing. The town was settling in for the winter.

At last, it was Thanksgiving morning and the cars began to arrive.

The first to drive in were Uncle Chet and Aunt Genevieve with their two children, Edwin and Ginger. Uncle Chet was Dr. Rory's younger brother from Rutland, Vermont. He and Aunt Gen farmed the old homestead, which they had purchased from Grammy Dunleavy, when she had decided to move to Wellesport to be near Dr. Rory. It was no secret that Grammy Dunleavy favored Dr. Rory, her firstborn, in the extreme. Every person ever born should have one person who thinks that they can do no wrong. God could work on that.

Uncle Chet had a warm and innocent heart though, and paid scant attention to Grammy Dunleavy's likes and dislikes. He and Gen asked little of life. They had their kids, their farm, and a small circle of devoted friends. Actually, they had quite a lot. The cousins were very much like Chet and Gen graciously building a great bonfire of enjoyment with precious little fuel.

It was a good two hours before the others arrived, with Uncle Ox and Aunt Flora as the headliners. Uncle Ox was a mountain of a man, more like an outhouse with arms and legs. He could grab the shirts of any two teenagers and lift them until their heads hit the ceiling. Yet with his wife, Flora, he was gentle and attentive, caught in the spell of her cheap perfume and thick make-up.

Unlike Uncle Ox, who kept a small herd of milk cows in the little hamlet of Brownsville, Vermont, Flora was from Boston. It has never been stated as such, out of respect for Ox, but Flora had been a stripper. Behind her back, she was called "Aunt Floradora." They married late. Uncle Ox had taken a trip to Boston on business, met Flora, and this odd mésalliance followed. They were married in Brownsville, with not one person from Flora's side of the family in attendance.

Uncle Ox had been in the Navy, and then the Merchant Marines, before he finally became a dairy farmer.

After he settled into an overstuffed chair and accepted a glass of scotch, the first order of business was to take requests from Zeke, Jack and Wibby. First they wanted to see the "eagle." Uncle Ox would parry their requests for a short time, and then he would roll up his right sleeve to expose a big, full-colored tattoo on his heavily muscled forearm. It was the "fouled anchor," with heavy chains wrapped around it. Superimposed over this, was an American bald eagle in flight, trailing a ribbon from its beak. The ribbon read, "DEATH BEFORE DISHONOR."

Great "oohs" and "ahhs" rose as he flexed his muscles causing the eagle to "take flight."

The next request was for the left arm. Uncle Ox would balk, and tell Wibby that she would have to leave the room. In the end he always relented, and pulled up his sleeve to expose a woman in a pose reminiscent of the World War II pinup shot of Betty Grable.

It was also in full color, and although there were no tattooed words, the curvaceous girl offered a beguiling message of welcome. Again he flexed his muscles, and the girl's rump would shake. Great shrieks of laughter would swell in the room, until Aunt Floradora came in. She scolded and belittled Uncle Ox for showing his tattoos. He lamely rolled down his sleeves, winked at the Dunleavy kids and said, "To be continued."

Aunt Floradora was beneath contempt for the way she savaged Uncle Ox, but he just laughed. Rather than disliking women for their flaws, he just looked on them as one of nature's amusing riddles. When Jack asked Uncle Ox once why he let Aunt Floradora talk to him the way she did, the gentle giant just smiled and said, "It's not easy being a woman. How would you like to wake up every morning not knowing who you're going to be?" Jack, of course, didn't understand what Uncle Ox was talking about, but he never forgot the comment.

After the arrival of Uncle Ox and Aunt Flora, a procession of aunts, uncles and cousins followed that God himself couldn't keep straight. All together, there were thirteen adults and sixteen children.

The men drifted outside to walk around the property, talk sports and, finally, to admire Zeke's car. Even in its unpainted condition, it was breathtaking to behold. It struck a chord, not because it represented great, good work on Zeke's part, and not because it was unusual to build an automobile, but because it truly resembled a 1929 Mercedes SSK Drophead Coupe. Which is to say that it didn't look like a Ford or a Chevrolet, but it really resembled the very last word in automobile design. It was clearly an exact replica of the most beautiful car ever made. Only now did others see it.

It inspired awe and it inspired something else—one of the seven deadly sins that is involuntary, envy. Beauty does this to people, and yet they understand it not at all. It magically transforms them into hateful people, before they are aware that they have changed at all.

However, there would be no time for the corrosive effects of envy today, because it was time for dinner.

Everyone marched into the house, and found their places at a long table, which spanned the dining room clear through the French doors to the front parlor, stopping just short of the piano, which faced out onto Main Street. Several tables had been joined together, the gaps filled with plywood to seat this group. Twenty-nine hungry people around one table—but not for long.

Dr. Rory, who was rightfully seated at the head of the table, held up a book, and announced that it was time for the annual weigh-in. Great whoops of laughter and embarrassed giggles from the women followed, as the whole group, in a great dancing train, straggled toward the barn.

In the corner of the second floor loft, remaining from the days of the big grain harvests on the property, was a set of scales, which at one time could weigh a team of Clydesdales. It had a large, flat steel plate that held the load, and a respectable inventory of steel disks that slid onto a hook. The hook in turn had a pointer, which let the attendant know when the weights and the load were in balance.

Like sheep being led to slaughter, aunts, uncles, and cousins lined up to be weighed before dinner. The results were fairly predictable, with the kids weighing from forty-two to one hundred and twenty pounds. Of the adults, Aunt Floradora weighed only one hundred and two pounds, with Uncle Ox using up all of the rusty steel discs on hand, and unofficially weighing a tad under three hundred pounds.

With laughter, embarrassment and loud chatter, the group returned to the house, and once again took their seats.

Dr. Rory offered the grace to Uncle Ox, who he knew would give it back to him, and then began by saying, "We thank you, Lord, for all the blessings you have bestowed upon us. Most particularly, we thank you for the food we are about to eat, and the family that you have given us to enjoy it with. And until we meet again, we humbly ask that you hold each and every one of us in the palm of your hand."

Dr. Rory was a sucker for the traditional Irish toast, and sneaked little bits of it in wherever he could.

Everyone said "Ah-men," and began passing around the bowls and platters of food. Talk and laughter filled the room for the better part of three hours, as everyone ate and drank.

Aunt Gen had brought a turkey also, so there was one at each end of the table. There were fourteen different types of vegetable dishes, not counting the cranberry and stuffing, and five different pies and rum pudding for dessert. Just when someone thought that they had had enough, they would lean back, have a cigarette, and a few minutes later, start in again.

Finally, Dr. Rory announced that it was time for the afternoon weigh-in. There were loud groans everywhere, with some of the women flatly refusing to participate. Sad to say, while they could resist the adults, they couldn't resist the entreaties of their own children, and the line to the barn was formed once again.

Jokes were made about being able to get up the stairs to the second floor of the barn, but finally everyone was weighed one last time.

All eyes were on Uncle Ox as he waddled up to the scales . . . and disappointed everyone terribly. He still weighed a tad under three hundred pounds, which nobody could believe. Dr. Rory kicked at the little bits of straw near the base of the scales, as if that were the problem. But it changed nothing. Uncle Ox's weight was officially marked in the book as— 300 lbs(–).

Dr. Rory himself was the big gainer—up until almost the end of the weigh-in—with the addition of six pounds. It was beginning to look like he would bear the imaginary stigma, until the next Thanksgiving, since there were only a few of the ladies left in line.

At length, and dead last, Aunt Floradora got on the scales, and set a new record with a weight gain of a whopping ten pounds. Everyone asked each other if that were even possible. Again, Dr. Rory fiddled with the scales in disbelief.

Tiny Aunt Floradora, apparently without anyone noticing, had eaten the meal of her life, with an actual weight gain of nine pounds and fourteen ounces.

Aunt Floradora was red-faced for the rest of her visit, and refused to ever get on the scales again, claiming that Dr. Rory had played a trick on her because he didn't like her. This, of course, was untrue, but her demeanor was adamantine. Any trip to the barn in the future would be made without her, which was probably the first and last time in her life she had ever said that.

For three more days, everyone laughed and ate. The men threw the football around, and the women went shopping. Sunday dinner was served at two, and afterwards all the guests left for home.

Thanksgiving came and went like this every year, and yet it always seemed new and fresh, because life kept changing without any of the participants really noticing. Old age is the dirtiest trick to sneak up on folks, but the Dunleavys and their relatives barely noticed.

17

Through early December, activity in Wellesport slowed significantly, with Christmas shopping and house decorating being the two big exceptions.

School took its predictable course, but the Wellesport Weasels couldn't seem to win a basketball game. It was all the town could talk about.

The school mascot had, in recent years, become the subject of heated discussion and downright disgust. Such was the mood of the citizenry that there was nothing but constant talk of an upgrade to an animal that could more easily generate school spirit. One had to conclude, that just after the Civil War, when the weasel was chosen as the school mascot, it enjoyed a little more favorable status than it did now. Almost a hundred years later, mothers cringed as they saw their own flesh and blood running up and down the basketball court, with "Weasels" emblazoned on their chests.

Sensing the need for action, First Selectman Cameron Cooper brought a motion before the board to commence a hunt for a more appropriate mascot. Since no one had ever heard of a town changing the name of its mascot before, they just assumed that they could make up their own rules as they went along. And that's exactly what they did.

So as not to appear heavy-handed, the selectmen decided that a contest would be held. Each person in town would be allowed to make one recommendation. A blue ribbon committee would choose the new mascot from among the entries. The winner of the contest would be the first entry received, with the winning mascot on it. The entry box would be emptied every night and the entries dated. The winner would receive dinner for the whole family at their favorite restaurant, with the winner's picture displayed permanently in the trophy case in the high school's main hall.

However, the contest had a short time period. The town was so sick of the Weasel, that the last entry would be accepted the day before Christmas, the Wednesday that school got out. The winning weasel replacement would be announced a week later.

It seemed pretty obvious to Zeke that if you could sell one name to enough people before the contest was over, then you would be the winner. Motivated more by the prestige, not to mention a touch of glory, he set out to do just that.

Wellesport's little library on Main Street had been moved a number of times, with trustees from the prison doing the heavy lifting. Owing to the small number of volumes, it was at best a day's work. There were many initiatives over the years to try to increase the number of volumes, but the Republican selectmen had all graduated from Wellesport schools and done well with their lives, so what was all this nonsense about more volumes? To a man, they felt that if the library shelved the classics, it had it all.

An expansionist group in town called "The Friends of the Wellesport Library" put heat on the Library Board, who in turn petitioned the selectmen, hat in hand. Still, little changed.

When Thomas Jefferson was a boy, he had read every book in the public library in his hometown in Virginia by the time he was sixteen. If he had taken that long in Wellesport, he would have been considered a dolt.

The crops were all in and the Christmas decorations were up, so young and old alike descended on this poor, little institution, looking for books on animals. Some of the old time farmers took out books on American colleges, in the hopes of stealing a mascot from somewhere in the Midwest. As long as they didn't settle on the Wellesport Crimson Tide, who would know?

Zeke figured that first out of the gate would probably be the winner. It wasn't just that there was so little time to lobby for your choice, but the mascot that made the first big splash was going to have the momentum—the good word of mouth. So the day that the contest was announced, Zeke ran the five hundred yards from the Dunleavy house to the library, and checked out the three best books on animals of the world.

Coincidentally, they were three of only six books on animals, and they wouldn't be due back for three weeks. The contest would be practically over by then.

Zeke started near the back of the book with "w." Alliteration would be a good selling point, although it was this implied need that necessitated the current contest.

Wallabies. Walruses. Warthogs. Wasps. Water bears. Water Lice. Oh good. The Wellesport Water Lice. Or how about the Wellesport Water Snakes? How about Wellesport Weevils? Nope.

Whales? Whelks? Whipworms? Wildebeasts? No wonder the school mascot was the Weasel with these choices.

Zeke kept on with the w's. There had to be one animal with a little charm that began with the letter "w."

Winkles?

Wolves? Possible, but not very original.

Wolverines? Good possibility. Fearless, and fearsome.

Wombats? Woodchucks? Woodlice? Woodpeckers?

How about the Wellesport Worms? He'd be lucky not to get expelled if that were his entry.

After pawing through all three volumes, he decided that he had to have the alliteration, and so Wellesport Wolverines it was.

The next step was to get his brother Jack to quickly carve a wooden block that he could use as a stamp. He would stamp up hundreds of cards with his entry on them.

He would drop one card in the ballot box early the next morning. The others, he would pass out as "vote-getters." The next day, Zeke began his pitch. He even drew up a black and white reproduction of a wolverine, and copied it on Dr. Rory's thermofax machine.

And it all worked exactly as advertised. There was so much momentum built up for the wolverine, it was a forgone conclusion that it would be selected as the new mascot.

Just as stated in the rules, the Dunleavys had dinner at Ucello's Oyster House shortly after the holidays, courtesy of the Wellesport Board of Selectmen.

***

On the first weekend in December, every year like clockwork, the people of Wellesport were treated to a truly Herculean event, unofficially sponsored by a team of Irish bachelor brothers, who lived two doors down from Grammy Dunleavy on Chestnut Street.

Binky and Billy Sullivan worked for the town maintenance department, were lifelong members of the Wellesport Volunteer Fire

Department, and spent all of their free time tying trout flies and reloading shotgun shells.

In the patriotic fervor that swept America after the war, the Board of Selectmen decided to give jobs at the maintenance garage to any veteran who couldn't find a better situation. Though it wasn't for public consumption, those hired could never be let go, because nobody fires war heroes. As a result, the veterans of the town maintenance crew spent an inordinate amount of time in taverns with impunity. In fact, it became great sport for others in town to watch the back windows of the local tavern when the chief of maintenance drove up. Bodies flew out the windows like soldiers fleeing a hand grenade in a wartime bunker.

While Binky and Billy could certainly have done better, each for his own reasons, decided to stay in Wellesport, and skip the big job search. They showed up at the maintenance garage right after the announcement, and were hired. The job didn't pay much, but this happy-go-lucky matched set of leprechauns had inherited their mother's house debt free, and so didn't need much money.

Years went by, their pay increased, they got seniority, and simply never left.

The house that they had inherited was a brown-shingled bungalow with a porch across the whole front, a massive television antenna on the chimney, and a roof that over the years had settled into the shape of a woman's picture hat. It was a run-down place, but perfect for Binky and Billy. They drank beer, took turns cooking, and watched sports endlessly on the television. Without complaint, they watched the Red Sox disappoint them as regularly as the seasons.

Their lives may have appeared circumscribed to their neighbors, but in one single department, everyone agreed that the boys reigned supreme—Christmas decorations. On the appointed weekend, they began at first light by elevating a magnificent twelve-foot tall blue spruce tree up onto the middle of the front porch roof, with block and tackle. This mammoth conifer was seated in a custom-built steel bracket, and braced at each point of the compass with guy wires until it was pronounced satisfactorily sturdy. Next, the tree was trimmed in the normal fashion with an overabundance of lights, tinsel, and ornate bulbs. Lastly, a star to shame all others, a sixteen-point affair with dozens of smaller lights of its own, was plopped on the top of the tree.

Toward the end of the forenoon, would come the crèche, with wise men, camels, sheep and cows and, of course, Jesus, Mary, and Joseph. They were all happily housed in a genuine stable of boards and bolts, saplings and straw, and topped off by another star of competing pedigree to its kin on the blue spruce.

It was getting late in the day now and Binky and Billy had completed less than two-thirds of their work, but they stopped for something hot to drink, and then redoubled their efforts.

The remaining scene, which would complete the display on the front of the house by filling in the rest of the porch roof to the right of the tree, was Santa and his reindeer. After bolting the sleigh down, one-by-one the boys hoisted eight good-sized reindeer to the roof, and buckled their harness. More guy wires were used to discourage the animals' flying proclivities; and at long last, they installed Santa in his sleigh with a huge bag of presents.

Their one remaining bit of business was to fasten long strings of bulbs on all of the house's architectural lines.

The wires and attached bulbs ran across eaves, up rafters, along the ridgepole, and down the corner boards. What lighting remained was used to encircle the whole house at the level of the sills. With the sky as black as soot around them, they made a couple of wraps around the chimney, and they were finished.

By the end of the day, word had usually spread through the town and whole families came to watch the "Binky and Billy Sullivan Show." As the cold night air found its way down Chestnut Street, adults began to shiver, and little children grew increasingly restless. Just when the assembled crowd of five hundred souls was ready to cancel in favor of next year's show, Binky threw the switch.

A loud cheer went up as the shabby cottage embraced the Christmas spirit with a vengeance. At the same time, it completely dispelled the notion that it wasn't worth the wait. Binky and Billy just smiled.

Dr. Rory got a big kick out of the Christmas lights around town, and an hour or so after Sunday dinner, maybe around four o'clock, he would pile everyone into his Buick, and tour all the streets and lanes of Wellesport. Everyone would discuss in great detail which decorations—besides Binky and Billy Sullivan's—were the best.

After about two hours of sightseeing, and just before they swung by Wellesport Drug for ice cream sundaes, he would ask who wanted to see the lights at their electrician's house. Mr. Volpe had a special knack with the eighteenth century houses, and had done the wiring on Dr. Rory's office when it was built.

Everyone cheered in agreement, and Dr. Rory swung the car down Chestnut Street. He came to a stop in front of a small, neat bungalow with not a single bulb, wreath or ornament on it. As far as the occupant was concerned, it might just as well have been Ground Hog Day.

Genuinely pleased with himself, Dr. Rory said, "Well, what do you think?"

Everyone groaned, and Ann Dunleavy leaned over and said, "Time for sundaes."

18

The weather had turned cold early, as everyone in Wellesport put the final touches on winterizing their homes, barns and outbuildings.

Some snow flurries had already dusted the lawns. As farmers worked to fix their machinery, their wives decorated the front doors and began in earnest their Christmas shopping. All of the shopping for the holidays could probably have been done in one day, but Christmas was the one truly guiltless time of the year for serious shopping, so most people spread the pleasure out over the whole month of December.

Wibby Dunleavy joined a choral group at Wellesport Elementary—a like-minded gaggle of eighth graders, who intended to go from house to house singing carols just before Christmas. They met three times a week to practice the old favorites, and to decide which homes they would grace with their music. There wouldn't be enough time to sing at every home in Wellesport, and they all knew it. Fairly effortlessly, it was decided that they would concentrate on Main Street and some of the side streets nearby. This was exactly as Wibby wanted it, because it would include her home, and the homes of Grammy Dunleavy, Marie Fortunato, and the Finellis.

As December moved along, the students at Wellesport High got antsier every day with the anticipation of a vacation. This year, Christmas would fall on a Thursday, and even the administrators knew the ridiculousness of asking students and faculty to return for a Friday session the day after Christmas, only to try the same thing the Friday after New Year's. It was decided that the vacation would run from December 24th until January 5th. Not that the head of the school system had much choice, but the students were ecstatic.

Twelve days before Christmas, after the nine o'clock Mass on Sunday, Dr. Rory piled everyone into Ann Dunleavy's station wagon for a drive out to Folding Hills. It had become something of an annual ritual, this drive to Milewski's Tree Farm. It began when Zeke was just five, and did not even understand what was going on, but had developed into a full-fledged contest to see who could find the fullest tree at Milewski's.

Some families got an enormous jump on the Dunleavys, selecting their trees in the first week or two of December. But with a two hundred year old house that would go up like flash kindling, Dr. Rory decided that having a dead pine tree in the house for about twenty days was plenty.

Bundled up for what proposed to be a long hunt, the Dunleavys fanned out over Stanley Milewski's acres of Christmas trees, each with a different conception of beauty. Dr. Rory and his wife just tagged along for the harvest.

As had been the way in every other year, the choice was narrowed down to two trees, and after wearing a path through the fields, with all concerned parties examining each finalist dozens of times, Dr. Rory finally had had enough. He reached in his pocket for what he called "Solomon's little helper." It was a five-dollar Indian Head gold piece that his father had given him shortly before his death.

The gold piece was a peculiar coin. About the size of a dime, it had all of its features indented into the coin, instead of in relief like traditional coinage. Apparently the United States mint tried this incuse design for about twenty years, in the hopes that coins would last a little longer. Unfortunately for the designers at the mint, it was learned too late that these coins were dirt collectors. Even under the very best conditions, grime built up in the crevices of the engraved parts of the coin, so the experiment was ended.

Dr. Rory took the coin out of a small leather pouch that he kept it in, and announced that, "Heads . . . it's the tree on the north; tails . . . it's the tree on the south." Without a lost second, the gold coin sailed straight up into the air, glinting in the morning sun, flipping and shimmering endlessly, until it hit Dr. Rory's open right hand. Like a Venus flytrap, he snapped it shut. Just as quickly, he opened his fingers, and slapped the coin onto the back of his left hand, eyeing everyone conspiratorially.

As the younger Dunleavys closed in, he removed his right hand, and Wibby let out a whoop. It would be her tree on the north this year.

Everyone trudged to the tree on the north, which suddenly looked moribund. It crossed Zeke's mind to appeal the decision, but in other years, such an effort fell on deaf ears, so he quickly dropped the idea.

Dr. Rory asked Zeke to do the honors, and handed him the saw. He dropped to his knees, and began cutting as low to the ground as he could. A few minutes later, the tree fell over, its days of sucking nutrients from the rich soil of Folding Hills ending in a flurry of steel teeth, sawdust and perspiration. The two boys carried the tree back to the car, where Jack used a combination of heavily practiced knots to anchor the prize to the luggage rack on the top of the station wagon.

Once secured, they drove back to Wellesport, talking excitedly about almost everything they saw—the houses, the hayfields, the trees, the stone walls and later on, presents, candy and food. It was the most exciting season of the year just for its ability to capture one's imagination. Could anyone miss the gaiety of such a crowded season?

***

The fields where Frenchie and Ruppert grew their crops were frozen, and covered with a light dusting of snow, the uneven mounds of dirt left exactly as they were the day the potatoes, onions, and beets were harvested. Throughout the winter months, Frenchie and Ruppert would spend their days with the coal crew, leaving the prison after morning yardout, and walking the quarter mile down River Road to the docks, where they would shovel coal. One shovelful at a time, the coal would be taken off barges, and put into the beds of trucks, which would bring the dirty fuel up to the prison. Entering through the side entrance of the prison, the trucks would go through the same inspection every other vehicle went through, whether coming or going.

As a truck entered the outside overhead doorway, it moved forward into a large "sally port." There, a crew of guards would inspect the truck's undercarriage, and any other part of the vehicle where contraband could be hidden. Then, all of the trustees' clothing would be checked for banned articles. It was a slow process, but absolutely essential.

There were really only four ways that a prisoner could obtain contraband. The least likely way was for a guard to bring it to him, although this had happened from time to time. Once in a while, a guard was even found to be supplying prisoners with drugs. Inasmuch as this was grounds for immediate dismissal, it was an infrequent event.

The second way was for a trustee to engage in the aforementioned behavior, but again the chances were slim. The position of trustee was so coveted, that few would risk it just to get someone drugs or a hacksaw blade. Add to this the likelihood that a few years would be tacked onto the trustee's sentence if caught, and it was obviously a low percentage play. Once in a while though, it did happen.

The third way a prisoner might import forbidden items was in the visitors' room. There was a long table, down the center of which ran a floor-to-ceiling, heavy wire screen. Nothing could pass from visitor to inmate, except what was turned over to the guards for inspection first. On a fairly regular basis, hacksaw blades were found in the soles of shoes—as well as other obvious ploys—but these attempts at smuggling in contraband were rarely successful.

The fourth and last way that a prisoner could expect to get hold of forbidden items was through the "sally port." Every inmate, at one time or another expected that he could smuggle something in through the truck entrance. Prisoners even expected to escape this way. They thought that they could simply lash themselves under one of the many trucks that came and went from the prison, but it really was the longest of long shots. The trucks were inspected too carefully.

Even with these few ways to get things in and out of the prison, there were still other methods that might be called variations on a theme. A trustee might be in one of the administration offices, and be left alone for a brief moment, just long enough for him to rifle the handbag of one of the secretaries. Dr. Rory Dunleavy was surprised to notice the first time he left the prison hospital that two vials of morphine were missing from his bag. It went on and on. Desperate men, with very little to lose, trying the impossible.

Henry Cutler lay on his bunk. For the moment he was not thinking about his kills, although he enjoyed that immensely. Instead he was running down his escape checklist in his head. Unlike the usual planning sheet, it might be called a checklist by elimination. He had examined his options, and even though he had already eliminated some avenues, he would still reconsider them, or parts of them, from time to time.

The first order of business he had already settled in his mind. Death row, run as it was, afforded him only one hour out of his cell each day. That one hour was in the exercise yard. One scant hour with a Winchester 30-30 trained on him the whole time. He guessed that the guard on duty hadn't fired the weapon in thirty years. Even if at one time he had been a good shot, could he still hit his target?

Cutler considered further. On the other side of the thirty-foot wall was freedom. He had found out recently that going under the wall was out of the question. He wouldn't have time to dig anyway. He couldn't go through the wall. Happily though, he could go over it. Best of all, he could do it with limited equipment. He knew there were ivy vines covering the outside of the prison, which he could use to rappel down the outside of the wall, when the time came. But how would he get up the inside of the wall without getting shot?

Henry Cutler felt reasonably sure that if the guard should be called into the guardhouse, he could be up the wall before the guard even noticed. This assumed, of course, that he had a rope.

He also felt that even if the guard could get off a shot, in his excited state, with Henry scrambling like a monkey, it was extremely unlikely that he would be hit. Still, could he take that chance?

Cutler had been doing his exercises religiously every night after lights out, and his upper body strength was nearing its peak. Just on the basis of pulling himself up and down on the wire, he figured that he would need only four seconds to get to the top of the wall.

That brought him to a whole new set of problems. A daylight breakout, accompanied by rifle shots, would alert the whole town. The chances of being caught were very high.

He decided that if he could get into the exercise yard after lights out, in addition to not getting shot, no one would see him on the other side of the wall, when he descended. His chances for escape would be enhanced enormously. The guard outside his cell was telephoned every hour on the hour, but if he timed it right, he would have the better part of an hour to make good his escape.

Toward this end, he put the finishing touches on his plan to get out of his cell after lights out. He had spent many years as a grease monkey, while he tortured and killed young girls in his spare time, and now a little known skill of auto mechanics was his salvation.

From sheer repetition, Henry had learned to look at a nut or bolt on a car engine, and say to himself, thirteen-sixteenths, three-eighths, or five-sixteenths. Simply stated, Henry Cutler's eyes could calibrate almost exactly the size of small objects in his mind. He had watched the guards carefully, and with a number of quick glances, he had memorized the teeth of the key to his cell. He would now set about making a replica of this key.

He didn't need to make a replica of the key to the exercise yard door, because once he was outside his cell, he would subdue the unarmed guard and use his key. So the only trick now was to get a key made for the lock on his cell door.

He knew a couple of people doing time at Wellesport, and unless Benko Sadck spent his spare time memorizing and cross filing the autobiographical data of the nine hundred souls now doing time at the prison, he would never pick up the connection between Cutler and Joseph "Doo-dah" Dymski. Doo-dah was at the Manning School for Boys with Henry Cutler but, in the criminal food chain, his decided lack of brains kept him at the bottom. Fat and unkempt, Doo-dah actually looked up to Henry Cutler. So, when Henry smuggled a small shopping list to his friend by way of a crumpled dinner napkin, Doo-dah was more than happy to help.

19

Christmas was a little less of an affair at the Dunleavy place than Thanksgiving, with Uncle Ox and Aunt Flora being the only two relatives free for Christmas dinner. To Aunt Flora's great relief, there would be no trips to the scales this holiday.

On Christmas Eve, the Dunleavys enjoyed a small dinner of cold meats and cheeses together with assorted cold vegetable dishes. Afterwards, they sat around the front parlor opening presents. Everyone was allowed to open two presents on Christmas Eve, with the rest left undisturbed until Christmas morning.

At eleven-fifteen, Ann Dunleavy would announce that it was time to get ready for midnight mass. Everyone went to their bedrooms to change into their best clothes, and at about eleven forty-five, they all left for St. Michael's.

Zeke Dunleavy was only sixteen but he was already well on his was to becoming an agnostic. The Catholic Church and its rituals left him cold and empty. In truth, a great many Catholics felt the same way. Simply to keep his mother happy, Zeke reluctantly continued to attend church.

After midnight mass, where the young priest gave a long and completely enervating sermon on the meaning of Bethlehem in our lives today, the Dunleavys returned home, and most everyone was in bed and asleep within minutes.

Dr. Rory and his wife Ann missed the days when they used to sneak all over the house to secret hiding places where presents had been squirreled away since July, careful not to wake any of the kids, who still believed in Santa Claus. When the kids were younger, Dr. Rory and Uncle Ox used to climb up onto the roof and jump up and down on the peak of the old house, as if Santa's sleigh had just landed. They also took turns dressing up as Santa, and giving out small presents to the children early on Christmas Eve. Santa would tell the children that he was just beginning his rounds, but had decided to stop at the Dunleavy's house first.

The kids got so excited that it took hours for them to fall asleep. In those days, the whole family went to the nine o'clock Mass on Christmas morning. Dr. Rory and his wife lay awake talking about the earlier days, and how much more fun it had been. Soon they were asleep.

These days, Uncle Ox and Aunt Flora arrived from Vermont about eleven on Christmas morning. Uncle Ox would settle into the big overstuffed chair hoping to see some of the football game, while Aunt Flora helped out in the kitchen.

Dr. Rory enjoyed the company of his brother, Ox for he was that rarest of human beings. Ox actually reveled in the successes of the people that he loved. He wasn't blessed with the brains of Dr. Rory, but he wasn't an idiot either. Nature had more than compensated him with a large and generous heart. Uncle Ox never judged his life against others, and he asked little of those he loved.

After Ox and Flora were married, Ox discovered Flora was a marvelous cook. Before he proposed to her, he didn't even know whether or not she could boil water. Ox had cooked for himself for so long, it mattered not a wit to him if he had to continue cooking. He married Flora just because he loved her.

When Ox later learned that Flora couldn't have children, he felt worse for her than for himself. Uncle Ox told his brothers that it was tougher on Flora, because "all women want to have kids."

Uncle Ox asked so little of life, and got so much by comparison.

A few days before the holiday, Zeke and Jack Dunleavy had once again ridden out to A. T. Rule & Sons in Folding Hills. This time, however, the turkey was only a scrawny eighteen-pounder. Zeke picked up the box by himself, and with Jack opening the tailgate, threw the box into the back of the station wagon.

Dinner was much quieter on Christmas Day, more befitting the occasion. Dr. Rory delivered the toast, which varied only slightly from his Thanksgiving toast, and everyone fit nicely right in the dining room proper.

When Flora asked for seconds on the turkey, Jack gave a sideways grin at Zeke. Dr. Rory glared at him, and he quickly assumed the frozen puss of a pallbearer.

After dinner, the men went into the den to finish watching the football game, and the women cleared the table and washed the dishes. While they cleaned up, Flora told the story of Uncle Ox's latest invention.

As a dairy farmer, Uncle Ox was sick of shoveling out the barn. It seemed that his whole life was spent shoveling cow dung. Finally, one night after dinner, he sat down at the kitchen table, and with all of the artistic bravado of a three year old, drew a picture for Flora of his latest brainstorm. He was going to build a water trough at one end of the barn, but it was going to be huge. Uncle Ox was talking about a water trough that was six feet tall, ran the width of the barn, and held about eight thousand gallons of water. This trough was actually "V" shaped, and the bottom was hinged the entire length.

At the opposite end of the barn, the lower three feet of the siding of the barn would be hinged as well, so that it could be swung up with the pull of a rope.

At the end of the day, after the cows had been milked, and all the tools and milking machines were stored away, Uncle Ox would open the barn siding, and tip over the trough sending a huge tidal wave of water through the barn carrying all the cow dung with it. He figured that he could even add a small amount of detergent or disinfectant to the water to ensure a sanitary barn.

It was Uncle Ox's plan to start with a small quantity of water, and work his way up to the right amount. Sadly, trial and error showed him that to really clean the barn, it took a tidal wave of all eight thousand gallons. Unfortunately, Uncle Ox's well could only produce one tenth of that per day, so Ox and his hired men were back to shoveling dung, nine out of every ten days. Some invention.

Still no one laughed harder than Uncle Ox. He had an unlimited capacity for self-deprecation, and he practically insisted that the other fellow get the better of any human comedy. He loved being the butt of a great joke.

Zeke and Jack loved Uncle Ox even more than their father did. Without even knowing it, they were witnessing a truly great human being, who was just a dairy farmer. How many times in the future would they look back on Uncle Ox with love, good will, respect, and just about any other legitimate emotion that one man can have for another. And yet, when he sat in their midst, he was just Uncle Ox—a glass of scotch, and three hundred pounds of laughter.

Promptly at eight o'clock in the evening, Uncle Ox and Aunt Flora would collect their things and begin the drive back to

Vermont. Dr. Rory promised to get up to see him and Flora in the spring, but everyone knew that when spring arrived, he would be too busy, or the kids would have some activity that would keep them anchored to Wellesport. The two brothers just laughed.

When they were growing up in Vermont, there was a farmer named Asa Pagan who was always telling people what he was going to do for them, when in truth, he never did a thing for anybody. To this day, when someone made an insincere or hypocritical offering, the two brothers would say to each other, "Pagan Promise."

They laughed and shook hands. Uncle Ox thanked his brother for his hospitality, Aunt Flora smiled and agreed. Then they were gone.

The weather turned bitterly cold on Christmas Night and, in two days, the skating pond, which was really just a brook that the town dammed up in October, had a six-inch thick slab of ice covering it. Zeke and Jack were both hockey players, and two seasons before, had built hockey goals out of two-by-fours and chicken wire. They put the goals into the back of the station wagon and brought them over to the skating pond, which was almost opposite the entrance to Soapy Doyle's place. With the nets out on the good smooth ice, the boys played hockey until it snowed on Friday.

After the ice was covered, it could take the better part of a day to clear the snow, and of course, nobody wanted to do it. Zeke tried to talk the other players into shoveling, but they all managed to manufacture great excuses. In the end, his only helper was Gino Finelli. Even Jack said he had something else to do.

The Wellesport Cove took a little longer to freeze, but by the end of the week, it too was a good thick plate of ice, now covered with snow. Jack Dunleavy and his friend Ed Nadeau decided, that since they could now walk it, they would pay a visit to their campsite on Hidden Island. While they were there, they could clean the snow off "Old Sparky."

Back in October, when they had boated and then floated the old oak chair out to Hidden Island, they had set it up with its back up against a large swamp maple. From a limb, which extended out over the chair, they hung the electrical reflector. It was uncanny how much it looked like the real apparatus. They had also gathered a number of old belts that no one would miss, for the arm and leg restraints, and damned if it wasn't a convincing copy of the real "Old Sparky"

After slogging through the snow a good fifteen minutes, they got to the small spit of land that extended out to the west, and almost completely obscured Hidden Island. It was only about fifty feet wide with very little foliage, but in the summer, it hid the earthen part of Hidden Island completely.

Back onto the ice channel between the two landmasses for just a short time, and they were pulling each other up the snowy clumps of grass at the edge of the island. Another very short walk, and they were at their campsite. Other people used it, but by hiding the reflector and the leather belts, others didn't realize what the chair was for. Nobody in their right mind would try to steal it. They might try to burn it, but no one would take it home.

In the wintertime, it seemed as if you could stretch your arm right across Wellesport Cove and touch the prison's long, high walls and the tall, round guard towers with their high-pitched conical roofs. The place resembled a castle, maybe in Siberia, Bavaria or some other remote location.

And quiet. Almost a thousand men lived behind the walls, and not a single sound to be heard. The only sign of life at all, was a gentle curl of smoke rising from the central chimneystack, some eighty feet in the air. Other than that, nothing.

The two boys cleaned the snow off of the old chair, and retrieved the reflector and restraints from a wooden box hidden in the brush. They threw the end over the tree limb, and then threw fingers to see who would go first.

Ed Nadeau won and sat in the chair. Jack buckled the arm restraints, the leg restraints, and then asked, "Henry Cutler, do you have any last words, before you are executed?"

His friend playing the part of Henry Cutler, and remembering the defeat of the Giants to the Colts a couple of days before, said, "I hope that the Baltimore Colts get stuck in quicksand . . . and I hope that the New York Giants win the NFL championship forever . . . and I hope that someday I get to see Laurie Cooney naked and . . ."

"That's enough last words," said Jack. "This isn't *Queen For A Day*." With that, Jack lowered the reflector over Ed's knit cap, and took his place off to the side, ready to throw the switch.

"Five . . . four . . . three . . . two . . . one . . . ZZZZZZZZZZZZZZZZZZZZZZZZ."

Ed Nadeau snapped his body back and forth, in a grotesque interpretation of the actual motions that Henry Cutler's body would go through, as two thousand volts of current singed his hair and burned his flesh. In the inimitable way of twelve year olds, it was all a great joke. They took turns strapping each other into "Old Sparky" and making up memorable last words, until they got tired of the game and decided to quit.

As they left Hidden Island, first they swung to the west, which put them right in back of the prison. They walked slowly as the sun began its descent. Suddenly, they stopped.

Guards began to pour out of the cove guard tower and fan out along the walls with rifles in their arms. For a moment, they both tensed up. Then it dawned on them that yardout was about to begin. There was one hour until sunset. They continued their walk toward the prison watching the guards, not one of which even glanced in their direction.

Without noticing it, they had walked almost to the shore, and were within twenty feet of two steel pipes—each about six inches in diameter. These pipes were the main sewage drains for the prison, and dumped raw sewage directly into the cove.

"Nobody's ever going to escape through these pipes," said Jack.

"Yeah," agreed Ed. "A mouse would have a tough time running through there."

They turned to the East and walked to the frozen dock, then up to Main Street toward home.

20

With the Dunleavy children, and all their classmates enjoying that time in life when not working produces no guilt, the Christmas vacation was wiled away playing hockey, trudging around town visiting friends, shoveling snow, and watching all their favorite television shows.

The Dunleavy boys would be outside all day long, while Wibby slept until noon, talked to her friends on the phone, and at length, took a trip uptown to buy records or maybe catch a movie.

There was a movie theater in Wellesport, The Ciné Wellesport on Route 5, but for the last six months, it had been showing *Cat On A Hot Tin Roof* with Paul Newman and Elizabeth Taylor. Most everyone in town had seen it twice, so it was into the city, just for a change.

There were three theaters in the city. The girls could choose between *Buchanon Rides Alone* with Randolph Scott, *The Roots of Heaven* with Errol Flynn or *Auntie Mame* with Rosalind Russell. They chose *Auntie Mame* in the early part of the week, and *Buchanon Rides Alone* on Saturday.

Each day, no matter what their choice of entertainment, they arrived home by four o'clock for *American Bandstand*. If the radio blurted out that the Russians had launched nuclear missiles with their nose cones pointed directly at Wellesport, Wibby and her friends would still be watching *American Bandstand* when they hit. Dick Clark would do the patter and spin the disks, while some obviously well-screened teenagers from Philadelphia would dance the many different versions of "The Bop."

Wibby and her friends would go upstairs, spin their own records, and practice "The Bop," taking turns being the boy. Some of them, Wibby included, became very good dancers. They talked about boys, and looked forward to the time when they would finally be attending the sock hops.

When Dr. Rory walked in the door after office hours on Friday of the first week in January, he had some shocking news to tell his little family.

Any story regarding the practice of medicine from Dr. Rory was like finding a gold nugget in your rose garden, and indeed, Dr. Rory was as closed mouth as a person could get on the subject, but this was a special case.

Earlier in the day, Dr. Rory had made a quick stop at the hospital to see one of his patients. He left his medical bag in the car, and while he was in the hospital, someone had smashed the back window of his Buick, unlocked the driver's door and stolen the bag. He explained that it was probably addicts looking for drugs. It had happened once before, just after he started in practice, and he predicted that it would happen again. He had actually gone to some pains to keep the bag with him at all times, but sometimes he just didn't.

They all filed out to the barn to see his Buick, which looked a little sickly with its broken window. They also studied the smudges, where the detectives had dusted the car for fingerprints. It was unlikely that they would catch the addict who stole the bag, but they had dusted for prints anyway. There were just a couple of small black smudges now, but interesting to the Dunleavy children all the same.

The same detectives found the bag about a week later, floating in a pond, in one of the city's many parks. The bag was empty, and not in any condition to be used again. Dr. Rory had already purchased a new one anyway.

***

The winter months were the easiest months for Benko Sadek. The prisoners were out of their cells for only about eleven hours a day—no baseball, no football. During yardout, the inmates just roamed around trying to keep warm in their P-Coats and knit caps.

The whole mood of the prison quieted down, with the chance of someone trying an escape just about nil. If someone did get out, they would leave tracks in the snow, and probably be caught just before they froze to death. Even the trustees spent less time outside the prison. No lawns to mow, no flowerbeds to tend, no crops to grow. If there was no shoveling to do, the only crew outside the prison was the coal crew, and their whole operation could be watched from the "Gate" guard tower atop the northeast corner of the prison wall.

All the same, Benko made his rounds, and looked in on Henry Cutler three times a day, sometimes more. He also had the guards toss his cell about twice a month, just to make sure he wasn't into any handicrafts. He would toss the cells of the other prisoners on death row as well, but it was just window dressing. It was Cutler that he wanted to watch.

So far, he could find nothing out of the ordinary and it gnawed at him. Cutler had a well-deserved reputation for slipperiness but, unless he was planning on disappearing into thin air, the Dep was stumped. When it came to the cons of the Wellesport prison, the state didn't pay Benko to be stumped.

21

During the good weather, Dr. Rory Dunleavy usually played golf on Wednesday afternoons, with a bunch of his cronies, at Deer Run, a semiprivate club in the Town of Rowley—twenty-minutes south of Wellesport. He had considered joining the Wellesport Country Club, but decided against it. Somehow to him, it smacked of elitism, a mindset he fought against.

He was the physician for the prison, Wellesport High School, and the volunteer fire department, the last two of which required almost no time, but solidified his image as a down-to-earth, involved citizen—all good advertising tactics.

However, it was the middle of winter now, and the best that he could manage was an afternoon of skiing in Massachusetts or Vermont. Once in a while, if no snow had accumulated on the ground near the Connecticut shore, he and his buddies would drive there, and play some winter golf on one of the public courses. With a steady winter's wind blowing off the ocean, and all the golfers bundled up like Eskimos, it just barely passed for golf. Still, it was a day in the country with a little exercise, and a lot of laughs. It suited them fine.

This week, however, he had called one of the members of his group to let it be known that he wouldn't be seeing them on Wednesday. He said that he had to spend some extra time at the hospital-meetings and things—you know. Couldn't be helped.

In fact, he had an appointment with the governor.

It was not easy to see the governor, and knowing full well that if he came right out and wrote to the man concerning the beatings that he was witnessing at the prison, the governor probably wouldn't see him at all. So, he came up with a roundabout plan.

At Joan d'Arc Hospital, there was a doctor named Mordecai Levy. His friends called him Mory. He was an anesthesiologist, who had grown up with Governor Belden. They had been schoolboy chums right up to the time when they both left for college. They went to different universities, but both went on academic scholarships. Dr. Rory had approached Mory, imploring him to arrange a meeting with the governor.

At first, Dr. Levy wasn't interested, but then, with a little more persuasion, he agreed to at least talk to the governor when he saw him next. That had been two months before, and now at last, he heard from Mory. The governor would meet with them briefly on Wednesday, January 21 at two o'clock, if that was agreeable to him. He would make time.

Finally, the day arrived and he arranged to stop at the hospital early to buy Mory some lunch before they went to see the governor. He reasoned that when the governor gave you a two o'clock meeting, and intimated that it was going to be a short one, the man had no interest in breaking bread with you.

Dr. Rory arrived at the hospital just before noon, and went directly to Mory's office, where he found him talking to himself, as he rummaged through some papers. Dr. Rory knocked gently on the door.

The small plump man wheeled around quickly in his chair.

"Ah. My good friend, Rory Dunleavy. A man on a mission. Please come in," he said affably.

Dr. Mordecai Levy was a "mensch." He was lovable beyond human understanding. Men and women both found him irresistible as a person. He made each moment of life seem fun and instructive. He, of course, talked incessantly, and if you ever got stuck in an elevator with him, you would have a decidedly different view of the man. All things considered though, he was a joy.

"Good morning, Mory. How are you?" asked Dr. Rory.

"What? No Doctor Levy? Oh . . . you young people are so disrespectful of us old farts. Why, just the other day, I was telling my dear Esther that if I had to do it again, I would have become a brain surgeon. No matter how old you get, people still respect you," the older man kidded his colleague.

"My dear Dr. Levy, please pardon my insolence," joked the younger man, bowing to make his point.

Mory Levy laughed and said, "You're forgiven, my son."

Then Dr. Rory said, "You know, Mory, we have plenty of time. Would you rather go out for a good meal before we meet with the governor?"

"Nonsense, the food here is fine. Come along." While it seemed that he was saving the younger doctor some money, and simplifying matters considerably, the old fox had an ulterior motive.

In the past month, he had become smitten with a middle-aged woman doctor, who was working on a research project in one of the labs. He didn't want to miss even a single opportunity to run into her. She was a tall, good-looking blond with aquiline features, and best of all, she was divorced.

On the face of it, Mory was not any woman's idea of a great catch, but the halls of hospitals all over the Northeast were littered with the bodies of greater men, who underestimated Mordecai Levy. His formula was simple. He made women laugh and feel good. From there, it wasn't a long leap into bed.

As they walked to the cafeteria, bantering back and forth about the demands of modern medicine, Mory's eyes darted back and forth, electric with anticipation. They stood in line with their trays, when who should dart into the queue behind them, but Dr. Evyln Levesque.

Mordecai pretended to have missed a salad that he wanted, and slid Dr. Rory ahead of him. As the svelte beauty edged closer, Mory Levy went into action.

"Ah, Dr. Levesque. How are you today?" he asked with a Cheshire cat grin on his face.

"Just fine, Mordecai. How are you?" she said sweetly.

"My dear. Please. My friends all call me Mory," he said pleadingly.

"All right, then. I'll call you Mory, too."

"Thank you. Thank you," he beamed. "You know, my dear, as a physician and a colleague, I must warn you against eating here. You'll ruin your lovely figure," he said as he scolded with his index finger.

She smiled in appreciation and, as the talk progressed, Dr. Rory began to think that he should be taking notes. His courtship with his wife, Ann, had been so straightforward that some of the fun that Mory was now enjoying had been completely missing. On the other hand, their ideas and values were such a good fit, that he had not thought to question whether they were having enough fun.

Mory invited the beautiful, blonde doctor to join Dr. Dunleavy and him, but she said that two other girls from the lab were on their way down. She thanked him, and said maybe some other time. Mory smiled in deep appreciation and said good-bye.

When they were shuffling toward their table and out of earshot, Mory said to Dr. Rory, "Lovely girl. Just lovely." Dr. Rory agreed.

They arrived at the capitol building, in the heart of the city, with about fifteen minutes to spare, and they took the elevator to the fifth floor where the governor's office was. When they arrived in the outer receiving room, the governor's secretary looked up from her typewriter and asked, "Can I help you?"

Mory stepped forward and said with his big winning smile, "Doctors Levy and Dunleavy to see the governor."

"He's been expecting you," she said with her own agreeable smile. "I'll check with him, if you just wait a moment."

When she left the anteroom, and entered the governor's inner office, Mory said "Lovely girl. Just lovely." Dr. Rory agreed.

After a few minutes, the secretary emerged from the inner office and said, "The governor will see you now." She left the door ajar.

The two doctors thanked the secretary cordially, and walked into the governor's office. As they did, Governor Belden rose, and came out from behind his desk to shake hands with them.

He was a slim, Anglo-Saxon Protestant of medium height, with the polished banter of a longtime politician. He had been president of his high school class and Phi Beta Kappa in college. In a sentence, he was good-looking, well liked and plenty smart.

"Mory. You old quack, how've you been?" said the governor, extending his hand.

"Trying to keep my money from political hacks like you," said Mory, showing his biggest grin of the day. They shook hands and hugged. They were obviously enormously fond of one another, treating each other to the crudest barbs, reserved only for the best of friends.

After they were done hugging, Mory said, "Governor, I'd like you to meet Dr. Rory Dunleavy."

The governor extended his hand, and smiled as he said, "It's a pleasure to meet you, Doctor. I'm surprised we haven't met before. Mory tells me you're our man at the prison. Is that right?"

"Yes. That's right," said Dr. Rory, a little confused. This was the first governor in a hundred and thirty years who refused to annually inspect the prison. How were they supposed to meet? Still, he said in a civil manner, "It's nice of you to see me, governor."

"Not at all. Not at all," said the state's chief executive, as he asked the two to take seats. Dr. Rory settled into a soft leather upholstered chair on the left of the governor, with Mory on the right, and the governor returned to the cushy chair behind his desk.

"So how can I help you, Doctor?" asked the governor.

"Well, governor. I asked to see you today, because of what I consider inhuman beatings that the prisoners are being given. Unnecessarily, I might add," he began slowly. He tried to explain the other methods that could be used on the prisoners, instead of these vicious beatings. As part of his presentation, he also apologized to the governor for even taking up his time with the matter, but explained that he had exhausted all the other responsible links in the chain of command.

The governor acted totally surprised and dismayed to hear of the beatings, and even at one point reached for a piece of paper and a pencil from a little holder on his desk. He began scribbling notes, as if he were receiving grave news about a sick family member.

He asked a few questions and then listened some more. After it seemed that Dr. Rory had completely vented his spleen, the governor said that he was going to look into the matter personally, and that he would get back to the doctor as soon as possible.

Then the governor rose to indicate that the meeting was over and said, "Say, Dr. Dunleavy, would you mind if I got a picture of you together with Mory and myself. I'm not going to be governor forever, and some day I'll want to look back. If you like, I can see that you get a copy."

"Oh," said Dr. Rory, "that would be fine."

The governor pushed the buzzer on his desk twice, and instead of the secretary coming into the office, a man with a camera around his neck emerged.

The governor got in the middle, putting his arms around both the men's shoulders. At the very moment that the photographer asked everyone to say "cheese," the governor shamelessly rose up to his tiptoes. The photo would only show the men from the waist up, so Governor Belden could use this cheap trick with impunity.

They all shook hands again, and the governor thanked the men for coming. They were in and out of his office in ten minutes flat.

When the men left, Belden crumpled up his notes of the meeting, and threw them into his wastebasket. Then, he began to prepare for his next meeting by memorizing the names and family situations of the next group of "tongue flappers," as he called them—wasting his time with their "flapping in the breeze" nonsense. "How long, O Lord?" he used to say behind their backs, with his face up to the heavens, and his hands outstretched.

Three months earlier, he had won reelection with the largest plurality of any governor in the history of the state, and he hadn't done it by worrying about prisoners who had lost their right to vote. He had done it with a warm smile and a good cameraman. As he saw it, hard work in politics wouldn't get you elected dogcatcher, but charm and pictures—lots of pictures—could get you anything. Accordingly, he had mastered what Dr. Rory and his brothers called the "Pagan Promise," the kind word and the group photo. And he always found a way to make himself look bigger than he was, just as he had done today. Most people were so caught up in their own appearance, they didn't even notice him spring to his tiptoes.

The governor toyed a little with the idea of calling Warden Stoner at the prison just to keep him apprised of things, but decided against it. He knew that general practitioners worked long hours, and as a result, Dr. Dunleavy would have little time to make trouble, even if he wanted to. On top of that, he would have a picture of himself with the governor hanging in his consultation room, with all of his patients thinking that he and the governor were personal friends. This guy wouldn't be a problem, he assured himself.

About a month later, Dr. Rory was going through the mail, when he found a manila envelope from the governor's office. Excitedly, he opened it, finding an eight by ten glossy photograph with a cover letter. He leaned back in his chair and read the letter. It stated that the governor had looked personally into the matter, had spoken to the warden and taken the necessary steps to correct "this aberration."

In subsequent visits to the prison, Dr. Rory realized that the governor had played him for the fool. Nothing had changed, and nothing was going to change. He was disgusted.

He realized that there were really only two choices. He could quit in protest, but that would accomplish nothing. Or, he could continue his work, and try to slowly alter things with Harvey Stoner and Benko Sadek. He chose the latter.

22

Henry Cutler felt like the prize catch of Wellesport. There were only two other inmates on death row. Both murderers. Both appealing their sentences. Neither had a prayer, but they could eke out a couple more years of life in the bowels of Wellesport Prison, for whatever that was worth.

Benko Sadek put the two others in the two cells closest to the exercise yard, and kept Henry Cutler in the cell farthest away from them. No good could come from any conversation between these three. Also, Cutler was given the first exercise period right after lunch, so that if there were any trouble, even during the short days of December, there would still be a couple of hours of daylight to deal with it.

Close tabs were kept on his visitors, and anything going into or out of his cell. Security was as tight as it could get.

Unfortunately, Benko Sadek was dealing with some imponderables that were beyond his control. At the top of the list was the decrepit condition of the decaying cells on death row. They were the oldest cells in the prison, and the only ones still made of brownstone and mortar. As if to underscore this problem, on the cell doors were the kind of locks that were operated with skeleton type keys.

The rest of the cells on the north and east cell blocks had been upgraded through the years, but with the prison scheduled for demolition in the autumn, nobody was putting an extra cent into the place. The roof over the north cellblock had been leaking for three years, and they just put buckets under the drippings. One of the walls of the piggery had actually collapsed, when one of the huge hogs undermined it with his constant digging. The whole place screamed out for attention, but all the money was going to the new prison, and there would be nothing for Wellesport.

During his yardout, Henry Cutler studied the situation for the umpteenth time. Part of the hour, he pretended to do exercises in the middle of the yard. First, he would do jumping jacks with his eyes moving around the yard. Over and over again, he asked himself whether or not the guard would be able to shoot him before he could get over the wall. His rifle had no scope, just the "blade and V" sight that came with the standard Winchester 30-30. A good marksman could get the gun in position, and squeeze off a shot in about two seconds, use the lever action to chamber another round, and get off another shot at about the four second mark. Despite this, if Cutler's calculations of his speed up the wall were correct, that would be the last shot the guard would get off. Henry would be over the wall and gone. In the final analysis though, a nighttime escape still made more sense.

He had already decided to head for the city. He wouldn't have a chance, if he tried to hide out in Wellesport or any of the other farm towns south of the city where everyone knew everyone else. He would stick out like a pumpkin in a pea patch. No, he had to get to the city, and he would do it without using the streets, sidewalks or public transportation. The way to avoid the search party was to swim the Wellesport Cove, and then sneak into the city, using the meadows by the Pompaucau River.

The police would without doubt search his mother's apartment. He hadn't kept close contact with Pearl and he wouldn't visit her now. He knew of a married couple in the city who had no children, and they both worked. His plan was to lie low until they left for work, break into their house, steal some clothes and food supplies, and make tracks for Massachusetts. He would walk along the banks of the Pompaucau, at night if possible, and within a few days, he would be in the Bay State. Once he was out of Connecticut, he felt that he could get a place in Springfield or Worcester, and perhaps achieve some level of anonymity.

He would let his beard grow the whole time that he was traveling, and try to keep clean by washing in the Pompaucau. He felt that it was a good plan, but he had to get out of the Wellesport Prison first.

After the jumping jacks, he did toe touches. Every time his head came up he studied the wall—thirty feet of brownstone and mortar. He needed a rope and some kind of a hook, he thought.

The rope was easy. When the time came, he would simply rip his sheets into six-inch wide strips, and tie them together. He knew, instinctively, that such a makeshift rope would support his weight.

Still, the hook was going to be a little tougher. The east wall near the front of the prison overlooked the empty women's cells, the execution chamber, and this one heavily guarded exercise yard, and so it did not have a catwalk and rail (and armed guard) like the north wall did. The east wall catwalk and the rail ended at the guard tower, where even now he could see smoke curling up out of the small chimney in the center of the high, conical roof. A small, pot-bellied coal stove kept the guards warm, and they retreated there whenever they could.

Cutler suspected that when his two death-row mates had their yardouts, the guard spent most of his time in the guardhouse keeping warm. When he was in the yard, the guard walked the wall with his rifle cradled in his arms. It seemed to mesh very nicely with the other special treatment he was receiving.

The problem with the lack of a rail was that the hook had nothing on which to catch. He could throw the hook up the wall all day long, and it wouldn't grab onto anything. Suddenly inspired, he remembered the ivy on the outside of the wall. It had been growing there forever, and almost completely covered the exterior of the prison. He supposed that the townspeople preferred the regal disguise, and maybe that was the same reason that there had never been any barbed wire on top of the walls. Aesthetics would come at a high price this time.

In his mechanic's mind, he decided exactly what the hook would have to look like to catch the ivy and, of course, now his bed sheet rope would have to be longer. He could visualize the hook catching the ivy. He could see the thousands of tiny runners gripping the brownstone, and easily supporting his weight as he pulled himself up the wall. Another problem solved.

It was late January now, and Henry Cutler began to give time some thought. He was a little anxious about the lack of it. If his lawyer should just say the hell with it, and not file his "Friend of the Court" appeals motions—ostensibly against Henry's will—then Henry might run out of time very quickly. When he was taken out of his cell for yardout, he could look past the guard's desk, and see the door to the execution room. He had no intention of getting any closer than he was at present.

Also, with regards to time, he knew that it might take him months to make a key for his cell, and that assumed that he got it right the first time. Now, he had to make some kind of a hook as well.

He walked around the exercise yard for the remainder of his hour, and then was ushered back to his cell, where he spent the rest of the afternoon making a small sketch of the hook that he would need.

When he tired of studying the drawing, he folded it flat, and slid it into a small slit at the end of his mattress. He noticed that whenever the guards tossed his cell, their view was always toward the back of the cell. If they allowed him to have paints, he could have covered the back edge of his mattress with bright orange pigment, and they would never have noticed. For that reason, it made an ideal hiding place.

Henry Cutler also went out of his way to convince the guards that he really was using his time to make his peace with God. He pretended to read the Bible assiduously, when in reality, inside the Bible were drawings of the key to his cell, and timetables for the different guards.

When his dinner tray arrived that night about six o'clock, it was first inspected by the guard who looked at it closely, and then looked at Henry and said, "Chopped beef steak. Your favorite."

"Yummy," replied Cutler trying not to give away the euphoria that he felt at that moment. He wasn't happy about the food though. His friend, Doo-dah, had slopped gravy around the edge of the metal tray, so that the trustee would know which dinner was intended for Cutler. A sharp guard would have caught it, but this one did not.

The tray was put on the floor and slid into Henry's waiting hands. He took the tray to his metal desk, sat in his chair and began to eat. As he ate, he sat kitty-corner so that he could see out of his cell and eat at the same time. He sipped some milk out of a waxed cardboard container as he looked at his bunk.

The steel frame under the mattress was a latticework of flat steel straps. They ran from side to side, and end to end of a heavy, steel frame. Each strap was about an inch wide and an eighth-inch thick, and the whole thing was held together with steel rivets.

Just as he was thinking about those steel rivets, he looked out of his cell to make sure he wasn't being watched. When he was sure that the coast was clear, he slowly lifted the chopped beefsteak to reveal a small flat file and a piece of flat metal. The metal was perfect for making a key to his cell, and the file, while small, would do just fine. He was ecstatic.

The first order of business was to find a place to hide the file and the piece of metal. After watching the guards toss his cell for months, he had a pretty good idea where not to put these priceless little gems, and finally settled on creating a hole in the old mortar, where he could insert them. He would save some of the mortar and mix it with some toothpaste to make a small plug, which he could use over and over again. All of this, he would do right where the mattress met the wall.

Even when they tossed his cell, they wouldn't get a good look at the spot that he had in mind. By his calculations, he could have the hiding place all set by morning, if he worked through the night.

Henry Cutler sat quietly in his cell pretending to read the Bible when the lights went out. He, and the other inmates on death row, then undressed by the light given off by the bare bulb in the corridor outside their cells. In a few minutes, he was in bed watching to make sure that Ryan was on duty. He was.

Ryan was a tremendous help to Henry Cutler, because of the old guard's bad hearing. When he checked in every hour on the hour, the inmates could hear him practically shout into the phone. The phone would ring, and Ryan would yell, "AAAAAHHHH, YALLOW." After a pause, he would yell, "SAY WHAT?" Another pause, and he would yell, "AAAAAHHHH, YOKAY," and hang up.

The racket that this old guard made used to wake Henry up and it ticked him off, but now it was time to reap the rewards.

He worked on his hiding place all night long, being careful to work as quietly as possible. One of his fellow boarders might decide to rat to Benko Sadek in exchange for some inconsequential privilege.

By morning he had his tools hidden safely away and was ready to start work. He wouldn't have enough light at night to make the key so he would have to make it during the day and evening hours.

He found that if he wrapped everything in clothing, he could file the metal almost at will. The grinding noise was barely perceptible.

He set his Bible in such a way that he could close it quickly, and cover the drawings of the key, if need be. On the back side of the drawings, he copied Psalms so that even if the Dep opened the Bible, he would see the Psalms first, and think that they were just scribblings.

Though the metal was soft, it still took considerable skill to file it into a key. Henry also faced the dilemma of sculptors throughout the ages—whatever you take off, can never be replaced. He would have to be very careful not to make the key too small. The one consolation was that the lock was old, and probably housed a sloppy mechanism. Under such conditions, sometimes they could be opened with a screwdriver.

As he worked on the key, he considered other parts of his escape.

Again, he kept going back to timing. The seasons were a serious consideration now. Winter was out, with its bare landscape and freezing temperatures. He would not even have access to a pair of gloves, and there was no telling if Wellesport Cove would be frozen hard enough to support him. Walking was preferable to swimming, but if the surface should give way and he was forced to swim in the icy water, he'd freeze to death before he had to worry about being captured.

The month of May, after new leaves covered the trees, would be a good time, but still the waters of the cove might be too cold for comfort. Walking around the cove was much too risky. It was considerably longer, and he had to assume that someone would be on his tail.

He settled tentatively on the summer months for a number of reasons. To begin with, the climate would be the best, and he wouldn't have to worry about the temperature of the water. If he got real lucky, there would be a rowboat to steal. Grabbing a motorboat didn't seem like a realistic possibility, but a rowboat—maybe.

Summer was also the time of the year when the inmates were the most active—mowing lawns, tending crops, digging ditches—all of which tied up guards. Most of whom took their vacations in the summertime as well. In effect, there were fewer guards at a time when they were needed most.

He decided, at last, that he was definitely going right after Ryan got his midnight check-in call. He might be able to unlock the cell before the call came, but either way, as soon as Ryan got off the phone, he would spring from his cell, jump him, and tie him up with pieces of bed sheet.

He had thought about simply killing the guard, but it wasn't necessary. He also decided that he couldn't afford to tear any of his sheets until he had Ryan subdued, and the exercise yard door key in his hands. What if he had Ryan bound and gagged in his cell, and then he found out that for some strange reason he didn't have the yard-door key on him?

He had observed the guard closely, looking at his keys, counting them, watching as the shift changed, and he was about ninety-nine percent sure that the yard key would be there. It was a calculated risk that he would have to take.

He reasoned, also, that the steel strapping from his bed would make a good hook at the end of his bed sheet rope. However, he wouldn't bend it until he had used it as a club to inactivate Ryan. To that end, he filed off the rivets of the piece that he needed, cutting most of the way through the steel using the edge of the file. Then, he covered his work with ground up pencil lead mixed with food scraps for a binder. It worked reasonably well.

The one last detail was the other inmates on death row. They would want to go with him. He thought first that he would con them into thinking that once he had the rope set on the wall, he would come back for them. Instead, he would just take off. However, this might anger them enough to start a ruckus, and reduce his lead-time.

He would tell them, before he left, to be cool. That this was only a one-man escape, and that if they, in any way, contributed to his capture, his friends in the kitchen would put rat poison in their food. They would respect that, and as usual, act in their own self-interest.

Even as he put the final touches on his plans, he kept telling himself to be ready at any time. Anything could happen in prison, and he wasn't going to get a warning if Benko Sadek decided to change his cell. Therefore, he had to be set to go whenever the opportunity presented itself. He had worked out the ideal plan in his head, but seldom does such a plan go off without a hitch, inside prison or out.

23

February brought with it the biggest fire on record in the city. The towering St. John's Cathedral, in the short span of five hours, burned straight to the ground. It was the most enormous fire, with reported sightings up to twenty miles away—one large Roman candle blazing into the night sky.

Arson was suspected, but no one really knew for sure. The authorities would naturally investigate.

Oddly enough, it was as if someone was just turning out the lights, when leaving a room. The middle class Catholics had been leaving the city in droves, and the attendance at the Sunday masses had dropped to a meager few. Just when the cathedral teetered on the razor's edge of uselessness, someone simply cleared the lot.

Still the archdiocese, against all intelligent reasoning, announced to the public, even while the cathedral was still smoking, that they would rebuild. The new cathedral would be bigger and grander than anything extant. It would be a tribute to Connecticut's love for God.

The church cast out her net, trolling for those who would lead the collections in each Connecticut River town.

No sooner had Mrs. Veronica Cooney installed the black crepe over her front door, than an aide of the Archbishop knocked and asked her to chair the Saint John's Cathedral Rebuilding Drive in Wellesport. It is uncertain whether the archdiocese felt that Mrs. Cooney was a model Catholic because she had thirteen kids, or whether the idea of thirteen little beggars going from door to door suited their purposes expressly. Either way, she accepted with great fanfare.

The fund drive did not mean that there wouldn't be extra collections every Sunday, but the little kids at the door collecting money for a completely unnecessary cathedral, proved a nice touch.

For Veronica Cooney, it was a dream come true. She would give speeches, hold luncheons, organize bingo games, and do anything else that she could clear through the archdiocese. The church, for its part, showed its tolerant side by allowing any means of raising money, short of women taking their clothes off at Knights of Columbus dinners.

This money-grab was repeated all over Connecticut, and the cash poured in. A good estimate would be that Holy Mother the Church raised two and a half times what it needed for the new cathedral, but the word refund was not to be heard.

When Jack Dunleavy arrived home from school one afternoon, his brother Zeke was already hard at work stringing wires inside the SSK; but he didn't mind talking, so the two started to chew the fat about nothing in particular.

Jack looked around the garage, and asked his brother where all the extra parts had come from, and Zeke explained that all sorts of strangers had been good enough to surrender old parts that they had in their barns.

Zeke needed them too. The SSK had gotten way beyond his own financial capacity, and he was practically reduced to begging. On the bright side, the end was in sight. Barring anything unexpected, he believed he could finish by summer.

He would need some extra help from Soapy Doyle, but Zeke was sure that wouldn't be a problem. Soapy had made it a point to stop by at regular intervals during the construction, and bless the proceedings with a few special profanities. As a result, he and Zeke had become good friends. In a truly stupefying inversion of logic, Soapy became the brains, and Zeke became the brawn of Dunleavy Motors.

As if that weren't bad enough, Soapy thought that whenever he gave Zeke some help, his stock would rise ever so slightly in the eyes of Dr. Rory. The reverse was really the case, considering that Dr. Rory was prepared to move heaven and earth to make sure "that thing" never passed inspection, much less cruised up and down the streets of Wellesport on lazy Sunday afternoons.

As the two brothers worked on the front end of the car, they watched as Chief of Police Hoagy Larkin, pulled up in front of the Cooney's house. They waited for a while, speculating which of the Cooney boys was in trouble with the law now. Zeke thought that it would be the oldest, Peter, but Jack was sure that it would be Billy, Jr.

Billy, Jr. was like a seedling off the tree of Henry Cutler. Different economic and family backgrounds to be sure, but these particulars aside, he smoked cigarettes, lied nonstop, stole from the local stores, and set fires wherever he thought he could get away with it. At only thirteen years of age, his future looked dim.

If he could lie a little better, he had a chance in politics, but his other skills offered no hope whatsoever.

Sure enough, when Hoagy Larkin walked out of the Cooney's house, he had Billy, Jr. in tow. In a grimy sweatshirt and chinos, Billy, Jr. walked with his head down toward the sidewalk—the handcuffs on his wrists portending very serious trouble. Except for the inmates who were being shuttled in and out of the prison, Zeke and Jack had never seen anyone in handcuffs before, much less a neighbor.

It reminded Zeke of a man named Riggs who lived somewhere on the west side of town. He went to prison for taking pictures of naked women. He had been a professional photographer, and saw the chance to make some extra money in the calendar art business. He hired some models to pose nude for him, sold the pictures to a printing company in New York, and promptly went to prison.

Now it was Billy Cooney. The last time that Hoagy had come for Billy, Jr., he and some friends had been leaning out the front windows of the house, trying to shoot out an electrical transformer atop a telephone pole with a BB Gun. When Hoagy took him away that time though, there were no shackles. The handcuffs were a bad sign.

Rumors spread around town that Billy Cooney was in the city on the night that Saint John's Cathedral burned down, and some friends of his were placing him right at the scene. The truth would not come out for many months, but that was the early scuttlebutt.

Veronica Cooney was asked to step down as chair of the fundraising drive to rebuild the cathedral, and she did so very quietly.

About a week later, Connecticut was buried under the most powerful load of snow and ice ever visited on the Northeast. The storm began on a Friday night, with the gentleness of sugar sprinkled on cake. It stopped on Monday morning with freezing rain, which pulled down trees and power lines in demanding crashes throughout the state.

The town of Wellesport was without power for seven days. The townspeople scrounged all over the place looking for firewood to keep their houses warm, and with which to cook—burning fireplaces that hadn't been used in decades. Boy Scouts did well; others did not.

The first day was a lark. It was the beginning of the winter school vacation and around every corner was a most commanding spectacle—crunched cars beneath oaks . . . maples pressing on houses. Ice encrusted power lines were tossed around like tinsel. The shovels and the plows went nonstop for days. Great big front loaders and dump trucks tried to free up the businesses, so people could buy batteries and cans of sterno for cooking, while homeowners labored to keep their houses warm enough so that the pipes wouldn't freeze.

The local electric company had worked out an agreement in advance with other utilities in neighboring states, whereby in such an emergency, linemen, trucks and other equipment would be exchanged. Into the state poured crews from Pennsylvania, New Jersey, New York and Maine. Men even came down from Canada. The linemen on these crews worked under almost impossible conditions to resurrect the infrastructure of the electric utility. They worked sixteen hour days, seven days a week, in the cold and wet, as sometimes house by single house, they brought the system back on line. It was a yeoman job. Here and there, they would bring power to two hundred houses with a single connection making progress look at times rapid. Inevitably, they got into the areas that had the largest and densest collection of old trees, and the battle returned to a house-by-house reconnect.

Probably as a direct result of the working conditions, the long hours and the tedium, two linesmen from Pennsylvania were electrocuted at four o'clock in the morning in a remote part of the state. It was no one's fault, but it was heart-rending for all who learned of it.

One of the last places in the state to have power restored was Wellesport. An aged town with an abundance of oversized trees, the village looked like what in wartime would be called "a direct hit." Of all the streets in Wellesport, Main Street was the worst. The town had always taken enormous pride in the way that a natural canopy of greenery enveloped and embraced visitors, as they strolled down the main thoroughfare of the old village. There were even penny postcards in Zemel's drugstore of this bucolic scene. It was not unusual for visitors to think that the eighteenth century houses, which where the homes of the townsfolk, were museums. They would ask, "Where can we get tickets to see the Ezekiel Ransom house?" What they didn't know was that that particular house was really the Doctor and Mrs. Rory Dunleavy house, where they were now raising their three children.

In any event, the linesmen made their way slowly down Main Street and, by an odd coincidence, a camera crew from one of the local television stations arrived to interview the neighbors, just as the electric crew reached the Cooney's house.

With a light bar pointed toward her torso, and a microphone the size of a canned ham shoved in her face, Veronica Cooney proceeded to tell the whole world that the power company didn't know what they were doing—that they should have begun in Wellesport, and worked their way out to the surrounding towns. On and on she went, begging the question, "Why does participatory democracy look so good on paper?"

The linesmen were not the only ones working overtime. The trustees shoveled the walks and driveways all around the prison, finishing with the walk leading to Warden Stoner's house. Then they left the prison in groups of four to shovel paths and driveways all over town.

The elderly people of Wellesport would not have had a fighting chance without the help of the trustees. The snow was just too heavy, and snow blowers were new and rare. School kids went door-to-door looking to make a few extra bucks with Zeke and Jack Dunleavy in the lead. It would seem that the trustees, and the school children were at odds, but there was more than enough work for everyone.

The prison's coal delivery arrived thanks to the coast guard's ice cutter, and Benko's coal shoveling crews kept scooping as if nothing changed. The prison would stay warm. There would also be lights at the prison, for an emergency generator supplied electricity. The steady purr of the generator's diesel engine and the warm glow it ensured were the only signs of life in the otherwise shutdown town.

***

While the whole state dug out from this horrific storm, Henry Cutler lay quietly on his bunk filing a key for the lock on his cell door. He had to be very careful. If he was discovered, he would never have enough time or freedom to gather together again the materials he now had, nor would he necessarily be able to implement the same plan.

Months would have been wasted, but more importantly, he would be too close to his appointment with "Old Sparky" and the mysterious electrician, "Mr. X." It was an appointment that he had no intention of keeping, so slowly and quietly he filed at the key.

Even though the metal was very malleable, it turned out to be a tricky alloy with which to work. He had no intention of cussing out Doo-dah though. His friend had risked a great deal to get these few small items to him, and he was grateful. Besides, when it came to finding little pieces of steel, a prison was no hardware store. God only knew where Doo-dah had gotten these items.

He would have to be careful not to break the key off inside the lock, leaving him standing there trying to pick the lock with his fingers.

Every time he heard the guard get up from his desk, he had to slip the file and the metal blank down the front of his pants, drop the clothing to the floor, and pretend that he was reading the Bible.

One time, a guard had stopped to ask him what part of the Bible he was reading. He started to talk idly about the Psalms as his eyes quickly looked to the top of the page to see just exactly what it was that he was reading, and then he said that today though, he was reading Ecclesiastes. Open any King James Bible to the center, and you'll be at Ecclesiastes. However, a shiver of fright went up his spine as he talked to the guard, for the pages of his Bible were covered with metal filings.

And yet, he had said to the guard as he turned back a couple of pages, he liked Proverbs too. As he lifted the pages in an effort to hide the metal filings, they all shifted into the binding. The guard hadn't noticed. That was too close for a repeat performance though.

He knew that Benko Sadek was most likely to toss his cell during his yardout after lunch, so he had to make sure that everything was tucked nicely into its cubbyhole in the wall, and covered over before he went outside.

Henry Cutler was surprised that the Dep hadn't bothered him too much. He expected that he would be prodded and probed at every opportunity, but except to check up on him frequently, the Dep had essentially left him alone. He gave this a lot of thought. Could this Dep be convinced that he couldn't escape from death row? Was Benko overconfident because there had never been a successful escape on his watch? Maybe both?

He decided that as soon as the key was done, he would try to secret both it and the file somewhere on his person, or in his Bible, so that in case Benko ordered a cell switch, he would still have some kind of a key with him. Whether it would fit another cell was anybody's guess.

When he did get outside for his hour of exercise, he would walk around the perimeter of the yard, only letting himself glance up at the southeast part of the wall, his escape route, when he was at the north part of the yard. At this point, he would be directly under the guard, who couldn't see where he was looking.

Again, he thought about the hook catching on the ivy. What if there was no ivy at that spot? Then he would have to move along the wall until he could catch some. Since his plan called for him to go after midnight, as a last resort, he could hook the rail on the north wall of the exercise yard. The only problem with this scenario was that the north wall catwalk and rail could be seen from the cove guard tower. Too risky. Besides, in the quiet of the night, the steel hook would make too much noise when it hit the rail.

He would be best to rely on the ivy. Besides, he had decided to use the sheets and the hook to rappel down the outside of the wall but, if for any reason the hook wouldn't release, he could still use the ivy to get himself to the ground.

After yardout, he went right back to working on the key. He would stare at his drawings, then file a little, look at the drawings, then shave off a little more. All the while, he listened for the footfall of his jailers. It was very slow going.

24

Aside from a few late snowstorms, the month of March was like the ninth month of pregnancy for the town of Wellesport, with the farm families raising annuals and various vegetables from seeds in their greenhouses, and others around town raising pretty much the same things on the stool caps of their south facing windows.

The victory gardens of World War II were still deeply ingrained in the lives of everyone. They were not necessary anymore, but they saved money, and gave such a sense of satisfaction, that almost every family still planted one.

The weather held other surprises. Interspersed between the laggard snowstorms were some unusually warm days. Saint Patrick's Day almost set a record, and at the very end of the month, there was a string of nice days. However, the grass was still a sickly washed out ochre and mint color. It would be another month before it turned the lush green of spring. In another month or so, buds would appear on the trees.

The Dunleavys were as busy as ever despite the uncertainty of the weather. Ann Dunleavy was reading the best-selling novel, *Anatomy Of A Murder* (a courtroom drama written by Michigan Supreme Court Justice John D. Voelke using his pen name, Robert Traver). Dr. Rory spent his evenings listening to *Aida, Rigaletto, Don Giovanni, Carmen, Tosca, La Boheme, Madam Butterfly* or the Bohemian composers Smetana and Dvořák that he loved so much. He was particularly drawn to music that painted a picture. For example, he never got tired of Bedrich Smetana's *Moldau* because he could close his eyes and actually envision the river flowing. Other times, he read his medical journals while he listened. For all his self-assurance, he lived in mortal fear that he would wind up a senile general practitioner, whose knowledge of medicine was easily surpassed by a licensed practical nurse just out of school. With this in mind, he made it a part of his daily routine to read the journals and try to stay current.

Between the medical journals, he read Frost, Wordsworth, A.E. Houseman, Oliver Wendell Holmes—the physician not the jurist—and Yeats, simply because he was Irish. Occasionally, if a good novel came along he would read it, but he rarely read popular fiction. It was an art form that he simply did not enjoy.

He was a bifurcated man in the sense that, in the presence of his patients, he rarely used a word of more than two syllables, but his own time was spent in places that these same people didn't even know existed. Even Ann Dunleavy chose not to swim in the deeper waters.

Sometimes, Dr. Rory himself tired of this loneliness, but kept his own counsel. He was a New Englander through and through. Just as he didn't burden other men with his problems or concerns, he never borrowed tools from neighbors, and prayed to God that they would have the decency not to ask to borrow his. He would quote Shakespeare—

> "Neither a borrower nor a lender be;
> For loan oft loses both itself and friend,
> And borrowing dulls the edge of husbandry . . ."

For a short time, a salesman and his wife, a New Yorker, had lived in the neighboring house to the north. This man had the manners of a pig, and the borrowing habits of a Bowery bum. Dr. Rory secretly cursed this "leprosy on the loins of mankind" and again, quite unnoticed by others, cheered wildly the day the man moved away. Not to put too fine a point on it, but Dr. Rory felt that you should paddle your own canoe until your arms fell off. Then, gripping the paddle firmly in your teeth, continue on your way.

One night in late March, Zeke, Jack and Wibby were watching *Wagon Train* on the television. Every week, Ward Bond would lead a long entourage of Conestoga wagons around in circles, and every week a new crisis arose.

Wagon Train was no one's favorite show, but people endured it because it was on just before *Leave It To Beaver*, which everyone watched.

Though Zeke could still enjoy *Leave It To Beaver*, his favorite show came on at eight-thirty. It was called *Yancy Derringer* starring Jock Mahoney and X Brands as Pahoo-Ka-Ta-Wah, his sidekick. It was the strangest show ever filmed, with a gambler seemingly floating from one dangerous card game to another, while his Indian companion ensured peace with a sawed-off shotgun hidden under his cape. Unknown to everyone, except the audience, the gambler was really a lawman ferreting out wrongdoing in New Orleans. Zeke pronounced it a classic of the silly western genre, but he watched it religiously.

Between commercials, Ann Dunleavy asked her children how they would feel about moving to Africa. She asked the question as if it were just some game, but when she mentioned making all new friends, and attending schools that were a bit more limited, everyone sat up a little. They talked all evening about Africa, even going so far as to get out the World Book Encyclopedia to look it up— during commercials, of course. They didn't know how to feel about it. She decided to ask them again in a few days.

What the children didn't know was that Dr. Rory had tired of sore throats and swollen glands, and he wanted something more exciting and challenging for his life. It was a spell that he went through from time to time.

He was making absolutely no progress with Warden Stoner or Benko Sadek. The treatment of the prisoners was as brutal as ever, which he just couldn't countenance. He was at a loss to understand why depriving the inmates of their privileges, combined with indeterminate sentences in solitary, wouldn't do the job. The prisoners only had four privileges—writing, visitation, recreation and smoking. When a person had so little, these things became precious.

It didn't matter. Benko Sadek would just stick his ruddy, twisted visage up close to Dr. Rory's face, and through the vapors of cheap whiskey, tell him to mind his own godamn business.

He thought about going to work in the emergency room at Joan d'Arc Hospital, but the pay was so poor that he wouldn't be able to put his children through college. Mired in doubts, he read a biography of Albert Schweitzer and thought that Africa would be just the thing—adventure, challenge, excitement.

A short time later, the talk of Africa stopped. Just like that. It had come on like a line storm, and ended just as quickly. Dr. Rory apparently decided that dreams of saving hundreds of thousands of people in far off lands were for others and thereafter he kept his own counsel. Africa was never mentioned again.

Easter came early, March 29th. The weather was balmy again, and crocuses were showing everywhere.

Ann Dunleavy had taken all of her children into the city to buy new clothes for Easter. The boys each got three-piece suits that were on sale at J. Kent & Co. for $49.95. They were a nice gray wool, but the boys still looked like a couple of "smoothies," as Grammy Dunleavy joked. Wibby got a beautiful Villager suit. Unlike her brothers, the suit, together with a very becoming picture hat with matching purse and shoes, made her look quite chic.

Ann Dunleavy bought herself a new wardrobe as well, but Dr. Rory wore what he had. He simply had no interest in clothing at all. He let his wife buy him the bare necessities from time to time. He could get excited about any kind of tool or machinery, and of course, new discoveries in medicine, but he just had no interest in clothing or the furnishings of such stores.

For her part, Ann Dunleavy worked patiently to make sure that when Dr. Rory left the house, his suit pants matched his jacket. She wasn't always successful. His ties were the biggest bone of contention. Every other leap year, when he couldn't play golf on a rainy Wednesday afternoon, Dr. Rory would have a change of heart, and decide that he wanted to be a clothes horse like the golfer Doug Sanders. Without telling anyone, he would sneak into a men's store somewhere and look around. With shirts selling for three dollars, he quickly changed his mind.

Before leaving the store though, he always managed to find a rack of ties that were on sale—four for a buck. Beauty being in the eye of the beholder, Dr. Rory would buy two dollars worth. It was pretty close to a lifetime supply. Wellesport really came alive after Easter with some people showing their faces for the first time since Christmas.

Their skin white as alabaster and their torsos a few pounds heavier, they came out of their houses as the daffodils and irises found their way up out of the ground. The days were much longer now and spring athletics were starting up at all levels.

Zeke played first base for the all-new Wellesport Wolverines baseball team, while Jack played the coveted left field position for the Wellesport Grocery team of the Babe Ruth League—Ted Williams played left field. Unfortunately for Wibby, Wellesport offered no sports for eighth grade girls. She would have to be content to watch *American Bandstand* and dance The Bop with her friends.

Before the actual season began for the Little League in Wellesport, there would be several weeks of practice, and then the teams would play exhibition games on school day afternoons inside the prison for the inmates.

Dr. Rory wasn't concerned with these exhibition games inside the prison. The inmates would be on their best behavior and there would be guards everywhere. A small part of him also felt guilty that he had been unsuccessful in curtailing any of the brutality of prison life. These baseball games were good for the prisoners and gave them something to look forward to.

Later in the summer, adults who belonged to club teams would enter the prison on Sundays, and play against the inmates' team, the Wellesport Gold Sox. This would continue right on through the summer as long as the prison wasn't on lock down. If there was any kind of trouble, and summertime was the season for it, the inmates would be locked down. No yardout and no ball games.

While the games were played, there was always a group behind the chicken wire backstop at home plate, playing cards and shooting dice. People liked baseball for different reasons. Spring was for some unknown reason, the time of the year when everyone decided to clean out their houses, and bring their useless and broken castoffs to the Wellesport dump to be burned. The Dunleavys were no different in this respect. Ann Dunleavy's station wagon was loaded up with the refuse of an entire year, not counting the small weekly disgorgements, and driven slowly to the dump in the southern part of town.

It was a disgusting place, attended by an unshaven, drunken dreg of a human being with a three-legged dog named Lucky. Repugnant smoke filled the whole place, as underground fires smoldered away night and day.

Dr. Rory would drive his wife's station wagon carefully over the shards of glass and general detritus of the lives of the seven thousand souls of Wellesport. Every imaginable consumer good was heaped in big smoking piles, as neighbors greeted each other quickly, and got out of this little glimpse of hell as fast as possible.

It was also in the springtime that Ann Dunleavy brought the dead light bulbs back to the utility company for the free replacements. Usually, only one grocery bag of dead bulbs accumulated during the year.

One of the toughest chores was to rake up the lawn, including the windfalls under the apple trees. What hadn't been sent home on the backs of Jack's football friends was now to be raked up and dumped over the bank toward the railroad tracks. The mush could still feed the wildlife and eventually it rotted away to nothing.

Dr. Rory announced that he was going to have the house painted. It looked just fine to everyone else, but he said that it hadn't been done in twelve years, and he had read that there was a movement afoot to take the lead out of the paint. He suspected, correctly, that this would make it less impervious to the assaults of the New England weather. No need to change the color. White was just fine. Black shutters, perfect.

***

While the general population at the prison played baseball during yardouts, and reveled in the warm weather and the longer days, the trustees had busy times ahead. The lawn and flower crews had to get the warden's rose trellises ready as well as the other gardens surrounding his house. There were two larger flowerbeds that lined the road at the main entrance to the prison that needed planting. In addition to this, the smaller flowerbeds at the cottages of the chaplain and the deputy warden would have to be turned and sowed.

As if that weren't enough, there were flowerbeds at greens and cemeteries in the town itself that needed work. The trustees had plenty to keep them busy.

The garden detail crews had been out early getting the peas and carrots in. Now the less hearty vegetables would be planted. Like any other farmers without much machinery, the trustees would be kept busy from now until late autumn with the production of food for the prison. At regular intervals, sometimes daily, they would truck the produce into the prison, and hand it over to the canning shop, where it would be put up for the following winter.

Of the food crews, Frenchie and Ruppert's field behind the warden's house was the biggest of the bunch and, in past years, they had handled it without breaking a sweat. Sadly, the two were getting older now. As they planted seeds one day, Ruppert said to Frenchie, "I wonder how much longer for the dandelions?"

"Pretty soon— maybe," replied Frenchie finishing the sentence on an up note, as most Canucks are prone to do.

"Hope so. I could use something to lift my spirits. Have you got enough sugar?" asked Ruppert. Though there was no one to listen, they kept their voices low. That was actually tough for Ruppert, who had a low and powerful voice like a tuba. He could whisper across town.

"I got me plenty of sugar. Just let's see some dandelions, eh?"

"I ain't going to miss 'em, don't worry," said Ruppert.

"I ain't worried," said Frenchie in a low voice. "I ain't worried, eh?"

***

In his death row cell, Henry Cutler put the finishing touches on his key. It wasn't a pretty thing but considering the tools and the working conditions, it was a masterpiece of the trade. He wanted to try it as soon as possible. He was beginning to worry more and more about time. Not that time had ever been on his side, but he felt particularly pressed for it now that the good months were here.

He had also begun to have bad dreams about sitting in "Old Sparky." Ghastly dreams. They would stop when he got out, he told himself.

The guard sat at his desk about thirty feet away from the corridor that ran between the cells. He couldn't very well try the key now. He would wait until later in the day when the guard was beyond his cell, and opening the door to the exercise yard for one of the others. He'd have about one minute each time the guard let one of them out into the pen.

When the guard brought Cutler back inside after yardout, he sat on his bunk, removed his shoes and placed them in the corridor outside his cell, as always. He hurriedly got the key out of its cubbyhole and stole up to the bars.

The guard was just opening the cell door next to the exercise yard door.

He checked the other direction. Nothing. He slid his hands out of the bars, with the key in his left hand, and slipped it into the wards of the lock. He turned it gently, trying not to make any noise. He couldn't turn it, so he jiggled it a bit while trying to turn it again. No good. He began to have a sickening feeling in the pit of his stomach, as he kept trying to make the key work. It was hopeless. The key simply would not turn.

Time was up. The guard was about to turn back toward his desk after locking the yard door. He pulled the key back into his cell, and walked over to his cot and lay down. Again, he pretended to be reading the Bible as the guard walked by.

When the guard was safely at his desk, Henry Cutler cussed to himself as he pulled out the key and the drawings. What was wrong with the damn thing? He had no idea, but he had better find out fast.

25

Considering that it was Soapy Doyle who gave Zeke Dunleavy that first big push out of the starting blocks, and into the automobile manufacturing business by selling him the Olds V-8, it seemed only fitting that he should be the one to push Zeke through the tape at the end of the race.

Zeke, having long since been tapped out, was selling futures contracts on his own labor to inch the SSK to completion.

Gino Finelli and his father had been a blue chip arsenal in the parts battle, and Zeke himself learned upholstery from his mother, but it was the vulgar yet lovable Soapy who offered to paint the SSK in early May. Out of the clear blue, on one of his visits, Soapy announced, "We'll spray paint this sumbitch in my godamn barn. What d'ya think?"

Zeke was again overwhelmed by Soap's generosity. He had long since learned to overlook Soap's limited and startling vocabulary. Naturally, he accepted.

Soapy would tow the coupe to his barn, cover the walls and ceiling with drop cloths, and put several coats of lacquer on it. Zeke would have to spend about a week masking all the places on the machine that shouldn't be painted—all the chrome, headlights, taillights, wheels, horns, exhaust manifolds and pipes. It was a long list.

One thing bothered Zeke though. With Soapy's place of work so completely tailored to his individual needs, could he do good work without his girls smiling down on him? Or would Zeus and Eros conspire to rob Soapy of his strength and skills, just when Zeke needed them the most? It sounded like superstition, but it troubled Zeke anyway.

Anxiety notwithstanding, on May 6th, the wrecker from S.B. Doyle & Sons pulled up in front of Dunleavy Motors, and out stepped Soapy ready to make good on his promise. He muscled a tow bar from the back of the wrecker, hooked it to the front of the SSK and towed it off to the finishing plant.

The choice of color was something of an exchange, with strong opinions from everyone including Wibby. She thought that all sports cars should be red. Dr. Rory, expecting the SSK would live to a ripe old age in the confines of his barn, chose a color that he could live with—white. Zeke's mother, remembering how her silence had been bought with the simple slogan "Safety Fast" thought that bright yellow would really make a statement. The statement, of course, was SAFETY, but she was disinclined to discuss her reasoning. Jack thought that British racing green was *de rigueur*.

Zeke felt that they all missed the point of the SSK. It wasn't only a sports car and it wasn't British. It wasn't a gleaming white vase for some woman's *étagère*. It was the very last word in a luxury sports car with shades of touring. Beyond that, it was automobile art of the highest order, a successful graft of the speed and precision of a Ferrari onto the elegance and style of a Rolls Royce. It was the natural survivor in the Darwinian race for all the marbles between Auburn, Duesenberg, Bugatti and Hispano-Suiza. In the automobile world, it wasn't merely regal; it was royalty, the genuine article.

So with Soapy's knowledge of paint and Zeke's sense of dignity, they humbled themselves before the SSK and exhausted the color possibilities.

"Probably oughta be some godamn shade of gray," said Soapy with the unerring authority of an authority on the subject.

"I was thinking of something in the blue family, no?" said Zeke tentatively. This whole conversation would take the delicacy of Dr. Rory probing an infant's ear with his otiscope. How to get the color that he wanted, without hurting Soapy's feelings, or worse? He felt reasonably sure that his friend would keep his word about painting the car, but he wanted Soapy's heart to be in it. He was only too aware that any idiot could spill enough color on his dream to call it a paint job. He wanted more; a finish that Narcissus could live with.

They continued the horse-trading.

"Hell. They paint godamn buses blue," countered Soapy, gazing vaguely off toward the Pompaucau.

"Well, no . . . I was thinking more of a very deep, grayish blue," offered Zeke hopefully.

"Damn right," said Soapy. "The kind of goddamn blue that used to be called 'slate blue.'"

"That's the one," said a relieved Zeke. "Slate blue."

"Godamn slate blue it is then. Come by my damn shop and I'll show you a sample of the sumbitch."

When Soapy left, Zeke couldn't help but ponder the riddle that was Soapy Doyle. Here was a man with a heart of pure gold who kept people at bay with a mouth that gushed raw sewage. He was doing everything he could to keep people from finding their way to his oversized heart. And all the time, they knew it anyway. How many other people were like Soapy? Showing the world a rough exterior to hide a kind interior, when it should be the other way around.

It has been said that small men talk about people and big men talk about ideas, but can any of us ever really stop thinking about what makes our neighbors tick?

Whatever the mystery behind the enigmatic Soapy Doyle, Zeke would be forever in his debt.

Jack Dunleavy was glad to see the leaves beginning to show themselves on the trees. Even if it was a warm spring day, he really didn't enjoy camping in a forest of bare trees. In the coming months, the Scout meetings would concentrate on the annual Jamboree to be held at the end of June, in the southern part of the state.

Except for a trip to the Philmont Scout Ranch in New Mexico, nothing had the magnitude of the annual Scout Jamboree, where troops from all over the state would march into a "wilderness" area carrying full packs, set up camp for three days, and compete head-to-head for ribbons. Completely self-sufficient, they would bring in food and supplies of every sort—pots to pans, tents to toilet paper.

They were not *really* self-sufficient though. A medical staff—complete with an ambulance—stood at the ready, and their water came from faucets scattered throughout the "wilderness," but it still had that Lewis and Clark feel about it. The Scouts sucked in the good, clean air of the countryside, and tried to replicate the meals of woodsmen of old, with mixed results, of course. The average Scout lost about four pounds in the course of the three days, the result of just eight bad meals that a dog wouldn't touch. Nevertheless, Jack had the time of his life lugging around water buckets that wouldn't hold water, and standing naked under showerheads that did.

In order to get ready for the big Jamboree, Jack and his friend, Ed Nadeau, decided that a week before the big event, just after school got out, they would schedule a practice run. The closest and easiest campsite affording some privacy was the one on Hidden Island. They would have to borrow some boats, but that could be arranged. To wile away the time, they would have a contest to see who could do the best execution act while strapped into "Old Sparky."

It was arranged. On the weekend of June 20 and 21, the Cobra Patrol of Troop 33 would leave the Dunleavy place on Main Street at eight o'clock on Saturday morning. Each Scout would carry the same pack that he would tote at the Jamboree. The packs would be all set up the day after school got out, with only the food to add at the last minute.

With the Dunleavy SSK receiving the final detailing, Dr. Rory decided that it was time to give Salvatore Rucci a call. He remembered back to the time when he questioned whether Zeke could actually build a car in two years, and here he was only nine months later trying to keep "that thing" off the road.

The Doctor hadn't talked to Salvatore Rucci over the winter, and he hoped that his patient was still the top man at the state's Motor Vehicle Inspections Division. He would give him just a friendly reminder that Zeke's coupe was never to pass inspection in this lifetime. Dr. Rory was convinced that Salvatore would help him in this matter. For now, he could rest easy, he told himself. All the same, could the automobile fail inspection forever?

***

After getting over his initial panic when he realized that his key was useless, Henry Cutler kept a sharp eye on the guard's keys to double check his calibrations. He kept looking at his own drawings and then at his key, until he finally realized what the problem was. When he filed the shaft of the key from the metal blank, he had not taken enough material off. The key could not be inserted deeply enough into the keyhole to allow the teeth to line up with the tumblers inside the lock.

He felt that he could remedy the problem with just a little more filing. To limit the filing to the least amount necessary, he shoved the thin file into the lock, and put his thumbnail on the file to get an accurate measure of the depth needed.

Then, transferring this measurement from the file to the key, he made a mark. Sure enough. The teeth of the key had to go a whole quarter of an inch deeper into the lock.

The condemned man lay on his bunk, just the way he had done throughout the cold months, clandestinely filing away. He was getting sick of the sight of the thing, but at the same time, he knew it was priceless.

A few days later, the key was ready.

Just as before, when the guard let one of the inmates out into the exercise yard, Cutler slipped his arms through the bars, slid the key into the lock and turned it gently. The aged tumblers turned over easily, and the door to his cell began to swing open.

It happened so fast, he didn't have time to panic. He pulled the door shut, and turned the key to re-lock the cell door. Just as the guard turned, he snapped his arms into the cell, got to his bed and opened his Bible.

Henry Cutler could barely contain himself. He was glad that his keeper didn't decide to stop and talk. His face was flushed, and he knew it. It was child's play now to open his cell door, club the guard over the head, and be gone into the night. He had to be patient though, for he still had to fabricate the hook from the steel bed strapping.

Now that Cutler had the means to get out, he was worried that Benko Sadek would have him switched to another cell. If that happened, the key would be left behind in a cell to which he would never have access. He had to figure a way to keep the key with him. His shoes were prison issue like everything else he wore, and were left outside his cell at all times, except during his yardout period. Leaving the key in the heel of one of his shoes was just too risky.

The only other items that would surely follow him to a new cell would be his papers, pencils, toilet kit, Bible and a few pieces of clothing.

His heavy winter P-coat was a possibility. He could secret the key in the lining, but with the arrival of good weather, the guards would probably take the coat for safekeeping. His other clothes were too thin to hide a key.

The toilet kit wasn't a good bet, either. They might just give him new things. That left his Bible. Prisoners have been hiding things in their Bibles since the advent of the printing press. It had become a joke within the prison. To get a new con into trouble, just give him a worn out piece of a file, and tell him to hide it in his Bible. Sure enough, two weeks later, he'd be in solitary.

Sadly, Cutler had no choice. He had been in the same cell since last September, and the hot months were coming. These were the months when the Dep, and all the other guards were the most nervous. If his cell were going to be changed, it would happen now.

He did catch a small break, however. The piece of metal was flat, unlike a real key and, as such, it would be easier to hide. He studied the construction of the Bible; a small, hard-covered book, which was about an inch and a half thick.

He pretended that he was Benko Sadek examining the book. He looked inside the front cover, and he looked inside the back. With his left thumb, he riffled the pages slowly. Then, he closed the volume and studied the front and back covers. Lastly, he examined the binding. At no time did his eyes catch the top edge of the tome.

The key, which he had to hide, was thinner than the hard covers of the Bible. By using a pencil, the file, and then the key itself, and working on a small opening at the top edge of the book, he was able to slip the key and the file into the back cover of the Bible.

Another advantage was that the key was not an item that he had to keep removing from the book. He could use ground up pencil lead and food scraps to cement it into place.

The file was different. He set the file up so that he could remove it when he needed it.

After watching the guards all these months, he was convinced that his key would fit any of the cells on death row. One less concern. When he finished cementing the key and the file into his

Bible, the book had a slight weight imbalance, but there was nothing he could do about it. He put the Bible on the desk and lay down on his bunk to think.

Tonight, he would devote less time to his arm exercises, and begin to file the rivets off the iron strapping under the mattress. Thank God for Ryan's hearing problem. Still, he had to be quiet because of his two ward mates—it was every man for himself in prison.

After lights out, Henry Cutler quietly pulled back the lumpy, old mattress and looked at the rivets for the first time in a month. They were low carbon steel, and he felt that he could file the heads off easily enough. He got out his file, and wrapped his extra clothing around the steel strapping to deaden the sound. Only then did he start to work on the rivets.

He was dismayed to find it much slower going than he had imagined. Just to test the iron strapping, he laid the file slightly on edge, and slid it slowly back and forth across the steel. Cutler exerted what downward pressure he dared; a broken file would end everything. Small steel filings were apparent immediately, which comforted him. He would shave down the rivets first and then file the softer steel of the strapping.

Time had to be expended to dress the rivets after each night's work with ground up pencil lead and food scraps, but he still made steady progress.

If all went well, he could be ready to go by the end of May.

26

Exactly one week after Soapy came to haul the SSK back to his shop to be painted, Zeke got the call to have a look. He grabbed an apple and began the walk to Soapy Doyle's place. As he rounded the turn onto the dirt road, he looked at Soapy's sign and mused that the sign should actually read "S.B. Doyle and Son—plus Zeke", because he was going to be spending the rest of his life working off his debt to his friend. He threw the apple core into the fields.

When he arrived at the barn, he stopped cold in his tracks. Before him stood a shining, shimmering, breathtaking dream of a car that he could not believe was his. Not only had Soapy caressed the SSK with a masterful paint job, he had also removed all of the masking tape from the chrome parts, the wheels, and the convertible top.

There it stood in the afternoon sun, gleaming and, twinkling like some Fourth of July sparkler, its sheen accentuated by the dull shadow cast to the far side of the machine. It was so much more than Zeke could have anticipated at the outset of the project.

He and Soapy walked slowly around the automobile in dumbstruck silence. Even Soapy, at least for the moment, couldn't coax up a single profanity for the occasion. Around and around they walked, like two old ladies in an art gallery, soaking up the redeeming glory of the beautiful automobile. In the surprisingly short span of nearly ten months, Zeke with the help of Gino, countless strangers and Soapy Doyle, had done what seemed almost impossible. And now here it was, sitting proudly before him. Too beautiful to touch. The Dunleavy SSK Drophead Coupe. For all time, one of a kind.

Finally, the silence had become unbearable, and quite beyond the hopes and dreams of anyone who created something of beauty, so Soapy christened the automobile with three words. He said, "Just godamn beautiful."

They couldn't walk around the SSK for all eternity, so it was decided that they would put Soapy's "repair" plates on the automobile, and tour around Wellesport with the top down.

As a means of partial payment, Zeke decided to let Soapy take the wheel for the maiden voyage. The "repair" tags would keep

Hoagy Larkin from issuing a summons, until Zeke could get the machine to the Inspection Station at the Motor Vehicle Department, and with the mechanical skills of Soapy Doyle on board, Zeke was in his glory.

Soapy drove the SSK about the speed of a sleeping turtle over the dirt road out to Main Street, where he explained to Zeke that, not only would it be more fun to tour the car slowly for the people of Wellesport to see, but also in any initial shakedown run, excessive speed wasn't a good idea.

They toured the town leisurely, inching their way up Main Street, waving to the people who, to a person, stopped what they were doing and just stared at the automobile. Some gave the victory fists of a prizefighter. Others just smiled and waved. The SSK was a *tour de force*, which quickly developed into a parade, as others got in their cars to follow the coupe. In no time at all, it was a full-scale motorcade, as now Zeke's alter ego temporarily assumed the duties of pied piper.

They toured the canopied streets of Wellesport in the late afternoon, with the sun settling in the western sky and the SSK taking on a dreamy look. Its classic lines and perfect accents of chrome highlighted the fabulous paint job, which now became redolent of mother-of-pearl—deep, mysterious, lustrous, luminous. The coupe was a fantastic contribution to a classic art form.

They toured long past suppertime, traveling in and out of streets that Zeke hadn't even remembered, as people continued to wave. Every once in a while, they would pass the property of a contributor to the dream—perhaps the farmer who had the old Prest-O-Lite headlights in his barn, and parted with them without even the mention of money. Or the home of the man who "found" four chrome wire wheels that just happened to fit the SSK chassis as if they were measured custom.

They took turns at the wheel, as they gathered up the diverse and pleasant accolades all over town.

Then, it was over. Just as quickly as it had begun, the chest-expanding experience of gathering up the garlands of mass approval ended. It was an experience that Zeke would never forget.

He was not by nature overly introspective, but in the slight letdown of the days that followed, he thought a great deal about the ride through Wellesport, and the bursting feeling he got out of the experience. In stark contrast, he thought of his own father who actually, single-handedly, all his life, saved people from the town's bone yard behind the Old Congregational Church. Would he once feel the glory that Zeke had felt on a single afternoon spent touring the town in a classic automobile? Are the joys of adulthood so neutered of raw pleasure as to render them almost worthless? It certainly wasn't meaningless straightening out the health problems of others, but couldn't the rewards be more uplifting? The hosannas a little louder?

The next step, Zeke had mixed feelings about. He wasn't sure what to expect at the Motor Vehicle Department. Was his machine going to be judged by the specifications of the new 1958 cars? Would his car fail inspection because of all the things that made it a classic? Would the headlights be too dim by today's standards, or would allowances be made?

Or, would the whole thing be like the electrical codes for houses, where each year, when the new and stricter codes were released, each building in town fell into noncompliance. The houses were exempted with the use a "grandfather clause." Would this same grandfather clause gently ease Zeke's newly built classic automobile onto the highways of America?

On Thursday afternoon, Zeke and his friend, Gino, using Soapy's "repair" plates, drove the SSK to the Motor Vehicle Department where a man named Salvatore Rucci inspected the automobile. He praised the car for its classic lines and stunning good looks, even taking a minute to admire the chrome wire wheels. He walked around the machine, checking the lights, blinkers, horns and windshield wipers. Fastidiously, he moved on to the suspension, brakes and steering. Lastly, he inspected the gas tank, radiator and bumpers.

Apologetically, he handed Zeke a bill of particulars, failing the vehicle in every category. It was a bureaucrat's wet dream, raining on someone else's parade.

Zeke was stunned. He couldn't possibly fix all of the things listed on this paper, nor did he want to. What would his dream look like with the bumpers of a new Chevrolet on it? He drove the car to Soapy's place to tell him the bad news. Throughout the ride, he figured that he would have to put the SSK in the barn under a tarp, and wait for a miracle to happen. Something had to be wrong with a system that wouldn't allow his coupe on the road, while countless other death traps cruised merrily along.

Soapy seemed unfazed by the bill of failings. He just said to Zeke, "Put the sumbitch in my godamn barn tonight. Then, you and I will take it to the damned inspection station tomorrow. But don't tell a godamn soul, y'understand?"

Zeke welcomed his friend's help and did as he was told.

On Friday afternoon, Zeke went over to Soapy's place as directed. Soapy was pulling the engine out of an old Ford, but he finished quickly and said cheerily, "Let's get the hell out of here."

They opened the barn door and settled into the SSK. With Zeke at the wheel and the top up, they headed out of the barn. He noticed that Soapy had a thick, impressive book with him. Clearly, it was some kind of a reference manual. He sat this volume on his lap as they left the Doyle property.

When they hit Main Street, Soapy pointed to the south and said, "Go that way."

Zeke looked at Soapy blankly, because the Motor Vehicle Department was to the north, in the city.

Soapy just smiled and pointed to the south. Obediently Zeke put the car in gear and drove south, with Soapy giving directions. After a drive of about twenty minutes, Soapy gave more detailed rights and lefts, until they arrived in front of the Motor Vehicle Department's Branch Station in Mattanuck. Zeke didn't even know that the place existed.

It was almost completely deserted, and they brought the SSK right into the inspections bay. Soapy got out with his thick book under his arm, and introduced himself and Zeke to the attendant. Zeke was surprised to learn that, in the course of the trip, he had somehow become Soapy's nephew, "his sister's kid," as he put it. The two older men gabbed for a while about the inspections division, the workload, and the bosses. All the while, Soapy sprinkled his sentences with more than the usual number of profanities and vulgarities, including some female body parts that Zeke wasn't even sure existed, at least, not in the context that Soapy was using them.

A few minutes later, the inspection began, with Soapy close behind the hapless inspector, moving his thick volume strategically from under one arm to under the other. All the while, Soapy carried on a vile soliloquy on the internal combustion engine.

The inspector, clearly wearied by the conversation, passed the SSK on all counts. Soapy thanked the man profanely, and they were off to the next building to get the machine registered. Having absolutely no trouble there, and with Soapy paying the fees, they were through with the ordeal in twenty minutes.

On the ride back to Wellesport, Zeke asked Soapy if the book was a compendium of regulations. Soapy laughed and said, "No, it's just an old motor manual for a car that isn't even produced anymore." Soapy went on to explain that books of laws and regulations were written by lawyers, and in truth, most bureaucrats only understood a part of what they were expected to enforce. And incidentally, there were thousands of gray areas. Therefore, an inspector lived in fear that someone would know more than him, and quite naturally, be intimidated by Soapy's book. As if to punctuate his remarks, Soapy let out a big laugh and said, "Never trust a godamn bureaucrat!"

***

Benko Sadek sat at his desk. He had never liked the paperwork part of the job and now, with the move to the new prison coming up, he had more paperwork to process than two men could handle. He bristled at the thought of trying to integrate nine hundred inmates into a new prison. Just working out the logistics of the transfer, forty miles away, was a nightmare.

Still, he was happy that he had been asked to be the Dep of the new prison. He welcomed the chance to put his mark on the systems of this new facility, but all the paperwork was a high price. On the other hand, he had just turned fifty-three, so retirement was out of the question. Harvey Stoner had opted for retirement in Wellesport, golf every day and tending his own rose garden in a small house on some dinky side street, but that just put a greater workload on Benko now.

He had visited the new prison several times, and most everything was to his liking. The security at the new prison was good, with a few exceptions. He had asked the chief engineer with the Bureau of Corrections to install three perimeter fences, instead of two, and to electrify the center fence. Signs could be attached to the fence advertising the fact. It wouldn't affect the prisoners unless they were trying to escape. The engineer, however, had rebuffed his idea.

While the prison was being planned, the American Civil Liberties Union had inserted itself into the process, and fought bitterly against the more stringent security measures. There would be no electric fences, and the guards would no longer carry blackjacks. There would be a bigger library, and larger exercise yards, with more yardout time.

It was going to be up to Benko to make the old way of doing things fit into this new system—a difficult adjustment for everyone in the beginning.

Besides all this, the state would no longer supply a cottage for Benko. He would have to rent something, which wasn't likely in the jerkwater town where the new prison was located. He could buy a house, but he had never been good with money, and wasn't sure that he could come up with the down payment. He decided that he could leave his living arrangement problems until the last minute, because he would have the use of his cottage in Wellesport into the new year if need be.

He wanted all of the equipment from the shops to go up to the new prison at the same time as the inmates. The less that their daily routine changed, the better. The new prison offered another feature that left him puzzled. The number of acres set aside for the growing of fruits and vegetables was about thirty times what he had in Wellesport, and far outstripped the number of trustees that he had available to work in the fields.

He had a choice. He could lower the standards for trustees, thus creating more field hands, or he could put the existing trustees up on tractors. The idea of Frenchie and Ruppert driving tractors was unsettling. Like so many things these days, he simply put the decision off.

At the moment, he wanted to move some inmates to new cells but he was too busy. He decided to change only Henry Cutler's cell. He would do that this week.

Frenchie and Ruppert were in the fields bright and early one Monday morning at the beginning of May, and were thrilled to see that the young dandelions were finally big enough to be picked. While Ruppert pretended that it was business as usual, Frenchie collected the young dandelions and put them into a brown paper bag.

When the bag was full, he walked to the back of the warden's house, and entered the cellar through the gardener's door. He squinted in the gloom of the unlit basement until his eyes adjusted to the dark, and then he poked around looking for a hiding place.

At the back of the cellar in the corner, was a sizable, old furnace, which probably wouldn't be touched until the oilman tuned up the burner in the fall. He walked over to this boiler, and slipped a ceramic pot behind it. Dumping in the dandelion stems, and some sugar and water, he then covered the whole thing with the brown bag.

As he left the cellar, he counted off four weeks in his head. He gave the date to Ruppert, and told him not to forget it.

"I ain't goin' ta furgit dat one," assured Ruppert with a smile.

27

Dr. Rory was faced with the greatest acting job of his life when he found out that Zeke's automobile had passed inspection. Indeed, was registered. Insurance was not required to register the SSK, but now he would have to buy some as long as Zeke was his son. The insurance company would probably raise his rates through the roof with a homemade car, but what could he do?

He found it personally humiliating to walk out into the drive, and compliment Zeke on his magnificent automobile. Reluctantly, he had to admit that it was an incredible feat. He realized that Zeke had acted with no duplicity in bringing the coupe to Mattanuck to be inspected. Actually, Zeke wasn't the family member whose behavior could not be held up to the light, but Dr. Rory pushed such thoughts aside.

Fatherhood was subterfuge itself; men didn't want kids, they wanted sex. Then, seventeen years later, a father found himself standing in his own driveway, fibbing like a rug merchant. There he was telling his son what a beautiful automobile he had built, when he had done all that was in his power to keep the machine off the road.

Another thing he hated to admit to himself was that the world he had once known—where everyone knew everyone else, and he enjoyed the power of a liege lord—was now slowly disappearing. Just a few short years ago, with the help of Salvatore Rucci, he could have kept Zeke's dream safely stowed away under a tarp in his barn. . . . forever. Now, with the population expanding so rapidly and spreading out, he was losing that control. His little kingdom was blossoming, and he was not. He would soon be a small fish in a big pond, and one of the reasons for coming to Wellesport in the first place would be gone forever.

So he stood in his own drive, smoking a Camel, and complimenting Zeke on a fine job. He would not sit in the automobile though, even though Zeke begged him to. Dr. Rory demurred by quoting Shakespeare—

"Be not the first by whom the new is tried,
Nor the last to cast the old aside."

Besides, it would be too much like George Washington trying on Lord Cornwallis' sword. He would confine himself to a few words of praise, and then go about his business. They settled a few details about insurance, garaging, continued good grades and so forth, and then Dr. Rory walked back into the house.

Zeke polished the car with a dust rag, and put it in its stall. He decided to leave the Dunleavy Motors sign just as it was. What harm?

June came on, and the farmers were hard at work in the fields. Business at the seed companies in town slowed down as they hit their low season. It always seemed odd, but their peak season was the dead of winter, when you couldn't plant seed with a backhoe.

Young children counted the days until school got out. This year, adding on for all the snow days, they would be free on the seventeenth of June, Bunker Hill Day.

Ann Dunleavy called up to New Hampshire to check with her mother about their summer vacation plans. They had made it a habit to visit her parent's farm in early July each year. It was the only time besides Thanksgiving, when she saw her folks, and she wanted her children to know their grandparents as much as possible.

What the kids had learned of farm life over the years was enough to ensure that they would not be the future farmers of America. They had learned to milk cows by hand, shovel hay and manure, fill feedbags, fix machinery and even how to pluck chickens. Except for the machinery, Zeke and Jack couldn't care less, and Wibby was afraid of the animals, bar none.

Still, they went every summer for a week. Dr. Rory could use more vacation time, but in truth, he didn't know how to use it. He would read for a while, and then begin pacing and looking out the window. He just wasn't built for leisure.

***

In these early days of June, Frenchie would sneak away from the fields, and into Warden Stoner's basement to test the dandelion mix behind the furnace. It wasn't quite ready yet. Maybe another couple of days.

He covered over the pot, and made his way back to the rows where he and Ruppert were weeding with scuffle hoes.

"She's cookin' up a storm, eh?" said Frenchie.

"How much mo' time?" asked Ruppert, the irritation showing in his voice.

"'Nother couple of days, eh?" said Frenchie trying to soothe Ruppert's frayed nerves.

"I dunno if I can waits no longer," replied Ruppert.

"Trust me. You can wait, eh?" said Frenchie in an effort to reign in Ruppert's thirst.

Benko Sadek sat in his office not believing what his eyes were telling him. He was holding a directive from the Bureau of Corrections, which stated that all food that was given to the hogs in the piggery had to be sterilized first. No more garbage and table scraps, unless it was sanitized. The cost of processing the feed was going to make it ridiculously expensive to keep pigs. The smartest thing to do was shut down the piggery all together, and not keep one at the new prison. The hog house at the new prison could be used for something else.

He decided to go to the piggery himself to give the order for all the pigs to be slaughtered and butchered for meals between now and moving day. There was a German prisoner named Otto, who had worked in the hog house for years. He would be upset to lose such a great job. Benko felt that if he told Otto himself, and explained to him that someone above his pay grade made the decision, it might be all right. Otto had always been a good inmate, so he would promise Otto the best job with animals that the new prison could offer. Perhaps if he handled it properly, he could keep Otto from going over the edge.

After he got done with Otto, he assembled a couple of guards, and set off for death row to move Henry Cutler to another cell. They all strode past Grand Central Station, through the east cell bock and laundry, and into the death row complex.

He had the guards open Henry Cutler's cell door. The Dep explained that he was moving Cutler to another cell as just a routine precaution.

They marched him across the corridor to the opposite cell, and the guards brought him his clothes, shoes, writing material, toilet kit, and Bible. As the items came into the new cell, Benko inspected each in its turn. He felt the clothing like a purchasing agent in a garment district. Next, he inspected the soap, toothbrush, and shaving brush. There was no razor. Cutler was given one to use each morning.

Lastly, he examined the Bible. He opened the front cover and looked inside. He flipped the book over, and opened the back cover and looked inside. Then, he riffled the pages slowly with his left thumb, while holding the volume in his right hand. He closed the book, and examined the front cover, the back cover, and the binding. He even ran the fingers of his left hand up and down the book's spine. Nonchalantly, he tossed the Bible onto the desk.

When the book smacked down on the desk, the file dislodged and slid out about a half inch. Cutler froze. He stole a glance at Benko Sadek only to realize that the Dep had not noticed.

"Making your peace with the Almighty?" asked Benko.

Henry Cutler's heart was pounding so hard that he didn't think he was going to be able to speak. At last, he managed to say, "Yes . . . Yes, I am."

Benko smiled his crooked smile and said, "I'll bet." He studied Cutler a little, and then asked, "You decide to change your mind about the appeal, yet?"

"No . . . No, I'll stick with my decision," he assured the Dep.

Benko didn't buy it for a second. He prided himself on knowing these punks. This loser would scream "uncle" as soon as he heard that "Mr. X" was on his way. Who was he trying to kid? He studied Cutler for a little while longer, then turned to leave. He watched as they locked the door to Cutler's cell. He shook the heavy steel door with his hand.

"Be seeing you," he said to Cutler. As he left death row, it occurred to him that just maybe he didn't know anything about Cutler. He thought that he knew him—that he was just another punk. However, in the whole prison, he was the only inmate who had carved up seven innocent, young girls. Maybe he didn't know Cutler at all. It bothered him. It was his job to know these punks, and to anticipate their every move. Yet, he was drawing a blank on Cutler. This killer was making choices that appeared to be against his own self-interest, and that was inconsistent with what Benko knew of these cons. It gnawed at him.

After Benko left, Henry Cutler slowly let out the air trapped in his lungs. He grabbed the Bible, and reinserted the file into the back cover. He had come within a half inch of his plan folding like a piece of fabric in the shirt shop. Now, he had to make sure that the key would work in the new lock.

Waiting again until the guard let one of his block mates out into the exercise yard, he tried the key. He pushed, pulled and jiggled it all over the place, but he couldn't get it to work.

Day after day, as the guard came to let him out for his exercise period, he studied the guard's key. It was a close match, but he could see that this key had a wider space between the teeth, so he set out that very night to file the gap on his key a little wider.

In two days, he was ready to try it again. When the guard locked him back in his cell after yardout, he went for his Bible and grabbed the refashioned key. As the guard let the first inmate into the exercise yard, he tried it again. The worn tumblers gave way as he turned the key. This time, when the cell door started to open, he was expecting it, and simply held it back, re-locked the door, and returned the key to his Bible.

Cutler breathed a sigh of relief, and immediately made plans to start in on the iron bed strapping that very night.

Time was beginning to weigh heavily on him, and his nightmares about "Old Sparky" were getting worse. He couldn't go a single night without dreaming of himself sitting in the electric chair, with sparks flying around the room, and his body convulsing under the force of the obscene voltage.

Having been moved to a new cell, it was unlikely that he would be moved again for a couple of months. He had to make his move before that time arrived.

That very night he wrapped the iron bed straps with his extra clothing, and started to file the rivets off the iron strapping.

***

Graduation from the Wellesport Elementary School was not anything that required a celebration in the eyes of the average resident. It was only the beginning of the long march toward productive citizenry and was treated as such. Jack and Wibby Dunleavy would attend Wellesport High in September, and their education would continue almost seamlessly. Their brother Zeke would be a senior and, although there was an unwritten code about seniors ignoring freshmen, they could find some comfort in the knowledge that Zeke felt such behavior was childish, even *déclassé*.

Assuming that Dr. Rory got over his defeat by September, Zeke would drive them to Wellesport High in the SSK, with Wibby uncomfortably smushed between the gearshift and the Jack's bucket seat.

Still, school days were way up ahead. There was a summer to consider first.

Just as they had done on all the other overnight campouts, Jack and his friends got together ahead of time, and stuffed the backpacks with everything they would need for the trip. They would only be going to Hidden Island, which could almost be seen from the attic windows of the Dunleavy's house, but this was a dry run for the Jamboree, so they decided to do everything up royally.

Ann Dunleavy did not like them camping on Hidden Island without any adults, but Dr. Rory intervened—he felt it would be all right.

After hours of the usual haggling about who would carry what, they finally had everything packed except the food. They would buy the food on Friday night, and be off the first thing on Saturday morning.

28

Frenchie and Ruppert had waited anxiously for their dandelion wine to complete the fermentation process, and at long last, the day had arrived. At least Frenchie thought that it had. With no hygrometer or other instrumentation, it was just an educated guess as to when it was ready for consumption.

With Ruppert's patience long since expended, the vintner in Frenchie decided that it was ready. Enough taste testing. Enough sampling. It was done.

Thankfully for the two inmates, it couldn't have happened on a better day, because the skies were misting lightly, and no one would think it unusual if Frenchie and Ruppert had to spend some of the day in Warden Stoner's basement, potting flowers or sorting seeds.

They decided to have just a sip in the early morning, maybe an eleven o'clocker, another sip after lunch, and some more at cocktail hour. All very dignified. They went into the basement, poured a little wine for themselves, and toasted each other's good health. However, just as they did, the skies opened up. And it was a biblical rain—the kind that turkeys drown in if they look up. There wasn't a damned thing to do about it either.

So, they rejiggered their time table—moving their eleven o'clocker up just a tad—all the time watching as the rain turned their fields into furrows of slop. They toasted each other's good health again while marveling at the rain. Eventually though, it became necessary to move their after-lunch drink up a bit as well.

They passed the whole morning drinking the dandelion wine, completely oblivious to the powerful effect the alcohol was having on two men who had not had a drink in many years. As if to put the lie to this fact, and convince themselves of the limited effect the wine was having on them, they chose to do some rototilling when the rain eased slightly.

Up and down, across and over, under and through, they rototilled. They destroyed the potato crop first, and then the onions, moving clumsily over the rows until Mrs. Stoner's rose garden was directly in the path of their destruction.

With the loud rototiller running at full throttle, its tines masticating great chunks of earth and plant, the beast chewed the beautiful, delicate blossoms like some wanton, diabolical demon. Frenchie sang *O Canada* as they slopped through the mud, falling and getting up, again and again, in a sea of drunken mayhem.

Benko Sadek was sitting in his office doing paperwork, when he got a call from Mrs. Stoner. The poor woman sounded half out of her mind with fear. He grabbed a couple of guards, borrowed a blackjack from a third, and stalked to the warden's house.

Frenchie was singing ". . .we stand guard o'er theeeeee" as the rototiller clawed its way toward the rose trellis, the only living thing still standing. Unfortunately, it never got to the trellis. Benko let loose the fury that he usually kept under wraps, clubbing Frenchie and Ruppert over their heads until their broken bodies lay face down in the mud. All the while, the rototiller rambled madly through the fields.

"Go get a pickup truck," Benko commanded one of the guards.

"Yes, sir," said the guard and left.

"Go turn that damn thing off," he barked, pointing to the tiller.

He stood over the two drunken trustees, with the rain soaking his clothing. He looked around, and seeing no one, he clubbed their limp bodies a few more times just to vent his anger. "Pantywaists," he said under his breath.

Frenchie and Ruppert were taken to the hospital where a nurse phoned Dr. Rory Dunleavy and implored him to come as soon as he possibly could. From the hospital, they would go to solitary for the maximum—thirty days.

Had it been worth it? The question could only be answered by another lifer and his answer would be . . . "yes."

***

On Saturday, as planned, the Scouts of the Cobra Patrol gathered at the Dunleavy's house for the march to Hidden Island. Mrs. Dunleavy had been good enough to get the food at the Wellesport Grocery the day before, a little insurance that the boys would have some decent meals. She had watched the effects of the camping experience for a good number of years now. Zeke's adventures of four, five and six years before were now Jack's, just as if he were a simple carbon copy placed under the original.

With the food stuffed into the packs, everyone hoisted a green canvas rucksack onto their backs and they were off—six happy, hopeful campers eager to practice their skills for the big Jamboree the following weekend. They marched on the side of the road, past the quiet houses of Main Street, with only a kitchen light visible here and there. Occasionally, a piece of farm machinery would slowly motor past them with a small wave from the driver, off to the fields for another day of back and forth, and back and forth, the very knell of life in a small farm community.

As they passed River Road, the conversation turned to the upcoming execution of Henry Cutler.

"My father says, 'They can't fry that bastard fast enough to suit God,'" said one of the boys.

"Same with mine," replied another.

"Why are they screwing around? Why can't they just do it already?" asked Arnie Hollis.

"His lawyer is doing some crap with the courts," answered another authoritatively.

"Didn't I read in the paper that he decided to waive his appeal?" asked Ed Nadeau.

"I think the lawyer can do it without his permission. It's called a 'Friend of the Court' something or other," offered Jack Dunleavy.

"It should be that if a killer decides not to appeal, they ought to fry him that day. Don't give his lawyer a chance to pull any shit," said Ed Nadeau.

"Yeah. They should have the chair in the courtroom, not in the prison," suggested Lefty Leiper, the wise guy of the group.

"Right. Do it in public, like my father said that they used to do in England. Everybody packed a picnic lunch and made a day of it. It was like the Christians and the lions. Great entertainment," offered Arnie Hollis.

They all remained silent for a few minutes as they let that bit of information sink in. They crossed River Road and started past the prison. It was set back about the same distance from Main Street as it was from River Road, and because the state owned all the land right up to where they now walked, there were no houses built on Main Street for about six hundred feet.

As the whole group paraded by the prison, they stared intently up at the guards on top of the walls, with their serious looks, and those ever present Winchester Model 94's cradled in their arms. It was morning yardout, and the guards were watching the exercise yard inside the prison closely.

The column of young, marching twelve-year-olds couldn't take their eyes off the watchmen, as if they had never seen them before. Stumbling a little here and there, they still remained transfixed by the stone figures with rifles atop the walls.

At length, they were past the prison, and at the end of a string of ten more houses, they were at a cul-de-sac, where Main Street ended at the boat dock and launching ramp.

They had made previous arrangements to use the Pheiffer's boat and another belonging to the Pheiffer's neighbors. They loaded their packs into the boats, and three to a dory, they began the row out to Hidden Island.

As they pulled on the oars, the June sun warmed their bodies, and at the same time, let them know that the weekend weather would be spectacular.

As Jack Dunleavy rowed, he turned toward the west and saw the sun glinting off the fortress-like back wall of the prison. The sun particularly sparkled as it fell on the high pitched, slate roofs of the circular brownstone guard towers across the back of the fortress. It looked every bit like the medieval castles in the stories that his mother used to read to him when he was small, sick, and home from school. The guards were still standing there with their rifles, just outside the towers.

The boats floated wide of the protective arm of land, and came to an abrupt halt as they grounded ashore at Hidden Island. Hurriedly, they got to their campsite, and began to unpack their gear. In the short space of a couple of hours, the tents were up and a fire was going. They dug a latrine on the north side of the island for serious business. Nobody was going to pretend that these scouts would hike the length of a football field to urinate when the island was covered with bushes, and swamp maples of every size imaginable.

In a short while, they prepared lunch of bologna and cheese sandwiches and bug juice. They spent the rest of the afternoon working on their fire-starting skills, and practicing first aid, as well as other disciplines that they would be tested on, the following weekend at the Jamboree.

When they first got to the island, the Scouts who hadn't seen "Old Sparky" yet, wanted to stage mock executions right away, but as the leader of the Cobra Patrol, Jack insisted that they put off the fun until they had gotten in the practice that they were there for. He wanted to take first place at the Jamboree, and he knew they wouldn't get anything done if they started playing games from the start. The fun with "Old Sparky" would begin after supper.

***

Without arousing any suspicion, Henry Cutler had turned into a dynamo of activity in the days since Benko Sadek had moved him to his new cell.

He had to laugh every time that he looked over at his old cell, because the trustees had folded the mattress on the bed exactly the way they always did when a cell was empty. It was precisely as he had suspected, and by doing everything by the book, no one even got a glance at the rivets that he had filed off of his old bunk. They were completely covered by the folded mattress. Benko Sadek's military training was a great help to Cutler without anyone realizing it—least of all, the Dep.

On his new bunk, he had the rivets entirely removed from a fifteen-inch piece of steel, and he had cut the flat stock almost completely free. It stayed in place with the smallest threads of uncut steel, which could be broken by twisting the steel back and forth by hand.

With his pencil, he marked the edges of his sheets at six inch intervals, so when the time came to tear them, there wouldn't be any second guessing.

Each day, when his time came for yardout, he walked around the perimeter of the yard, going over all the details of his plan. He could see that the weather was perfect. It hadn't rained for three days and the ground was firm, so he wouldn't leave any tracks.

Better still, the weather looked like it would hold for at least another twelve hours.

The quietest evening at the prison was Saturday night. The inmates had worked hard all week, and on Sunday they would receive visitors, and have a glorious four hours in the yard, among other things. Everyone, including the guards would be in a quiet mood tonight. God help the inmate who forced a lock down on a Sunday. But that wouldn't affect Henry Cutler, because he planned to be long gone by sunrise on Sunday.

The key to the cell was, of course, all set. Barring any last minute changes, Ryan would be on duty tonight at midnight, and he probably wouldn't even hear Cutler as he approached his desk with the steel bar raised high over his head.

Originally Cutler had planned to use Ryan's own blackjack to club him over the head, but he was afraid that it might be fastened in some way to the guard's belt, and they would just get into a messy scuffle. He decided instead, to use his own blackjack. He could bend it into a hook after Ryan was trussed and gagged.

He figured that after Ryan's midnight check-in call, he could be tossing the hook over the wall within ten minutes.

29

Henry Cutler lay in his bed, with the covers pulled up high, so as to hide the fact that he was still fully clothed. His shoes were outside his cell, but he would get them later.

The two hour wait, from lights out until Ryan got his midnight call, was an eternity. The covers over his clothing were causing him to sweat like mad. Still, he waited.

At last, he heard the low ring of the phone, and Ryan in his sleepy, phlegmy voice said, "AAAHHHH, YALLOW." Then as usual, he waited a bit and said, "SAY WHAT?"

Cutler thought that this guy was as predictable as the seasons.

Then Ryan said, "YOKAY," and hung up.

Cutler removed the covers, and swung his feet softly to the floor. He pulled the mattress back a bit, and reached down to grip the iron strapping where he had cut it. Rocking his hand back and forth, the steel bar broke loose from the bunk. He smiled, and let the mattress back down carefully.

He tucked the iron bar down the front of his pants, and moved quietly toward his desk where he retrieved the key from the back cover of his Bible. Stealthily, he made his way toward the front of the cell.

Very slowly, he moved his head up to the bars, so that he could see Ryan. The old fart was sitting sideways at his desk, with his elbows on his thighs, nonchalantly cutting his nails.

Henry Cutler slid his arms through the bars, and with the key in his left hand, inserted it into the lock. He rotated it as gently as he could until the tired tumblers kicked over. The door began to swing open a little. He held it in place. He had gone over this plan hundreds of times, and never even thought what to do with the key. After a moment, he decided that it didn't matter. He would leave the key in the door.

It was time to go. He began to open the door, but in the quiet of the night, the hinges started to squeak. He froze. How could he not have noticed it before? It was the difference between the subtle noise level of the daytime, and the dead quiet of night. It came down to a choice—either he could move so fast that Ryan wouldn't know what hit him, or move slowly, taking advantage of the guard's deafness. What was it going to be?

He chose to go slowly, watching Ryan all the time. He could always rush him if he had to. He eased the door open just enough to squeeze his body through, and tiptoed toward Ryan, while sliding the iron bar from his pants.

Moving as carefully as he could, he hoped to completely surprise the guard. His heart was beating out of his chest, and rivulets of sweat were running down his face. Ryan just continued cutting his nails.

Presently, Henry Cutler was right up behind Ryan. Raising the iron bar high in the air, he struck the guard on the back of the head with all his might, following up with a second quick blow. But it was unnecessary. With his right hand, Cutler steadied the old guard's body, so it wouldn't make a racket as it slumped off the chair and onto the floor.

Cutler grabbed the ring of keys, and then gently lowered the body to the floor. Watching the guard's stomach for a second, he tried to determine if the man was still breathing. He was not.

It hadn't been part of his plan to kill Ryan, but it didn't bother him a bit that he had. In fact, it saved him precious time, because now he wouldn't have to tie him up.

Cutler reached for the guard's wallet and opened it. Seven dollars. He grabbed the money and tucked it into his pants pocket, thinking that it would come in handy once he was out.

He darted back to his cell, and pulled on his shoes. Methodically, he bent up the piece of flat iron by wedging it into the bed frame, and prying until the thing had the shape of a fancy question mark. Next, he tore up his sheets and tied them together. Lastly, he tied the end of the sheet rope to the small loop of the iron hook.

Gathering up the sheet rope and the guard's keys, he said under his breath, "So long, Benko," and ran for the exercise yard door.

Just as he expected, the other prisoners started making demands. He told them to quiet down before they woke up the whole place. Then he told them what he had practiced.

He explained to them that the method of his escape would only allow one person to get out, and that that one person was going to be him. For good measure, he told them about his friends in the kitchen who would put rat poison in their food if they interfered in any way with his escape.

It surprised him how completely they bought it. They just never said another word. They were going to the electric chair, and they were silenced by the threat of a little rat poison? Tough guys, he thought.

There were six keys on the ring. By sight, two were eliminated immediately. He tried two others without results. The next key was the one. Opening the door slowly, and peering into the exercise yard, he could see that there was a light on. However, it was lunacy, because there was no one to observe what was being illuminated.

Cutler made his way to the wall and laid out the sheet rope on the ground, so it wouldn't get snarled. Then, he swung the hook and about six feet of sheet around and around like a cowboy swings a lariat. When it finally felt like it had enough speed for the steel hook to fly over the top of the wall, he let it go.

It sailed up and over the wall taking most of the sheet with it. The bottom portion of the sheet rope had been pulled up too high for him to reach. He jumped up and down several times, but couldn't get to it. Running from the other side of the yard, he put a foot on the wall, and vaulted high into the air.

He touched the sheet rope but couldn't grab it. Three more tries also ended in failure.

In desperation, he went back inside and got the guard's chair. Precious time and energy were being wasted as a result of this one stupid mistake. He braced the guard's chair against the wall so that it could be used almost like a ladder. By getting his feet on the arms of the chair, and then placing one foot on the top of the back, he was at last able to jump high enough to snag the end of the sheet rope.

Gripping it tightly, he dropped right to the ground with it in his hand. The hook was not grabbing the ivy. He twisted the sheets in the hopes of spinning the hook.

After wasting some more valuable time messing with the sheet rope, the hook finally grabbed the ivy. Now those thousands of pull-ups would pay off.

Cutler scooted up the sheet rope like a circus aerialist. But about half way up the wall, the hook began to drag through the ivy, and his body settled slowly to the ground. He had a difficult decision to make now—attempt to hook the ivy again with maybe the same result, or move over and try to hook the rail at the top of the north wall.

The second option would almost certainly work but it was dicey. It was sure to make more noise, and he would almost certainly be seen, silhouetted atop the wall bathed in the light of a three-quarter moon. In addition, he would be completely exposed while trying to make his way around the empty guard tower where the east and north walls met.

On the other hand though, the ivy didn't seem to be able to hold his weight, a miscalculation for which he didn't intend to be penalized any longer.

Cutler ran over to the north wall, and peered up at the top of the railing, thirty-three feet above his head. The hook was going to make a racket no matter what he did. Sitting on the ground and removing his shoes and socks, one by one he pulled the tubular fabric over the hook and tied it into place with a piece of bed sheet.

After jumping back into his shoes, he swung the hook just as before, but this time he made sure to let out only thirty-three feet of line. Cutler wanted the socked hook to hit the rail exactly once and catch. Sorry to say, it didn't happen that way. The socked hook hit the rail twelve times before it finally caught.

By the time the hook was set, the better part of the hour was gone. The one o'clock check-in call to Ryan's desk was going to go unanswered, and he had better be on his way by then or else.

With the hook on the rail now, Cutler went up the sheet rope as fast as his arms could get him there. Arriving at the top of the wall, he waited to check things out. Thanks to the bright light of the moon, he could see the guard in the cove guard tower atop the back wall of the prison. Things were actually lighted dishearteningly well. He hung on the wall studying the guard tower that required circumvention. It would be tough.

Then he noticed the door to the guard tower. The handle had no lock. Were his eyes deceiving him? Then it made sense. The towers were accessible only by passing first through the cove guard tower, and then by the guards walking to the tower to which they were assigned. There would be no need to ever lock them. They were inaccessible, and there was nothing to steal from them anyway.

Cutler lay on his back on top of the wall, and slide over to the guard tower. Reaching up with one hand, he opened the door, allowing himself and his equipment to tumble inside the small room. Opening the window, he dangled the sheet rope down to the ground, securing the hook to the pot-bellied stove, which was bolted to the floor.

It was odd. The one part of the plan on which he had spent no time at all, and it went like clockwork. Go figure.

Lowering himself to the ground, he cursed the moonlight while scurrying for the Wellesport Cove. Cutler had to travel through the backyards of about ten houses on Main Street in order to achieve some sort of cover, but when dogs started to bark, he stopped to reconsider.

After giving the matter a little thought, and considering that it was one o'clock in the morning, he decided just to run like hell for the cove.

Henry Cutler had made several mistakes and miscalculations during his escape, but this would prove to be the costliest.

A full out run through the backyards of any neighborhood in America, even with the help of a three quarter moon, was fraught with peril. In Cutler's case, he hadn't gone two hundred feet, when his legs got tangled in a tin can scarecrow and a chicken wire fence, which until moments before, had enclosed a promising victory garden. The racket had every dog on the street barking, and the residents who lived near the prison stirring.

It took him a good five minutes to untangle himself from the chicken wire and tin cans, increasing the level of alarm with the mounting noise. Cut and bleeding, he was off again. Cutler couldn't possibly know that in those few minutes, telephone calls had been made and Ryan's body found, along with the empty cell. Further calls had been made to the State Police, the Wellesport Police, and the Connecticut National Guard. And, of course, Benko Sadek had been informed.

30

The telephone rang in Benko Sadek's hallway next to the staircase. It rang five times before the half-drunk deputy warden could rouse himself and get to it. He rubbed his face as he talked on the phone.

At one o'clock in the morning, Benko knew it would be a call from the prison, so he answered the call informally.

"Yeah. What is it," he said. Then he listened.

"Killed him?" he questioned, as if not believing his ears.

"Have you called the State Police and the National Guard?" he asked quickly.

"He went towards the cove?" Benko repeated out loud.

"No. No alarm. Get Bogin to meet us at the dock with his motorboat. And I want him there this minute. Got it?" He hung up the phone angrily.

The Dep went into the bathroom, and splashed water on his face several times before drying off with a bath towel. Moving fast now, he dressed without bothering to put on underwear, and strode to the back of the cottage.

He yanked open a closet door in his kitchen, reached in and fished out his own Winchester Model 94. From the top shelf, he retrieved a box of cartridges. These items were laid on the kitchen table, while he put on a light jacket and his fedora.

Benko opened the box and slid five cartridges into the rifle's magazine, dumping the rest into his coat pocket. He grabbed a flashlight and hustled out of his back door. The guard who had telephoned him stood waiting on the bottom steps with the butt of his rifle resting on his thigh.

The two men swept toward the cove, over the same route that Henry Cutler had taken. As they walked, Benko had the guard fill him in on the escape. Each detail stoked his anger until he could barely contain himself—not only because this was the first successful escape on his watch, but because one of his men had been killed. He felt that he finally knew everything that he needed to know about Cutler, and he determined to get to him before anyone else did. He would punish the inmate who supplied him the file and the metal later. Tonight, he would deal with Henry Cutler.

The two men walked briskly. The flashlight shone on the garden, the big tangle of chicken wire and the crumpled scarecrow. In no time, they were at the town dock.

Waiting in his motorboat, was Jim Bogin, another guard. The boat was a sturdy affair with an outboard motor on the back. Bogin lived about two houses away from the cove on the west side, and kept his boat at a small makeshift dock. He used it for fishing mostly—tonight, for hunting.

After Benko and the other guard got into the boat, they set out to the north with the Dep pointing when he wanted the direction of the boat altered.

A few minutes later, he spotted the campfire on Hidden Island. Squinting into the distance, he saw the figure of Henry Cutler silhouetted against the campfire as he strangled a smaller figure. With the help of the moonlight, the whole scene was incredibly well lit.

The Dep gave Bogin the signal to kill the engine, and the boat settled quickly into a fairly stable drift. He stood up in the boat, chambered a round, and then told his two boat mates to hold perfectly still.

Benko Sadek raised his rifle.

***

The Scouts of the Cobra Patrol had finished practicing their Jamboree skills in the late afternoon, and cooked dinner over the open campfire. They had combined several packets of freeze-dried trail food to make beef stew. It had the consistency and taste of cabin chinking. They each ate a little and then filled up on cookies. Mrs. Dunleavy had taken the precaution to add several packages of fig newtons, and other cookies with fruit filling, expecting correctly that their cooking would not be edible.

Immediately after dinner, and right on until sunset, they staged mock executions with "Old Sparky." The more experienced actors performed the best, with the newcomers struggling with their last words. Each one of them treated it as some kind of a wish list. Each speech began with "I want . . ." In exasperation, Jack Dunleavy tried to explain to them that it wasn't some Jeannie in the bottle thing. It was supposed to be a statement. Maybe something like what Nathan Hale said. "I only regret . . ." Still, most of them couldn't make the distinction, and the last words just pyramided into more and more outrageous wish lists. It seemed that everyone wanted to see Laurie Cooney naked.

On toward midnight, they sat around the campfire, telling stories, discussing the demolition of the prison and Henry Cutler's execution. Around one o'clock, Jack suggested that they turn in, but Ed Nadeau came up with what he thought was an even better idea. He felt that their mock executions lacked realism, because with two thousand volts blasting through the condemned man's body, the chair should be rocking back and forth violently. Even at this late hour, he wanted to try another execution, but this time, he would direct the whole thing.

They dragged the chair out from the trees, and placed it near the campfire so they could see. They then lashed a stick on the back of the chair so they could suspend the electrical reflector over the head of the condemned man. Following Ed Nadeau's direction, they wedged long saplings under the chair, from the back. By slipping a small log under the saplings for a fulcrum, they would have the levers that they needed to make the chair jump and jiggle.

Arnie Hollis volunteered for the trial run of the new "Old Sparky," which he considered no big thing. Arnie would jump off of a suspension bridge on a dare.

They carefully strapped his arms and legs to the chair, and placed a brown shopping bag over his head. The electrical reflector was pulled down over the bag, and the two boys holding the ends of the saplings got ready. Jack Dunleavy held a big stick that was the juice lever.

With Ed Nadeau acting as the warden, he turned to the others and said, "Witnesses will now take their seats."

"In accordance with the orders given to me by the Criminal Courts of the State of Connecticut, you, Henry Cutler, will be put to death this day in June, 1959. Do you have any last words?" queried Ed Nadeau.

From under the brown sack and the electrical reflector came the voice of the condemned man.

"I want peace on earth and goodwill towards men, and I still want to see Laurie Cooney naked."

Everyone exploded in laughter and loud guffaws. Ed Nadeau stepped back and said, "May God have mercy on your soul." He gave the signal for the juice.

With that, Jack Dunleavy threw the switch and they all started screaming into the night air— ZZZZZZZZZZZZZZZZZZZZZZ."

"Old Sparky" began to rock and tilt madly, with the condemned man screaming at the top of his lungs, his body shaking in fits and spasms. The sapling levers added a fantastic realism to the whole thing.

From Jack Dunleavy's viewpoint, the prisoner twitching with the bag over his head, the reflector, the chair rocking violently and the sparks of the campfire snapping and spraying in all directions . . . it all seems frighteningly authentic.

***

Henry Cutler had been unable to find a rowboat that wasn't chained and locked to the dock, so he tucked his shoes into the front of his pants and waded into the cove. Owing to the tremendous load on his mind, he hadn't even noticed whether the water was cold or not. He simply slipped into the water, and began swimming north across the cove.

Cutler tried the crawl, but it was too tough with his clothes on, so he wound up doing a combination breaststroke-sidestroke. After a long and tiring effort, he pulled himself up on the spit of land that protected Hidden Island. After resting for a short time, he waded the small channel that brought him up to the island itself. He had seen the sparks from the campfire while he was swimming across the water, but all the foliage prevented him from seeing anything else. Checking out the camp was his first order of business. If there were only a couple of people, he might be able to steal their money and some food, as both were going to be essential if he was going to make good his escape. As difficult as getting out of the prison was, he knew that staying out would be even tougher.

Henry Cutler inched his way toward the campfire, with only the sparks visible to him. Then, he got to a clearing that afforded him an unobstructed view of the camp.

Silhouetted by the campfire with the attendant embers and sparks flying through the air, Cutler saw "Old Sparky" tossing and reeling wildly in the night. Strapped into the seat was a jet-black form with a bag over his head, screaming piercingly as the sound of electrical current emanated from the little mouths around him— "ZZZZZZZZZZZZZZ."

Henry Cutler went completely berserk. He jumped up off the ground and ran toward the boys, shouting, "You little bastards. I'll kill you . . . you little fuckin' bastards."

As abject terror gripped the scouts, "Old Sparky" came to a sudden stop and Arnie Hollis, still strapped in, wet his pants. Henry Cutler grabbed Jack Dunleavy by the throat, and began to choke the life out of him. As he squeezed, his face contorted into a demented grin. The act of choking a small body filled him with a familiar pleasure. It evoked memories of control and superiority, which he had felt as he snuffed the life out of his seven previous victims. He dropped his head back, allowing his demented grin to envelope his face, as the moonlight turned his features into a grotesque mask.

Then a single shot rang out, echoing eerily in the moist night air.

Henry Cutler's body fell on top of Jack Dunleavy, who could see and feel the man's blood and brains oozing out all over his scout shirt. He wiggled madly, trying to get out from under the dead man's bloody body, with his wide-open eyes and the stink of death on him. His own body felt as it did when his sister Wibby buried him in beach sand. He wiggled and squirmed until he finally got out. Ed Nadeau screamed, "Jack, over here."

He raced toward his friend, who was hiding in the bushes like the others, save poor Arnie who was still strapped into the electric chair. The others lay down in the brush, trembling, not knowing what to do.

A short time later, Benko Sadek came ashore with his rifle still in his hands. The two others followed. The boys still didn't come out, even though they knew who the deputy warden was. They were just too frightened.

Benko approached the body of Henry Cutler—now lying facedown next to "Old Sparky"—with his rifle to his shoulder at the ready. But Benko had seen dead bodies before and wasn't concerned. He used his foot to roll Henry Cutler's body over onto its back. Barely audibly, he said under his breath, "Pantywaist." He then turned to cut the straps and free a petrified Arnie Hollis.

By now other boats were converging on Hidden Island. First there were more guards, then the State Police. Later, a whole army of National Guardsmen. Then, the townspeople. Among them were Dr. Rory and Ed Nadeau's father. The other fathers followed.

One of the guards in the second wave put a tarp over the dead body of Henry Cutler and everyone walked wide around it.

Jack Dunleavy was surprised when Dr. Rory hugged him. It was the first time that he could remember his father ever hugging him. It felt good but strange. Dr. Rory took the bloody shirt off his son and threw it into the fire. He removed his own coat and covered his son with it.

He looked in the direction of Benko Sadek, who was giving orders to some of his guards, but said nothing. He took Jack off of Hidden Island with some of the other Scouts and their fathers. They would get the camping gear later.

When they got back to their house, it was close to three o'clock in the morning. Dr. Rory gave Jack a sedative to help him sleep, and he put him to bed. As he waited for his son to nod off, Dr. Rory told Jack that they would talk about the whole thing in the morning.

Before falling into a drug-induced sleep, Jack Dunleavy asked his father only one question. He said, "Who shot?"

Dr. Rory thought for a moment how distasteful it was to be in the debt of a sadistic animal that he loathed. It brought bile up in the back of his throat, but like it or not, his son would be dead now if it wasn't for the actions of the Dep. Finally, quietly, he said, "Benko Sadek."

In another instant, Jack Dunleavy was sound asleep. Dr. Rory knew that the boy would sleep deeply for about ten hours with the pill that he had given him. Early the next morning, he would drive out for a quick follow-up appointment with Shelly Oleski and her thriving toddler, and then he would ask John Gale to cover for him.

He would also call his brother Ox to see if he and Jack could visit him at his farm for a few days. It might provide just the right amount of diversion, while Jack sorted out all that had happened on Hidden Island.

Jack Dunleavy awoke at four in the afternoon with Dr. Rory sitting in the chair in his bedroom reading a book. Jack rubbed his neck, and then remembered the night before.

"How're you feeling?" asked Dr. Rory.

"I feel OK," replied his son. "It all seems like a bad dream."

"I know," said Dr. Rory reassuringly.

"Listen, Jack, your Uncle Ox has been pestering me for the longest time to bring you up to his place for a visit. There's some great trout fishing nearby, and Ox knows all the good holes. What d'ya say you and I go up there for a few days?"

Jack agreed and, after they had something to eat, they got into Dr. Rory's Buick, and headed for Uncle Ox and Aunt Flora's place in Vermont. They talked all the way up, with Dr. Rory gently nudging the conversation toward the familiar if he felt that it was getting too heavy. They fished, milked cows, and laughed some with Uncle Ox for three days—all the while enjoying Aunt Flora's good cooking.

After Uncle Ox and Aunt Flora turned in at night, Jack and Dr. Rory talked by the fire about everything imaginable. When asked what he wanted to do when he finally got out of college, Jack said that he wanted to do something creative—perhaps something to do with conservation.

Dr. Rory allowed that was a fine choice.

"Remember," he said, "it's a tiny segment of the population that gets to do the creative work of the world. All the rest of us just spend our lives straightening out other people's problems."

It would take all summer and then some for Jack Dunleavy to settle into anything approaching his life before the shooting, but the trip to Vermont had provided a good beginning. It seemed that Dr. Rory spent more time with Jack in that one summer than he had in the previous twelve years combined. By packing his summer with activities, all of the Dunleavys tried to ensure that he would be able to resume his life without the events on the island haunting him forever. Also, he and his friends compared notes about what had happened that night, and in a manner of speaking, the blind led the blind off Hidden Island.

Dr. Rory's second son was learning the Irish way of dealing with tragedy—bury it as deeply as possible, and never discuss it again. If, at some future time it surfaces, just submerge it deeper still. The Dunleavys were typical. They dealt with the painful, the ugly and the difficult by not dealing with them at all.

Summer faded quietly, and in September, Jack and Wibby started at Wellesport High with the considerable cachet of being chauffeured by a senior in a slate-gray Dunleavy SSK Drophead coupe. The prisoners were bused to the new facility forty at a time, and a wrecking crew tore down the Wellesport prison right on schedule. The thirty-acre prison tract became a huge empty field, which the town bought from the state for one dollar.

Benko Sadek followed the prisoners to the new prison as their deputy warden while Warden Stoner retired to play more golf. The papers ran lurid stories about the shooting on Hidden Island with pictures of "Old Sparky" placed next to pictures of the real "Old Sparky," but not a single voice was raised in protest of the fatality.

A blue ribbon panel picked personally by Governor Belden conducted a hearing to ensure that there were no laws broken by state employees. For two weeks, the panel discussed the escape and shooting, enjoyed nice luncheons courtesy of the taxpayers, found no wrongdoing of any kind, and then dismissed itself.

In the fall of 1959, the Connecticut Valley Railroad went bankrupt for the tenth and last time. The gandy dancers never passed through Wellesport again.

The End